Weep a While Longer

Weep a While Longer

For Kate — & Chive

Happy reading!

Penny Freedman

29.12.44

PENNY FREEDMAN

Matador
9 Priory Business Park
Kibworth Beauchamp
Leicestershire LE8 0RX, UK
Tel: (+44) 116 279 2299
Fax: (+44) 116 279 2277
Email: books@troubador.co.uk
Web: www.troubador.co.uk/matador

ISBN 978 1784620 165

British Library Cataloguing in Publication Data.
A catalogue record for this book is available from the British Library.

Typeset in Book Antiqua by Troubador Publishing Ltd
Printed and bound in the UK by TJ International, Padstow, Cornwall

Matador is an imprint of Troubador Publishing Ltd

Acorns day nursery is an invented place, inhabited by invented people, but I would like to dedicate this book to the children, parents and staff of The Oaks from 1973 to 1983.

Other places and people in this book are also, of course, entirely fictional.

Penny Freedman studied Classics at Oxford before teaching English in schools and universities. She is also an actress and director. She has a PhD in Shakespeare Studies and lives with her husband in Stratford-upon-Avon. She has two grown-up daughters.

Her previous books featuring Gina Gray and DCI Scott are *This is a Dreadful Sentence* (2010), *All the Daughters* (2012) and *One May Smile* (2013).

Benedick:	Lady Beatrice, have you wept all this while?
Beatrice:	Yea, and I will weep a while longer.

Much Ado About Nothing 4.1

1

Tuesday 17ᵗʰ July

Veiled Remarks

'I don't understand,' Jamilleh says, 'why the shops' people are saying me always, *Your right.*'

'*Your right?*' I ask.

'Yes. The shops' workers, they say always this.'

'Are they saying us *You are right?*' asks Farah.

'No, is a question,' chips in Juanita. 'It goes like, *Your right?*'

Light dawns. I laugh. 'Athene,' I ask, 'do you know what they mean?'

Athene turns stormy dark eyes on me and gives a little huff of impatience. 'It's like, *Are you all right?*' she says through barely parted lips. 'Always everybody is asking this in England.' She yawns. She is bored, as she has a right to be: her English is much better than the others' and she doesn't get much out of these classes. Also, she doesn't like the Iranians: the Greeks' view of themselves as Europe's bastion against the Islamic world doesn't really encourage mutual tolerance and understanding. And then there's the current meltdown of the Greek economy: since her husband is here doing a government-funded MBA, I guess she's wondering how much longer they're going to be here.

Farah and Jamilleh stare at her, affronted – as they so often

1

are – by the treachery of the English language; Juanita smiles in dawning comprehension and Ning Wu, the fifth student in the group, has decided to conform to stereotype and look inscrutable. I write on the board:

Are you all right?
You all right?
Yorright?

'It gets squished up,' I say, 'because people say it so often.'

'So they are asking me *am I all right?*' Farah asks.

'Well, no. They actually mean, *Hello, can I help you?*'

Her face brightens. 'In the book,' she says, 'this is how they say.'

'The book?'

'The book we were study with Mrs Jenny. *Emma Goes Shopping*. In this book the shops' people say, *Good morning. Can I help you?*'

'Yeees,' I say, 'that's what shop assistants say in books, but very rarely in real life. Except perhaps in posh shops.'

They laugh. *Posh* is a recent addition to their vocabulary and they like the alliteration of *posh shops*, and the way I say it.

This is not, in general, an easy course to teach: popularly referred to as *The Wives' Course*, it was given an official pc makeover to *The Spouses' Course* a couple of years ago and then became uber-pc last autumn, when a young Brazilian woman, taking an MA in Women's Studies, demanded that her boyfriend be allowed to attend. So it is now *The Partners' Course*, though Rio, the partner in question, swiftly lost interest and found himself a job in one of the campus food outlets, where his English is, no doubt, improving by leaps and bounds. Everyone in the current class is, in fact, a wife. The numbers are always small and the course never pays for itself, but it is a kind of pastoral care for overseas students at Marlbury University, founded on the premise that men who have brought their families with them will study better if their wives are happy and, rather more tenuously, that happiness and speaking English are coextensive. There's a flawed syllogism in there somewhere:

Students are happier if they are better integrated
Speaking English helps people to integrate
Ergo, learning English makes students happy

Anyway, the Student Union gives us a grant to run it and it's a dogsbody course, usually taught by the newest recruit to the English Language department, and as head of department I wouldn't normally be anywhere near it, except that I could see Jenny Marsh was really struggling with this particular group back in the autumn. Athene, Juanita and Rio, the Brazilian guy, were ganging up on Farah and Jamilleh, who spoke very little English at that point. They were suffering from severe culture shock and reacted fiercely to any perceived slur on their religion or culture. Ning Wu, from Shanghai, got caught in the crossfire and came to me to complain, so I swapped a nice quiet Cambridge First Certificate listening class with Jenny and took them on myself. It's been hard work, and as I look at them even now Ning Wu is still sitting in the middle between Farah and Jamilleh to my left and Juanita and Athene to my right, like a one-woman UN peacekeeping force. We've found common ground, though: Acorns, for a start, the university day nursery, where my students all send their children and where I am frequently to be found dropping or collecting Freda, my four-year-old granddaughter. We rub along; I keep it light; we have a laugh.

We are laughing now at *posh shops* when Farah's and Jamilleh's faces freeze before my eyes and their smiles stretch into masks of panic. At the same time I'm aware of a noise to my right and I spin round to see a young man coming into the room. I run at him, flapping wildly. 'Out! Out! Out!' I scream like a demented farmer's wife seeing her hens threatened by a fox.

He stares at me. 'I was just trying to f —' he says.

'Ouut!' I scream again and push him bodily from the room, slamming the door behind him.

I turn with my back against the door to find Farah and Jamilleh frantically bundling themselves into their jilbabs and khimars.

Damn, damn, damn, damn, damn. We were doing so well. About six weeks ago, you see, there was what can only be called an epiphany. It was early June and the first really warm weather of the year. Juanita and Athene were flashing brown shoulders in sleeveless T-shirts and they looked with pity at the Iranian women and asked if they had to wear *those hijabs* even at home. 'Of course not,' came the answer. 'At home we wear whatever we like. At home,' Farah told us, smiling, 'we are beautiful for our husbands.' And then it was Jamilleh, I think, who looked around, said, 'Well, we are all women here,' and started to pull off her headscarf. In a couple of minutes, they had both divested themselves of what I then, in my ignorance, would have called their hijabs and their long grey coats. The rest of us gazed in astonishment as they emerged, vivid, from their grey cocoons, two entirely Western-style young women with tight-fitting jeans, sleeveless tops, chunky jewellery and salon-improved hair – Farah's lowlighted a rich red, Jamilleh's highlighted in dark gold.

'And now,' Farah told us, flushed with her own courage, 'we teach you this is not hijab.' And so we were instructed. We learned that hijab simply means *modest dress*, though it can also refer to the headscarf, which is more properly called the khimar, as it is in the Qur'an, apparently. So the long, buttoned coat that Jamilleh had just taken off is not a hijab, nor is it a chador: the chador, we should understand, is the black cloak worn largely by peasant women. Farah and Jamilleh, smart young women from Tehran, wear the jilbab or, at the expensive, designer end of the market, the *manteau*, as in the French for overcoat. I was rather delighted to discover that there is fashion snobbery even in Islamic dress. I'm not sure how much the other students took in of all this but I lapped it up; always a glutton for new linguistic information, I've tucked it away and I'm waiting for an opportunity to show it off.

Since that occasion, as soon as we've all gathered and the door has been closed, they have shrugged themselves out of their outerwear as casually as anyone else takes off a coat and the dynamic of the class has felt subtly changed. It seems like a gesture of trust and I feel privileged, in an odd sort of way, to be trusted. Until today. Until three minutes ago when a wretched, rash, intruding fool blundered in and wrecked it. Because they're not going to take the risk again, are they?

I apologise and soothe my fluttered chicks as best I can, and then, since there is no point in trying to go back to the listening exercise we were doing, and from which we had diverged anyway, I ask whether they're all going to the end-of-term tea party at Acorns this afternoon.

'Our sons will sing,' Farah tells me solemnly.

'Oh yes. I've heard. We're getting an entertainment.'

'Just the big childrens.'

'*Children*.'

'Children. The children who will start school soon.'

This includes Freda, and if there's any performing going on, she likes to be right in there. I am commanded to attend since Nico, her baby brother, has earache and is keeping her mother at home.

'Do you know what they're singing?' I ask.

'Of course! They are practising all the time. *The Veals on the Bars.*'

'I'm sorry?' I ask, startled.

Farah looks at Jamilleh and they start a rotating, pumping movement with their arms and sing:

The wheels on the bus go round and round,
Round and round, round and round.
The wheels on the bus go round and round,
All day long.

Juanita laughs.

'*The wipers on the bus go swish, swish, swish,*' she sings, and the others join in, hands flapping – except Athene who, when they move on to *the horn on the bus goes beep, beep, beep,* gives a tragic groan and bangs her forehead on her desk. Laughing, the others carry on, through the driver on the bus, the baby, the mummy, the granny and several other verses.

I suppose the staff of Acorns know what a powerful role they play in the spread of British culture. I could wish, though, that they'd chosen something more authentic. This sounds ersatz, invented for *Playschool* presenters, I suspect, whereas I like those old, slightly strange rhymes with echoes of plague and religious persecution – something with a bit of grit. This little rhyme has done its job, though, and we depart cheerfully.

'See you later,' I say and they, as they have been taught, carol it back.

I have plenty of time for tea parties this week, since term is over, our regular students have scattered to the globe's corners and the new students for the summer vacation courses don't arrive for a couple of weeks. In fact, my five wives are probably the only students on the entire campus being taught this week; Juanita is going home to see her family at some point but the others are staying through the vacation, so the show goes on. Actually, even if I were busy I'd make the effort to go to an Acorns party, just to wonder at the brilliance of the women who work there: their calm, their resilience and their boundless good humour in the face of the egocentricity, irrationality and general stickiness of small children never fail to humble me.

So here I am, sitting on a plastic chair in the garden at Acorns, being force-fed fairy cakes and jellies made by the children this morning.

'We did plenty of hand washing,' Caroline, who runs the place, reassured us as we sat down to our feast, so I've decided to stop wondering how much snot I am likely to consume.

There are about twenty of us here, mainly the mothers of the self-styled 'Big Ones' who are going to entertain us later, and the children take their hosting role very seriously, pressing food upon us. I sit with Jamilleh and Farah and a couple of their friends for a bit but I get irritated by the suspicious way they are looking at their uneaten fairy cakes. We have been through this. I couldn't swear that the gelatine in the jellies wasn't pig-related, I conceded, but fairy cakes, I told them, were quite safe: flour, butter, sugar, egg – no chance of pig products getting anywhere near them. So why are they sitting there looking as though they've been given unexploded bombs to hold? I get up and go to join Juanita, who is feeding orange jelly with tinned satsumas in it to her two-year-old. 'I love tinned satsumas,' I say. 'Don't you?'

Juanita, whose husband is doing an MSc in Sustainable Agriculture, says, 'I prefer them right off the tree.'

'I suppose,' I say. 'But tinned satsumas are a thing all of their own – a different fruit almost.'

She looks sceptically at the spoonful she is holding. 'I suppose,' she says.

A small boy appears at my side, proffering a brilliantly

7

green jelly with grapes in it. I hesitate as I have already overdosed on fairy cakes, but when he says, 'I maked it myself,' there is no possibility of refusing it. I'm not a pushover for small children but I do love listening to them, hearing them juggle the language, contemplating the extraordinary thing that's going on in the brain of a three or four-year-old. Parents want to urge them on – to tidy up and correct, to turn speaking into performance. What they don't appreciate is that even the slowest child's brain is performing probably the most remarkable feat it will ever undertake. And getting things wrong is actually evidence of how well they're doing, because they're not just parroting. This little boy who 'maked' my jelly – Liam, he's called, he tells me – has never heard anyone say 'maked', but his brain has picked up the pattern of English verbs adding 'ed' for the simple past tense and it's sticking with that for the moment in spite of any empirical evidence to the contrary. Later, of course, the patterning will become more sophisticated and irregular verbs will find their place but for now it's the patterning that enables him to be creative.

I take a spoonful of jelly while Liam watches me anxiously. 'Delicious,' I say.

'I choosed green,' he says, 'because green is my favourite colour.'

'Well my favourite colour is blue,' I say, 'but you can't get blue jelly.'

'No.' He contemplates me solemnly for a minute. 'That's sad for you,' he says and gives my arm a pat before running off to continue his catering duties.

Soon after I've downed my last grape we are called inside for the entertainment. Two rows of chairs have been arranged in a semicircle round the performance area, with a gangway down the middle. This seems to have produced a mini-apartheid and I decide to join Farah and Jamilleh in the front row on the ethnically more interesting side of the audience.

Particularly interesting to the Iranians is a woman sitting behind us in full Islamic gear – black from head to toe, dark eyes just visible between headscarf and face veil. Farah and Jamilleh twist round to get a better look at her and then have a rapid, muttered conversation in Farsi..

'Do you know her?' I ask, sotto voce. 'The woman in the burqa?'

'Not burqa,' Farah says.

'Not?' I glance over my shoulder again.

'Niqab,' Jamilleh says. 'Burqa is top to bottom. One thing.' She makes a sweeping two-handed gesture from her head downwards.

I am embarrassed, convinced that the woman must know that we're talking about her, but Jamilleh is oblivious, consumed by the need to educate me. 'Niqab is veil for face,' she says. 'Separate. Headscarf, veil, dress. All separate.'

'So where do they wear niqab?' I ask. 'Where is she from?'

She shrugs. 'Maybe Afghanistan, maybe Saudi Arabia, maybe Somalia.'

'And you don't know her?'

'No.' She smoothes the folds of her rather fetching purple headscarf and leans back in her chair. 'It is clothes for peasant,' she says.

We are hushed by the appearance of Caroline, who welcomes us and ushers in from the room beyond the group of three small boys who are to be 'our first performers this afternoon.' With a minimum of the coaxing and fussing that usually accompanies any performance by small children, they launch into 'The big ship sails on the alley-alley-o'. They are somewhat overwhelmed by the vigorous piano accompaniment, but one of the trio – the boy Liam, in fact, maker of green jellies – has the strong, pure voice of a potential choirboy, and he it is who keeps them afloat (if you'll forgive the metaphor since, as we all know, *The big ship sank to the bottom of the sea*).

They are followed by a group of girls, including Freda, who has been clam-like about the nature of her performance. They sing a song about 'Auntie Monica', which I haven't come across before and which makes me vaguely uneasy:

I have an auntie, an Auntie Monica
And when she goes out shopping
They all cry 'Ooh-la-la!'
Because her feather's swaying,
Her feather's swaying so,
Because her feather's swaying,
Her feather's swaying so.

This is then followed by her hat swaying, her muff swaying and her skirt swaying, and it's all accompanied by vigorous swaying of hips and torsos by these tiny girls which seems to owe rather too much to pop videos. 'The big ship' is just the kind of nursery rhyme I like – threaded with tragedy and open to speculation. What was the ship that inspired the song? Is its sailing on *the first day of September* a clue? Who was the captain who said *it will never, never do*? And what was *the alley-alley-o*? (I would say that it's a rhyme that has *ballast* but I really must give up the marine metaphors.) 'Auntie Monica', though, raises speculation of a quite different kind. The feather and the hat, together with the French associations of *Ooh-la-la* produce, for me, a picture of a Toulouse-Lautrec Parisian tart, and as for the swaying muff – are we really comfortable with that?

Catching Freda's eyes on me, I hastily repress these thoughts and arrange my face in an expression of unalloyed delight. Freda is an unabashed performer, working the song for all it's worth, and my pride in her is only slightly moderated by mortification when she gives a very hard elbow jab to the mite beside her, who gets her verses muddled and puts the skirt before the muff.

I enjoy 'The wheels on the bus' mainly because I love watching Farah and Jamilleh mouthing the words. This is followed by 'Heads, and shoulders, knees and toes', 'Five little peas' and a rousing finale from the full chorus of 'If you're happy and you know it clap your hands', in which the audience is exhorted to join. We then applaud vigorously and Caroline asks if we will please wait outside for a few minutes while the children gather their belongings and 'calm down a bit'.

Acorns was originally a harmless bungalow, minding its own business, pleasantly situated with a view of school playing fields, but some years ago it fell prey to the inexorable advance of Marlbury University, *Moving Forward*, as billboards announce on building sites throughout the town. Starting as a teacher training college in what was originally no more than a large house in a quiet area of the town, it is now officially a university – charter and all – and it has spread in all directions, engulfing surrounding buildings and consuming them like some giant phagocyte. Mostly these buildings have been replaced by standard edifices of glass and concrete, but Acorns has been allowed to remain almost unchanged, its rooms distributed between babies, toddlers and preschoolers. Its gardens, front and back, remain too, barriered now by six-foot fences and a bolted gate, solid enough to keep escapees in and predators out. In the front garden stands the huge oak tree which gives Acorns its name and most of us make for its afternoon shade as we wait for the children. Making rather effortful conversation with my student Ning Wu, I notice, idly, a woman and child arrive with a dog on a lead. The woman is a redhead, wiry and pale, in a sleeveless white top and skinny jeans; the girl is about seven, in school uniform, and the dog is one of those ugly, flat-faced beasts that you can't imagine anyone loves.

The children come trickling out, burdened by end-of-term detritus – spare pants, painting overalls, Wellington boots and artwork that has recently adorned Acorns' walls. Freda, I have learned, is often the last one out on these occasions. I used to panic at her non-appearance, believing that she had been abducted in plain sight, but now I know better: she will be engaged with someone else's problem – hunting a lost boot, advising on the ownership of a pair of knickers, consoling the creator of a damaged piece of pasta art. The leaving-well-alone-gene missed the females in my family altogether – the sin of the mother punished even unto the third and fourth generation.

Choirboy Liam emerges and carries his burdens to the woman with the ugly dog. I feel a brief pang to think that she wasn't there to hear him sing, but it is quickly dispelled by the drama that follows. As the woman is struggling to push Liam's belongings into the plastic bag of shopping she is carrying, the dog manages to yank his lead from her grasp and he rushes, barking furiously, at the niqab woman, who is walking up the path to the garden gate. She tries to get away from the dog, who is on its back legs, pawing at her black robe, but she is hampered by the group of mothers and children who are blocking the gate; the dog's owner yells at him; her daughter hoots with laughter; I am delighted to find that the dog is called Billy because it's the kind of dog you'd expect Bill Sykes to have; the dog Billy pays no attention to anyone but keeps barking and pawing; the niqab woman gives him a hard kick and the child tugs at her mother's hand.

'She's getting him! She's getting him!' she protests.

'Billy! Billy!' the mother calls again.

The woman finally drags her robe away from his paws and pushes her way through the gate; someone manages to slam the gate closed with the dog inside; his owner retrieves him, rebukes her daughter, who is laughing again, grabs Liam's hand and leaves. Jamilleh slips out of the gate behind her and everyone returns to the business of departure, with the extra zest that a bit of drama always imparts.

Where's Jamilleh gone?' I ask Farah, who is minding Jamilleh's son.

'To see if she's OK.'

'That's kind. Do you know her?'

'No.'

I see a flash of irritation. I have made a mistake. I have assumed that all Muslim women in Marlbury must know one another, which is pretty crass.

By the time Freda finally appears, bearing the important news that there are seven pairs of unclaimed knickers in the staff room, Jamilleh is back, looking cross.

'Is she all right?' I ask.

She shrugs, exchanges an unfathomable look with Farah and says one word in Farsi.

Peasant, I suspect.

2

17.07.12: 18.45

Crime Scene

DS Paula Powell made her escape from the screaming mayhem that was her seven-year-old nephew's birthday party and walked home relishing the cooling air of the early evening and enjoying the blessed quiet. It was impossible to tell her sister that she really didn't yearn for children of her own, that involvement in the noisy, sticky lives of her nephew and niece was not the only brightness in her otherwise bleak and barren life, that pursuing her career as a detective sergeant in the Marlbury police force was not a poor second best to the joys of marriage and motherhood but what she loved. It was impossible to say it without rubbishing her sister's life, without denigrating the children of whom she was, actually, very fond. She took out her phone to check for messages and found three from DC Sarah Shepherd, each more frantic than the one before, their arrivals unheard in all the screaming. A bubble of elation rose in her chest. She called Sarah back.

'Sarah?'

'Paula. Thank God. I really need you here. Ian's on holiday, David's not back for another week and I'm first on the scene at what looks like a homicide and a suicide. Dr McAndrew's here but otherwise all I've got is one uniform keeping the rubberneckers at bay.'

'I'm five minutes from my car. I'll be with you in twenty.'

'You've got the address, haven't you? It was in my message.'

'Yes. Eastgate estate. What a surprise!'

'I think you'll be surprised by this,' Sarah said, and Paula heard her voice wobble.

'Keep Dr McAndrew there with you till I come,' she said and started to run, simultaneously cursing herself for the spindly-heeled sandals she had put on in honour of the party and congratulating herself for emptying into a flowerbed the two glasses of lethal punch that her brother-in-law had pressed on her in the course of the afternoon. She hoped the buddleia growing nearby would be able to cope with it.

At home, she changed her shoes, checked that she had all her protective gear, listened again to Sarah's message and drove the familiar route to the Eastgate estate, generator of – probably – fifty per cent of Marlbury's crime. Most commonly it was uniformed officers who found themselves there, recovering stolen goods, pursuing vandals and joy-riders, called out to domestic violence or drunken stabbings. Recently, though, Eastgate crime had gone up a notch. Situated as it was between London and Dover, Marlbury had become a convenient link in a chain that trafficked both people and drugs, and Eastgate was playing its part. The police knew that the owners of some impressive houses with high hedges in salubrious parts of the town were playing their part too, but they were more difficult to trawl for, so it was the Eastgate minnows they picked up time and again, expendable food for the big fish. It was the Met's decision to prioritise breaking this chain that had led to DCI David Scott's being seconded as liaison to them for three months, leaving her, Paula supposed and hoped, as senior investigating officer on this case.

The planners who designed Eastgate in the 1950s had gone for maximum density; high rise was not an option within sight of the abbey's celebrated tower, so the houses were rammed together, shoulder to shoulder, their narrow front gardens now crammed with vehicles and wheelie bins, since neither drives nor side gates had been thought necessary. In the great 1980's council house sell-off, no-one wanted to buy a house here, so there had been no gentrification and precious little in the way of redecoration. Eastgate was, these days, the place where the council put problem families; here they could make problems for each other and everyone else could breathe more easily.

There was no difficulty finding the house: the hubbub of voices led her there and changed its nature as she drew up, got out her gear, locked the car and started to elbow her way through the crowd, her shouts of, 'Excuse me. Police!' producing cheers and whistles. She wished she had taken a moment to change out of her flimsy little sundress when she changed her shoes. In spite of her consciousness of being watched as she walked up the short front path, she had time to notice that someone looked after the front garden and the bins were tucked away behind a wicker screen.

In the narrow hallway she came face to face with Lynne McAndrew.

'DS Powell. Good,' the pathologist said. 'I'm just about done here. Your colleague is struggling a bit.' She pushed open a door behind her so that Paula could see, through the kitchen window beyond, Sarah Shepherd pacing the tiny garden, a clump of tissues pressed to her mouth. At the same time Paula was aware of a smell wafting from the kitchen, sweet and fetid at the same time. She looked at Lynne McAndrew.

'Yes,' McAndrew said. 'I think it was the dog that finished her off.'

'The dog?'

'You might as well look at it now, though it's hardly your priority, of course.'

She led the way into the kitchen and Paula's eyes were drawn immediately to a bright pool of red in the sink. She approached cautiously and for a moment could make no sense of what she saw, convinced somehow that since this was a kitchen, what she was looking at was something culinary. A dog lay in a puddle of blood, its head thrown back, and under its chin was a deep, dark, red hole with the neck vertebrae glinting white within it. Feeling the saliva rush into her mouth, she fought down nausea. 'Nasty,' she said as briskly as she could manage. 'Let's go back into the hall.'

In the hall, she said, 'So its throat was cut. What else am I expecting to see? Sarah – DC Shepherd – said a homicide and a suicide?'

'One upstairs and one down. I've finished and the SOCO team aren't here yet so they're all yours.'

Paula hesitated. 'I'd quite like a view from you first. Any pointers?'

Lynne McAndrew gave her a long look. 'How much of this sort of thing have you seen?' she asked.

Paula bridled, immediately defensive. 'That depends on what this sort of thing is.'

'Violent death.'

'I've seen ... well, there's much less of it than you'd think from watching TV, isn't there? You have to be a traffic cop to see it on a daily basis.'

'Right. So you want me to prepare you. It's not pretty, I warn you, but I've seen a lot worse. There's a child. A girl. Aged six or seven. In her bedroom, on her bed, smothered with a pillow. No blood but not a pretty sight. You can see the struggle still. And there's cyanosis – the face is blue.'

'Right. And?'

'And there's a woman – young, late twenties probably – with two slit wrists. Lots of blood.'

'OK. So one scenario is a woman at the end of her rope who kills her daughter – and her dog – and then cuts her wrists. Or we're looking for a partner or ex-partner and this is a revenge thing. But he's tried to make the woman's death look like suicide and that would be surprising, wouldn't it? Those kind of men – they want people to know it's them. Their pride's been hurt and they want to get it back by showing what big men they are. They usually kill themselves afterwards or go on the run. Does it convince you as a suicide?'

'It does and it doesn't. The wrist slitting was quite professional – no sawing away across the tendons but a deep incision into the artery. And the incision on the left wrist is deeper than the one on the right, which makes sense if she was right-handed. On the other hand, wrist cutters often don't do much to the second wrist at all. People will instinctively start with the knife in their stronger hand and then when they come to do the second wrist they're not only using their weaker hand but they've got blood gushing out of it. There's some bruising, too, that needs thinking about.'

She paused and looked around for her case. 'I'll take a better look at her when I've got her in the lab. If she killed the dog, I'd expect to find canine blood mixed in with her blood. And she'd had a lot to drink – reeked of gin. I'll be interested to see the toxicology.'

She stood with her hand on the catch of the front door. 'I should have preliminary results by the end of the day tomorrow,' she said. 'But if you're going to be the SIO on this then it's about time for you to go and look for yourself, Detective Sergeant, isn't it?' She closed the front door behind her.

3

Tuesday 17th July

A Crime Seen

I pedal Freda away from the nursery in the child seat on the back of my bike and drop her off at her home, the tiny terraced house that Ellie, my elder daughter, and her husband, Ben, are not quite managing to pay for on two teachers' salaries. I stop long enough to commiserate over Nico's earache, to give an account of the afternoon's festivities and to impress on Ellie, at Freda's insistence, the unparalleled panache of her performance of 'Auntie Monica'.

'I'm sorry I missed it,' Ellie says, and she means it. I feel bad. I should have offered to stay with grizzly Nico while Ellie went to watch Freda. 'There'll be other times,' I say feebly.

I get back on my bike and head for home, wondering whether a salad would be a good idea for supper, after all that cake and jelly. I know that there is something wrong the moment I turn into my road and spot, outside my house, an acid green Smart car which belongs to my younger daughter, Annie, and, behind it, a beaten-up Volvo with a flat front tyre. I know what this is and I feel a fool. *A couple of people to stay for a couple of days*, Annie had said, and I gave a breezy agreement when twenty years' experience of Annie's talent for manipulation and dissimulation should have warned me to

19

demand details – names, dates and terms of residence, not to mention setting a few house rules. I get off my bike and take a look at the Volvo, which looks alarmingly roomy. How many of them are there?

The house is quiet as I enter but, dazzled for a moment by coming in from bright sunshine, I trip over several backpacks artfully arranged in the hall. Rubbing a bruised shin, I go down the hall to the kitchen, find the back door wide open and see, sprawled on the grass outside, a group of five, lounging together in a rough circle, wine glasses and cigarettes in hand, two bottles and a couple of packs of Kettle chips nestling among them. I take a deep breath and step outside.

'Hello,' I call in a tone that neatly combines greeting and challenge. They turn to look at me, Annie's eyes bright with reciprocal challenge, the other faces bland and smiling. They are under the impression that they have been invited, aren't they? They are envisaging clean beds and regular meals for however long Annie has offered them. I move down the garden towards them and one of the boys jumps politely to his feet, which is disarming enough, but when he then says, 'Would you like a glass of wine, Mrs Gray? I'll get you a glass,' and speeds back to the house, I am ridiculously charmed even though I know quite well that it is my wine they are drinking.

'The drive down from Oxford was vile so we really needed a drink,' Annie says defensively, as if reading my mind, 'and we did buy the crisps ourselves.'

The others laugh uncomfortably so that the lifetime habits of hospitality force me to say, 'Oh, you're welcome to the wine. It's lovely to see you all,' thus wrecking any possibility of establishing dates, terms of residence or house rules. I do get names, however, though I'm not sure I shall be able to attach them reliably to their owners. There is a Dominic and a Matt and a Lauren and a Kate – nice middle-class names for nice middle-class young people – and I should probably explain to you why they're here. They are fellow students of Annie's at Oxford, and the week after next they're going up to the Edinburgh Festival to perform – on the fringe of The Fringe – a play written by one of them – Matt, I think. It's a three-hander, I gather, and it's about love and sex, treachery and trust, life and death, hope and despair and the search for identity – as these things generally are. Annie is taking part in it and she has persuaded our local theatre, the Aphra Behn, to let them put it on next week in their small, sixty-seat studio theatre. There was a meltdown at the theatre about eighteen months ago and the new stage manager is a young woman who was a couple of years ahead of Ellie at school, so Annie has got a foot in the door. I assume they'll be staying with me till that's over and they're heading for Edinburgh.

I must get Annie on her own and ask what arrangements they're proposing to make about eating because I'm not going to cook for six every evening, but I sip my glass of wine and they start talking about the play and the problems they need to iron out, and I make some suggestions which they take up with flattering alacrity, and I have another glass of wine and eventually hear myself say, 'Is pasta all right for supper?' and I toddle indoors to find the ingredients for pasta *con tutto giardino*. Annie used to call this my *Ma forgot to shop supper*, since it involves raiding not so much the garden as the vegetable rack and the fridge for edible vegetables. They don't need to be in their prime; even the wilting and withered can be put to service when thrown into a good tomato sauce. Annie had better not complain.

Everyone is very appreciative of supper, in fact; more wine is drunk and everyone helps to clear up in a slapdash sort of way. Then they go off to the sitting room to watch television and I stay behind to restack the dishwasher because nobody knows how to stack someone else's dishwasher, and then I can hear that they're watching something with a lot of hysterical studio audience laughter, which I shall hate, so I stay in the kitchen and sit at the table and read the paper until I'm roused by a shout from Annie. She puts her head round the door and says, 'Murders on the Eastgate estate. On the national news.'

I follow her into the sitting room in time to see the pictures on the screen: a school photo of a girl and a slightly blurred holiday picture of a young woman. 'I saw them,' I say. 'I saw them this afternoon.' And then, stupidly, 'How can they be dead?'

'… Believed to be those of Karen Brody, a part-time student at Marlbury University, and her seven-year-old daughter, Lara,' I hear, and then the picture changes to one I also recognise. This one is live, though. It's Detective Sergeant Paula Powell of the Marlbury police, smartly dressed in a crisp shirt and jacket for the telly, saying, 'This is just the beginning of the police investigation. At this stage we are treating the deaths as unexplained. We don't know, as yet, whether anyone else was involved.'

So, with David still away in London, Paula's in charge. Good luck to her. She'll want to get a result before he comes back and stamps all over her case. I ought to help. I look at the others, who are all staring at me now, rather than at the screen. 'I'm going to ring the police,' I say. 'She was there this afternoon, at the nursery. With a dog. And a little boy.' I look at the television screen as though I might conjure up his face too. 'He's called Liam. What's happened to him?'

4

Wednesday 18th July

I Witness

It wasn't as easy to get to talk to Paula Powell as I had assumed. I imagined them working through the night on the case, but when I rang the station it turned out that all I could do was leave a message. I made my information sound as important as possible: *an eye witness to Karen Brody's last hours*, I said, and I left my name and mobile number. Now I shall just have to wait.

Paula Powell and I have a complicated relationship. I quite like her, actually, but I'm sure she fancies David, who is her boss and my part-time lover, semi-partner or half-hearted other half (we are particularly semi-detached at the moment since he has spent the last three months in London as part of some drugs super-team). Paula, no doubt, thinks I'm too old for him, and I think that if he fancied her he would have done something about it and it isn't me who's holding him back. So there we are. She took me to hospital once, when I got my fingers and other bits of me burned while helping the police with their inquiries, and she was quite kind, but when we meet on those odd occasions when I'm invited to escort David to some work-related *do*, she's pretty chilly. I, of course, am charm itself.

I'm in my office thinking about coffee time when she rings.

'Gina?' She sounds cautious.

'Paula!' I sound delighted.

'I got a message that you wanted to talk to me.'

'Yes. You must be pleased, getting this case. A good time for you, while David's away.'

'Well, a young woman and a child are dead. *Pleased* is hardly the word I'd use.'

'No, of course not.' I can feel myself blushing. What made me say something so crass? Or think it, for that matter? 'Stupid thing to say. Sorry.'

There is a silence and I'm not sure how to proceed. Eventually she says, 'Your message said something about being an eye witness.'

'Yes. I don't know, obviously, when they were killed, but I saw them alive and well at about three thirty yesterday.'

'Where was that?'

So I tell her. I pride myself on my gift for précis so I launch in quite briskly but she stops me when I get to Liam.

'A boy?' she asks sharply. 'Are you sure?'

'Of course, I'm sure. That's why she was there.'

'Well, there was no sign of another – never mind. Go on. You said there was an incident?'

I tell her about the dog attacking the niqab woman and she surprises me by asking, 'What did the dog look like?'

'The dog? It was one of those squashy-faced things. A bulldog type. You're surely not worrying about whether the dog was illegal are you, when –'

She cuts me off. 'And the woman? What did she look like?'

'As, I said, she was wearing a niqab, so –'

'A niqab? What's that?'

'It's Islamic dress. Black. With a face veil.'

'A burqa, you mean, then.'

'Well, technically a niqab is different. It's a separate face

24

veil that covers everything except the eyes. And there isn't the grid thing over the –'

'I'm going with burqa. Everyone knows what that is.'

I say nothing; she says nothing.

'So,' I say, 'I assume you're looking for an ex-partner, aren't you?'

'Why do you say that?'

'Isn't that usually who it is when women and their children get killed?'

'Who says they were killed?'

'So it was an accident, then?'

She gives a short laugh. 'People don't generally slit their wrists by accident.'

I can hear that she regrets them the moment the words slip through her lips. She tries to eat them, but it's no good. 'They're … they're unexplained deaths. Murder, suicide, accident are all possible. We're not issuing any details at the moment and it would be very unwise to speculate on –'

'It's all right, Paula,' I say. 'I can be discreet.'

She rings off.

Slit wrists. I walk over to the common room for coffee thinking about this. I feel chastened. *A young woman and a child are dead.* Of course they are. And I saw yesterday a young mother already so desperate that she was about to kill herself and her child. Should I have known? Did we all blithely turn a blind eye to desperation? I don't think she looked like a woman on the edge, but when I consider this I realise I don't know what that does look like. She looked clean and she'd brushed her hair and the little girl looked neat and tidy. She was a bit detached, maybe; I don't remember seeing her talk to anyone. She didn't panic, though, when the dog went mad. She looked in control. But then suicide is a kind of taking control, isn't it? I realise that I don't know anything about it.

By chance, my colleague Malcolm is having coffee in the common room and is sitting alone. He usually is sitting alone, in fact, because he's something of a bore, and I would normally avoid him, but today I take my coffee and go and join him because I have remembered that he volunteers as a Samaritan and should be able to tell me about suicides. I've always thought it was interesting, this night job of his. My theory is that he's a bore because he's a shy man but thinks he ought to make conversation and has no gift for it; listening he's probably very good at.

I've bought myself an almond Danish with my coffee because I can see that Malcolm has a pastry and I wouldn't want to make him feel greedy. Also, this means that I can have one without having to self-justify with talk of missing breakfast or having no time for lunch. I sit down opposite him and he eyes me warily. It is true that when I do seek him out it is generally to exhort him about something.

'Well, we seem to have lost the sun,' he says.

I take a bite of my Danish.

'Lovely yesterday,' he goes on doggedly. 'Twenty-three degrees my car registered when I was driving home, but it was only sixteen this morning.'

Does he prepare these conversational gambits, noting the temperatures so he can weave dialogue around them? I go for a clumsy segue.

'Dismal summer altogether,' I say, through a mouthful of almond pastry. 'Depressing. I should think you're busy at the Samaritans, aren't you?'

He looks a bit startled but he rallies. 'Well, the recession, you know. We're always pretty busy these days.'

'I suppose you are.' I take a sip of my coffee. 'I guess you've heard about this young woman on the Eastgate estate?'

He looks uncomfortable. 'On the radio this morning,' he says, taking refuge in a mouthful of cinnamon bun.

'It's a nasty business, isn't it?' I say. 'What do you think happened?'

His discomfort deepens. 'I really don't know,' he says, and looks at his watch.

I know he's not teaching because my wives and I are the only people doing any learning and teaching this week, so I don't allow him to escape.

'I suppose,' I say, 'that she might have been one of your callers – if it turns out to be suicide, I mean.'

'Gina, I really can't disc –'

'Of course not. I know you can't talk about your callers. And it's all anonymous anyway, isn't it? So you wouldn't know if you'd spoken to her, would you?'

He hesitates. 'Well, no,' he says.

'So I was just wondering. I mean, we don't know, obviously, what happened, and it may be she was killed by an ex-partner, but when women kill themselves and their children, why do they do that? I can see that someone could be desperate enough to kill herself even though she has children, but why take them with her? I mean, I think about Sylvia Plath. Before she gassed herself, she put milk and bread and butter in the children's room so they would have something to eat when they woke up, and she stuffed towels under the kitchen door so that the gas wouldn't get out. That I can understand.'

He takes off his glasses and rubs his eyes. 'It's complicated,' he says. 'Mothers who kill themselves often feel that they're failures as mothers. They'll say that the children will be better off without them, but if you're deeply depressed you can't find solutions – you can't see your way through a problem, you can't make arrangements. And if they feel worthless then they can feel that the children are worthless too. Any problems the children have get exaggerated in their minds so that they feel that they'll be better off dead too.

Plath's case is remarkable but she was a remarkable woman. When you read about her last weeks, all the testimony shows that she was fighting her depression all the time and analysing her own state of mind. The discipline of her suicide, the planning – that's very rare. And there's no suggestion that she had been drinking. That's rare too.'

I gaze at him in wonder. Who knew that he could be so eloquent? Boring old Malcolm?

'Suicide is an aggressive act too,' he goes on, 'so killing the children can be revenge on a partner who has abandoned you. That's more common in men as a motive, but women do it sometimes. And sometimes mothers are angry with the children – feel oppressed by them and their responsibility for them.'

'I talked about Sylvia Plath but I've just remembered, Ted Hughes' second wife killed their child as well as herself, didn't she?'

He nods. 'So, there you are.'

'It must be so hard to listen to a caller who is in that state,' I say.

He puts his glasses back on. 'It is,' he says, 'but at least you're doing the job you're there for. We spend a lot of time talking to people who are just a bit sad.'

'But if you've got someone on the phone who's actually talking about killing their children, you have to do something, don't you? I mean, you'd have to call the police to trace the call and—'

'It doesn't work like that.'

'What do you mean?'

He sighs. 'If you thought there really were children at risk, then you'd get a colleague to call the director to decide what to do. But, for a start, you can never be sure that someone is telling you the truth. We get a lot of fantasists. When we're training volunteers we tell them cautionary tales, like the one about the branch that called out air-sea rescue for a guy who said he was about to jump off a cliff, but there was no-one there. People tell you all sorts of things. You have to try and find out what they really want to say.'

'All the same, you must want to do something, surely? I can't—'

'You would make a terrible Samaritan,' he says.

I am astonished. Malcolm has never said anything this personal to me in the ten years we have worked together. And even as I open my mouth to protest I know that what he says is completely true: Samaritans listen rather than talk; they are non-judgemental and they don't tell people what to do. On all counts I would be hopeless. I have to laugh.

'Really?' I ask. 'When I'm so lovely?'

'Sorry,' he says.

'The thing is, Malcolm,' I say, swallowing the last of my coffee, 'I saw Karen Brody here yesterday.'

'What?' He looks around as though her new ghost might be lurking somewhere among the tasteful furnishings of the common room. 'Here?'

'Well, here as in the university nursery. She was collecting her son and she looked – you know – fine. Clean clothes, clean hair, had obviously walked here with a dog. And her daughter looked clean and tidy too. The only odd thing, I suppose, is that she wasn't at the concert the children did, especially when—'

'It's a danger sign,' he says, interrupting my flow.

'What is?'

'When someone seems to be pulling out of a depression. If someone starts clearing up, sorting things out, making plans. Sylvia Plath's friends thought she was getting better because she was making plans for the future.'

'Why? Why is it a danger sign?'

'Because when you're deeply depressed you don't even

have the energy to kill yourself. A bit of energy is dangerous. It may just give you enough drive to do it.'

I walk back to my office by the scenic route – that is to say via Acorns. I would like to go into the garden and try to recreate yesterday's scene, but the gate is locked and the fence is too high to see over, so I stand outside and consider the walk Karen Brody made to and from the Eastgate estate, presumably via her daughter's school. You would need energy for that, with a dog as well, and a tired four-year-old to urge along on the homeward journey. As I'm standing around thinking about this, I hear voices in the garden, and then the gate opens and Paula Powell emerges. Good. Following up on what I told her.

'Hi!' I say, with a friendly little wave.

'What are you doing here?' she asks with an unfriendly scowl.

'Just heading back to my office,' I say, breezily.

'Where from? The Student Union?' she asks, sarcastically.

She heads for her car; I fall into step beside her.

'Anything useful?' I ask.

She says nothing.

'Well, good luck with it,' I say brightly as she opens her car door.

'The boy's not hers,' she says before she gets in and revs away.

5

18.07.12: 11.30

Next of Kin

Gritting her teeth, Paula Powell sped out of the car park. Taking a deep breath, she said to Sarah Shepherd, sitting beside her, 'Don't on any account give that woman any information whatsoever. She'll wheedle it out of you if she possibly can so clam shut. I don't want her anywhere near this. What are those addresses again?'

Sarah glanced down at the two addresses written on the pad lying in her lap. One was for Karen Brody's father, a widower; the other was for Leanne Thomas. 'One in Albert Road,' she said. 'That's the father. And one on the estate. Kendal Way. That's Karen Brody's sister, Leanne Thomas.'

Paula ran over the information Steve Boxer had pulled off the computer that morning: Douglas – or Doug – Brody, Karen's husband, had been known to the police in Liverpool since he hit puberty; he had been in and out of prison and now he was serving an eight-year term for armed robbery. Karen Brody had grown up in Marlbury, had gone to college in Liverpool and settled there, and then had come back, with her daughter, eighteen months previously when her husband had gone to prison. She had just recently moved into a house on the Eastgate estate, where her sister, Leanne, also lived.

Liam was Leanne's son, which explained why he wasn't another victim. Liam's mother suffered from depression, the woman at Acorns had told Paula, and his aunt, Karen, often brought him to nursery and picked him up. So Liam had been dropped safely at home yesterday, Paula assumed, before Karen and Lara went home. And found an intruder waiting for them?

'If Doug Brody's in prison,' she said, 'that rules him out, obviously, but we'll need to go and see him.'

'Has he been told, do you know?'

'The prison governor broke the news to him yesterday. We'll see him in a day or two.'

'She could have had another boyfriend, couldn't she? If her husband's been in prison for eighteen months?'

'She could. I'm wondering about Doug's armed robbery, though. We need to find out if the money from the robbery was recovered. If it wasn't, someone could have been after it and punished Karen for refusing to say where it was.'

'Wouldn't she have told if her daughter was at risk?'

'Probably, but she might not have known where it was.'

She stopped the car first at the address she had for Stanley Thomas. The house, on the outside, was neat but bleak. It was in a terrace of pleasant, solid, between-the-wars houses but where the other front gardens were a high summer flurry of colour, his was gravel from fence to fence, with not a bloom in sight. Inside, too, when he reluctantly allowed them space to sidle in, everything extraneous seemed to have been pruned. They glanced into a sitting room which had no ornaments, no books, no photos, no pictures on the walls. Had he erased all signs of his dead wife because he hated her, Paula wondered, or because he loved her?

He ushered them into the kitchen and half answered her unspoken question. 'Spend most of my time in here,' he said. 'Hard enough to keep the place clean and tidy now the wife's gone. Best to use the one room.' So he had decluttered, she assumed, to a ferocious degree, terrified that the dusting, polishing and gardening would overwhelm him. They sat on hard chairs and looked at each other across a small table in the painfully tidy kitchen but he did not offer them a cup of tea.

He was a thin, stooped man of about sixty and he was all grey: thin grey hair, steel-rimmed glasses and pale eyes, a lean, greyish, seamed face. She looked at the face for signs of grief but found it hard to read.

'I'm so sorry about your daughter, Mr Thomas,' she said, and he took off his glasses and polished them hard with a handkerchief – clean and ironed, she noticed.

'That bastard'll be behind it somehow or other,' he said, 'you mark my words. Nothing's gone right for her since she met him. Nothing. And now this.'

'It's her husband you're talking about? Doug Brody?'

'Husband? She called herself Brody for the girl's sake but they weren't married. Wouldn't expect scum like that to do the decent thing.'

'And were they on bad terms before he went to prison? Are you suggesting he might have wanted Karen and Lara dead?'

'I'm not suggesting anything.' He put his glasses on but kept hold of his handkerchief, kneading it between his fingers. 'I don't know what terms they were on, do I? She was up in Liverpool. We never saw her. Barely a phone call. She was ashamed, of course, as well she might be.'

'How did she meet Doug?'

'She went up to Liverpool for her nursing studies. Wanted to get away from Marlbury. Said it was boring. Wanted somewhere with a bit of life, she said. Well, she soon found out what life's like, didn't she? Pregnant at nineteen and only that scum to rely on.'

'Was it your suggestion that she came back to Marlbury after he went to prison?'

'Her mother wanted her back. She wasn't well. Cancer. She wanted Karen. They were always close.'

'But your other daughter, Leanne. She was here?'

'Oh yes, she was here. But her mother babied her, that one. You couldn't rely on Leanne. Karen was the one – the one we were proud of. We expected things, we –' He broke off and blew his nose. 'What has any of this to do with anything?'

'I'm just trying to get a picture of Karen's life – and what sort of state she was in emotionally. We don't yet know, you see, whether –'

'Don't try and tell me she killed herself. That's what that policewoman tried to tell me, the one who came yesterday. And killed Lara? She'd have done anything for that child. And she'd no reason to kill herself. That bastard was behind bars and she was making a new start, doing well at the university. She was a bright girl was Karen.'

'When did you last see her, Mr Thomas?'

'Saturday. I went round there for tea. It makes me sick to think of both my daughters living on that estate, but she kept the house nice did Karen.'

'And how did she seem? Was she depressed at all, or worried?'

He looked down at the handkerchief in his hands and folded it and put it away before he answered. 'I said to her she looked pale. I asked her if she was all right. She said she had some things worrying her. I didn't ask what and she didn't tell me. But that doesn't mean she was going to kill herself, does it? We all have worries. We don't ... do that.'

'She didn't give any hint of what was worrying her?'

'No.'

Sarah Shepherd spoke for the first time. 'Did she have a boyfriend? I mean, a new boyfriend, other than Doug.'

'Not that I knew.'

'She didn't mention anyone? In the past year and a half?'

'No. That scumbag. He was the only one.'

Leanne Thomas's flat was on the second floor of a small block at the far end of the estate. The stairs to it were litter-strewn and smelly and her front door was scabby and pockmarked. There was no bell or knocker so Sarah banged hard with a fist. No-one came but they could hear a television inside so she banged again and shouted, 'Leanne. Open the door, please. Marlbury police.'

Eventually they heard the shuffling of feet and the sounds of keys turning and bolts being released.

'What's with all the security?' Paula asked as the door was opened.

The young woman behind the door shrugged. 'Can't be too careful round here,' she said. 'Did anyone see you come in?'

'Why?'

'Never mind.'

The flat inside was better than the approach to it suggested. It was cramped and cluttered with toys and magazines, and there were clothes drying on a rack in the sitting room, but the window was open, and there was no smell of cigarettes or drink. There were some pop concert posters on the walls and a supermarket-style bunch of flowers in a vase on the coffee table. Leanne herself was a strikingly pretty girl, Paula thought, hardly a woman – not more than twenty probably. She was wearing tracksuit bottoms and flip-flops and her hair hadn't been brushed, but she was slim and blonde and would look good dressed up.

'Sit down,' she said, flopping down onto the sofa. 'I suppose this is about Karen?'

'Yes.' Paula glanced at Sarah, who detached herself to sit on a chair at the table in the corner, while she sat in the only armchair, opposite Leanne, and examined her for signs of grief, as she had her father. She was pale, but not puffy-eyed. Wary, her eyes were, and a bit scared, she thought. 'I'm very sorry about Karen,' she said.

'Yeah.' Leanne pulled her legs up onto the sofa and hugged her knees. 'Well, you have to say that, don't you? It's in the script.'

'Were you and Karen close?' Paula asked.

'Course we were. We were sisters, weren't we?'

'Not all sisters are close.'

'Well we were.'

'Karen was a few years older than you, wasn't she?'

'Yeah. So?'

'And she was away for a long time in Liverpool. Did you use to go and see her up there?'

'Yeah. What's wrong with that?'

'Nothing. Nothing's wrong. I'm just trying to get a picture. We need to know what was going on in Karen's mind. Was she missing Doug, for example?'

'Missing him? Nah. She was over him. She was obsessed with him in the early days, even when he screwed up, but now, no, she just wanted the best for Lara. She was doing this course at the university – medical secretary. She wanted a proper job.'

'Was she worried about anything?'

'Worried?' Her voice was sharp. 'What'd she got to be worried about?'

'I don't know. You tell me.'

'She wasn't worried.'

Sarah Shepherd asked, 'She used to look after Liam for you, didn't she?'

'A bit, yes. What's wrong with that?'

'She used to take Liam to nursery?'

'Sometimes. When she was going into the uni anyway.'

'Where do you work, Leanne?' Paula asked.

'I don't.' She lowered her head onto her knees. 'I'm on antidepressants. I can't work.'

Depression. That was what Caroline at the nursery had said, Paula thought, but this girl didn't look depressed. Discontented, maybe, and bored. *Her mother babied her*, her father had said. *You couldn't rely on Leanne.* No, Karen was the one they all relied on – Karen, who had plenty of problems of her own.

'It must be expensive to send Liam to nursery if you aren't working,' she commented.

'Karen paid. It's only a couple of afternoons a week. I need a break from him, stuck in here.'

'So Karen had plenty of money?'

'She had a student loan and she was a good manager.' She laughed. 'You think she was spending the money they robbed? 'Fraid not. No. 'Fraid not.'

As they got up to leave, Sarah Shepherd asked, 'So where's Liam today?'

Leanne snapped to her feet, immediately aggressive. 'Downstairs with Carole, my neighbour. Anything wrong with that?'

'And Liam's dad?' Paula asked, 'Is he around?'

'Oh, Liam's dad!' Leanne said, putting on a performance of scratching her head in puzzlement. 'Do I know where he is? Can I even remember what he looks like? No, I don't think I can.' She sank back onto the sofa. 'He's long gone,' she said. 'Long gone.'

They let themselves out.

6

19.07.12: 09.15

Handover

'Really, sir, I feel I can handle it. There's no need for DCI Scott to —'

'This is not a matter for discussion, DS Powell. I am sorry that the information found its way to the press before I had a chance to speak to you but DCI Scott has been released from his secondment and he takes over this case as of now.' The chief superintendent's tone was brisk. 'The forensic evidence is pointing in the direction of a double murder and one of the victims is a child. This is not a case to be led by a DS, however confident she may be of her abilities.'

Putting down the receiver, Paula Powell looked for something to hurl. She was sitting at David Scott's desk and her hand lighted on a paperweight that looked like excellent hurling material. She put it down, however, because it was a golden amber and had a fossilised creature of some kind trapped inside it, and because this wasn't David's fault. Instead, she said, 'fuck' several times and went out into the main office to talk to Sarah Shepherd.

'Off the case?' Sarah asked, looking at her face.

'Overruled. David's taking over.'

'But we're still on it?'

'Well, there's nobody else, is there, except us and Steve and the two uniforms? I suppose we'll get some reinforcements but there'd be no reason to drop us.'

'We'll want an incident room.'

'Yup.'

'We could get one set up ready.'

Paula looked at her. 'OK, I get the message. Show willing. Don't sulk. Be a team player. It's what women do all the time, Sarah. And where does it get us? Bloody nowhere. We just go on being used as dogsbodies and the sodding men walk off with all the prizes.'

Sarah stood up. 'I've written up my interview with Karen Brody's neighbour,' she said. 'David'll want that. I'll go and find Steve and tell him what's going on.'

When David Scott walked in two hours later he found Paula brisk, polite and patently furious. 'Sorry about this,' he said and got a resigned shrug in reply.

He looked round the incident room. 'You're well set up here,' he said. 'Good. What are you working on, Steve?'

Steve Boxer looked round from his computer screen. 'Known associates of Karen Brody's husband,' he said.

'Has anyone talked to the husband?' Scott asked Paula.

'Not yet. We've not had —'

'Fine. Fine. Looks like a job for me.' He looked at the file she had handed him. 'Come into my office,' he said, 'and talk me through all of this.'

'Coffee?' Sarah Shepherd called out as they were leaving.

'Fantastic!' Scott called back.

In his office, he pulled a chair round to his side of the desk so that they could look through the papers together.

'OK,' he said. 'The chief super emailed me some of this so I read it on the train. Karen Brody, age twenty-six, found dead, with her seven-year-old daughter, Lara, by a neighbour – Tina

Smith – at approximately 1800 hours on Tuesday evening. Lara Brody was suffocated and Karen Brody bled to death from wounds to both wrists. Initial picture looks like a murder and a suicide by a depressed mother but there was no history of depression and forensics suggest otherwise.' Flicking through the file, he pulled out a copy of the forensic report and glanced through it. 'One: Karen Brody's DNA and fingerprints were on the pillow used to suffocate Lara, and on Lara's clothes, but the pattern doesn't suggest the kind of force that would be used to press a pillow down hard enough to stifle a seven-year-old. Two: Karen Brody's blood alcohol level was very high – consistent with her having drunk at least half of the bottle of gin found in her house. Her saliva was found on the neck of the gin bottle but no fresh fingerprints on the bottle, and the glass that was with the bottle showed traces of gin but no traces of her DNA or anyone else's.'

'In other words,' Paula said, 'someone forced the gin into her and poured some gin into the glass to make it look as though she'd used it.'

'Which brings us to point three: her T-shirt was soaked in gin round the neck area and there was bruising around and inside her mouth, suggesting that the bottle was forced into her mouth.'

'There was other bruising as well,' Paula said. 'Look.' She pointed at the forensic report.

'Recent and older. Bruising from several days before, mainly on the upper arms. As though someone had taken hold of her and shaken her. And bruising to the side of her face, suggesting she had been slapped hard.'

They looked at each other. 'All of which,' Scott said, 'suggests a violent partner or ex-partner, but her husband, Doug Brody —'

'Karen's father said they weren't actually married,' Paula interrupted.

'OK, partner. He is Lara's father, though?'

'As far as we know.'

'Well, we should check that. Anyway, he's serving eight years in The Scrubs, so he didn't do it himself, but let's see who Steve comes up with in the way of criminal associates. And we need to find out if she had another boyfriend.'

'Her father and her sister both say not. I was planning to talk to other people who were on her course with her at the university.'

Scott shuffled through the pages on the desk. 'Medical secretary course,' he said. 'I doubt she met many men there, but someone might know something.'

'I was going to put Sarah onto that,' she said.

He opened his mouth to say something, changed his mind, and smiled. 'Good idea,' he said. 'So, you and I will go and see Tina Smith's boyfriend. She told Sarah that he works nights and had already gone to work when she went round and found Karen and Lara dead. And he couldn't talk to Sarah because he was asleep. I think we'll go and wake him up. And this afternoon we'll go to The Scrubs and talk to Doug Brody. Can you give the governor a ring and let him know we're coming?'

'We need a local search,' Paula said. 'I put the resources we had into a house-to-house in the street but we got nothing. The guy must have had a lot of blood on him, though, with the dog as well, so he'll have wanted to get rid of stuff.'

'Dog?' Scott queried.

'The family dog was killed. Throat cut, probably with the same knife as was used on Karen.' She looked at him. 'It's all in there,' she said accusingly, tapping her report. 'And it's further evidence that it wasn't a suicide. No dog-owner who cared about their dog would kill it like that. They'd find a more humane way.'

'OK,' Scott said. 'Well, I missed the dog. On our way to The

Scrubs this afternoon you can tell me what else I've missed. If there is more?'

Paula hesitated. 'No,' she said. 'I think that's about it.'

'I've asked for reinforcements to join the team. We'll get them onto the search. Let's hope the bins on the estate haven't been emptied yet.'

In the incident room, they found his reinforcements, two DCs hovering behind Steve Boxer, looking at his computer screen.

'Anything on Doug Brody's friends, Steve?' Scott asked.

'Lowlifes, small-time. Brody was always small-time too, before the latest. Started at fourteen. Car thefts, petty burglaries, a bit of dealing, the odd affray. Armed robbery was in a new league for him.'

'Where was the robbery?'

'Petrol Station in Liverpool. Not clever. He wasn't masked and he was caught on CCTV.'

'Liverpool? So why is he in The Scrubs?'

'He requested a transfer down south when Karen and Lara moved here. He was moved five months ago.'

'And the money?'

'Never recovered.'

'When was he convicted?'

'December 2010.'

'OK. Check his associates. See if any of them have been in this area. Paula and I are going to The Scrubs to see him this afternoon so we'll check on what visitors he's had.'

He turned to the two DCs. 'Morning,' he said. 'DCI Scott.'

'DC Mike Arthur, sir,' the older of the two said.

'DC Darren Floyd.' The younger man was good-looking, Scott registered, but surly, he thought.

'Eastgate estate,' he said. 'You're looking for a knife, though I doubt you'll find it, and bloodstained clothing or whatever he used to clean himself up. Gardens, sheds, bins, the usual. DS Powell here will give you the details. Start with the bins.' He saw a flash of disgust on the face of the younger of the two men. 'That's both of you on the bins,' he said, looking him in the eye. 'They keep their bins in the front gardens on the estate and this guy left through the front door – SOCO found bloody footsteps on the front path.'

'And no-one saw him?' the older DC asked. 'At six o'clock on a summer evening?'

'This is the Eastgate estate we're talking about,' Paula Powell said. 'Thirteen Windermere Road you're going to. You won't miss it – it's got the usual decorations.'

'*Windermere Road*. Someone's idea of a joke,' Darren Floyd muttered as the two men left the room.

'We'll see you there,' Paula called to them. 'We're off to have another talk to the neighbour.'

At Eleven Windermere Road, Scott and Powell found that the bell didn't function but some hammering on the door brought a woman to open it. She was carrying a small child and had another, about the same age, Paula thought, tugging on the leg of her jeans. She looked tired, belligerent and older than she probably was.

'What?' she asked, and when they showed their IDs she glanced involuntarily back into the house.

'Tina Smith?' Scott asked.

'I talked to the other one,' she said. 'I made a statement.'

'You did,' Scott said pleasantly, 'and it was very helpful. We'd just like to check a few things with you, and to talk to your boyfriend, Jason.'

'He can't tell you nothing. He wasn't here.'

'Still, we'd like to talk to him.'

'Well you can't. He's not here.'

'Where is he?'

'He's at work.'

'I understood from what you told DC Shepherd that he works nights,' Paula said. 'That's why he wasn't here on Tuesday evening.'

'Well …' the woman's pale face flushed '… yeah, that's right. So now he's asleep.'

'I think,' Scott said, 'that we'd better go inside, don't you?'

Reluctantly, Tina Smith stood back to let them in and they went into a small sitting room where a teenage boy was lying on a sofa pushing buttons on a mobile phone.

'School's finished,' Tina said defensively. 'He's on holiday. Go in the kitchen, Gary,' she said. 'We're talking in here.'

As the boy shambled out, Paula said, 'Don't go out, though, Gary. We'll need to talk to you later.' She just caught his mumbled obscenity as he left the room.

'Right,' Scott said as they sat down. 'First, let me say that I realise that you had a very nasty shock finding things as you did on Tuesday.'

'You're telling me,' she said. 'Not that I got any sympathy.' She was sitting on the sofa with a child either side of her, both leaning into her, both sucking their thumbs, both gazing at Scott with solemn faces.

'Shock can do funny things,' Scott continued, 'and we don't always remember things clearly as a result, so I would just like to take you through your statement to DC Shepherd and see if there's anything you want to add or change.' She seemed about to protest but he carried on. 'You say you went next door at about six o'clock because the TV was too loud and you wanted it turned down.'

'Yeah.'

He smiled. 'With a teenage boy in the house and the two little ones I guess it gets quite loud in this house sometimes, doesn't it?'

'Gary's a good boy,' she said. 'Quiet.'

'Did you often have to complain about noise next door?'

'No. That's the thing. These houses, the walls are like paper but we never heard it usually. The dog sometimes. She'd just got it, two or three weeks back. It was her sister's but her sister couldn't cope with it. Can't cope with nothing that one. But anyway, I'd had a sodding awful day with these two grizzling and fighting and I wanted them in bed and asleep. I was just giving them their tea and I could hear this racket and I knew I'd never get them off.'

'Your … Jason wasn't here?'

'He went out just before.'

'To work?'

'Yes.'

'Where does he work?'

'Well …' her head went up and they all felt the presence of Jason sleeping above them. 'It's … you'll have to ask him.'

'I will. Let's go back to you. You went round to complain about the noise. Did you leave the children here?'

'I got Gary to mind them.'

'And how did you get into the house?'

'The door wasn't locked. I knocked and yelled and then I tried the handle and it opened.'

'And where did you go first in the house?'

'Into the sitting room. I called out like, and then I went in there 'cos that's where the TV was.'

'And what did you find.'

'Her. She was like slumped on the sofa and there was all this blood.'

'Could you see that her wrists were cut?'

'I didn't get close. I just saw all the blood.'

'And then what did you do?'

'I ran out. I thought someone might still be there in the house. I ran out. And then I rang you lot.'

'You didn't look for Lara?'

'No.'

'And you didn't go in the kitchen?'

'No. I know what happened. I seen it on the news, Lara and the dog, but I never saw them. I just ran out.'

They all turned at the sound of feet on the stairs and the door was pushed open to reveal a man in sweatpants and a T-shirt. The two children, Paula noticed, leaned further into their mother, eying him warily. Jason Watts was a big man, muscly and shaven-headed. You had to avoid stereotyping in this business, Paula knew, but she was prepared to bet that his night job involved throwing people out of clubs or pubs.

Jason surveyed them. 'What's this?' he asked, looking not at Scott and Powell but at Tina.

She got up and edged past him through the doorway, the two children scuttling after her. 'They're here about Karen, Jase,' she said, not looking him in the eye. 'You'll have to talk to them. I don't know what to … you know …' her voice tailed off and she disappeared.

Scott and Powell stood up. 'DCI Scott and DS Powell,' Scott said as they flashed their cards. 'We'd like to talk to you about your movements on the afternoon and evening of Tuesday 17th July. Shall we sit down?'

Jason remained standing in the doorway. 'This is my house,' he said. 'No-one asked you to sit down.'

Scott walked across to the window and looked out, noting that DCs Arthur and Floyd were at work on the bins next door. 'That's fine,' he said, 'but I wonder why you want to hide behind that door.'

Jason Watts swaggered into the room. 'I don't hide,' he said. 'Ain't no-one can accuse me of that.' He sat down on the sofa, spreading his arms along the back. 'Go on then,' he said. 'Park your arses if you want to.'

'Where is it you work?' Scott asked as he went back to his chair.

Paula could see the colour rise in the man's face, under the tanned skin. 'It's not like work,' he said. 'Not like a job. I just help out a bit.'

'And where is that?' Paula asked.

'It's just a club,' he mumbled.

'And you do what? Bartender? Bouncer?'

'Whatever, bit of everything.'

'Name of the club?'

Jason Watts shifted uncomfortably. 'Look, it's not a job as such,' he said. 'Not like official.'

Paula exchanged glances with Scott and he gave the slightest of nods.

'Jason, if you're working while claiming jobseeker's allowance, we're not interested,' she said. 'We're not out to make trouble for you but we're investigating two deaths here and we need your full cooperation, and if we don't get it then we'll have you for obstruction. OK?'

He leaned forward, his hands on his knees. 'And I'm supposed to trust you, am I?'

'No choice, I'm afraid,' Scott said breezily, standing up. 'So you give us the name of the club, we'll check when you got there and we'll go on from there.'

Jason stood too. 'The Caz Bar,' he said, throwing it out like a challenge.

Paula suppressed a snarl. The Caz Bar was Marlbury's newly opened lap dancing club, operating in a basement beneath a hairdressers only a stone's throw from Marlbury Abbey and given the go-ahead by the town council despite howls of protest from all sorts of people from the shocked elderly to student feminists. Paula herself had taken part in a protest march and vigil outside the town hall.

Scott made a show of writing down the name. 'How did you get on with Karen?' he asked. 'Did you like her?'

'Not much, if I'm honest. Too up herself with no good reason.'

'Did you ever do odd jobs for her?'

'Like what?'

Scott looked at the blank incomprehension on his face. 'Did you ever go into her house at all?' he asked.

'No. Why would I?'

'Just being neighbourly?'

Jason shook his head in pitying disbelief. 'You people,' he said.

Driving to Hammersmith in sullen drizzle, Scott said, 'If I'd realised, we could have done this interview this morning before I left London. But at that point I hadn't read up on the case.'

Paula said nothing. He let the silence linger for a moment and then said, 'I should have phoned you.'

'It would have helped,' she said.

'Yup.' He decided not to say he was sorry again. She wasn't experienced or senior enough to be SIO on this case and at some time she'd probably acknowledge that. She was disappointed, of course, but she was going to have to get over it. He drove on in silence.

When the great prison gates opened for them and they drove in between its ornate towers, the officer on duty said, 'The governor would like to speak to you, sir, if you'd go up to his office.' He indicated a direction in the far corner of the courtyard.

The governor, new since Scott's last visit to the prison, was a lean, shortish man with a leathery, creased face that suggested that he spent his leisure time tramping moors or climbing mountains, as well one might, Scott thought, if one spent one's working days in a place like this. He greeted them briskly and said, 'I wanted to warn you, Brody reacted badly to the news. Became violent, had to be restrained.' He gave a blink of mild embarrassment. 'Fairly roughly, it turns out, but he attacked an officer and that calls for strong measures.'

'Where is he now?'

'In the infirmary. Purely precautionary. He took a knock to the head and he's under sedation.'

'And we're seeing him there?'

'Unless you have any objection?'

'No. As long as we have privacy.'

'Of course.'

Brody was in a room hardly bigger than a cubicle. He was propped on pillows with his head turned away from the door and as they entered he didn't move to look at them. Two chairs had been set at the near side of the bed. 'Mr Brody,' Scott said, sitting down.

Brody didn't move and Scott was able to take in the dressing taped to the side of his head and the scabbed knuckles of his right hand. Paula, who had moved to the end of the bed, was able to see a bruised cheekbone and a black eye. They waited and eventually Brody turned his head to look first at Paula and then at Scott. Close to him as he was, Scott was taken aback, in spite of the governor's warning, by the fury in the man's eyes. The face was puffy and slackened by sedation but the eyes were so venomous that he felt glad of the panic button on the wall and the two officers posted outside.

'Let me say first of all,' he said, 'how sorry we are for your loss.'

Brody's mouth moved as though he was trying to speak, but he said nothing and Scott saw that he was trying to gather enough saliva in a dry mouth to spit at him. He decided to be brisk and get this over with.

'We believe,' he said, 'that both Karen and Lara were murdered, and we are, of course, making every effort to find their killer. The killer may be someone you know, so we need you to tell us anything you can that might help.'

Brody's eyes continued to bore into him but he said nothing. Scott wondered if he was too drugged to be able to speak. 'The money from the bank hold-up,' he said. 'You've never told the police where it is. We think Karen could have been killed by someone who wanted that money.'

Brody made a rough wheezing sound which they recognised after a moment as a rudimentary bark of laughter. 'Haven't got it,' he slurred. 'Didn't take it.'

Paula came and sat down beside him. 'Prisons are full of people who 'didn't do' what they're in for, Doug,' she said. 'If we're going to find out who killed Karen and Lara, you're going to have to level with us.'

Brody shifted the heat of his gaze to her. 'Fucking idle. Fucking stupid,' he said, and now Scott could hear the Liverpool in his voice. Gina, he thought, would know the technical terms for those clotted consonants and curdled vowels. Gina. He would have to let her know he was back in Marlbury. But not today. Not while he had all this to get a hold on. Momentarily distracted, he realised that Brody was still speaking.

'Too fucking stupid, too fucking idle to do their job. Easier to finger me. Plenty of previous. Easy fit-up.'

'You were recorded on CCTV, Doug, committing the robbery.'

'Mistaken id –' he broke off and shook his head as though 'identity' was too much for his drugged tongue to manage.

'So, if it wasn't you, Doug, who was it?' Paula asked, leaning in towards him.

His mouth worked for a few moments. 'Your job,' he said finally. 'I couldn't say.' He closed his eyes and turned his head from them.

As they were leaving the room, they heard a sound from the bed and turned. Brody's face was turned to them, contorted in a rictus of grief. 'I wasn't there for them,' he said. 'I wasn't there.'

Having talked briefly to the senior prison officer on Brody's wing, they drove out of London, beating the early Friday exodus.

'This shouldn't be too bad,' Scott said.

'Plenty to talk about, anyway.'

'Really?' He glanced at her.

'Well, we know that Brody requested a transfer to the Southeast so that his wife and daughter could visit, and that they didn't miss a single visiting day.'

'Which could mean that they were terrified of him and he was pulling the strings.'

'Except that he's genuinely distraught. Don't tell me he was putting that on.'

'*And I must be from thence,*' he said.

'Shakespeare?' she asked.

'Macbeth. It's what Macduff says when he hears that Macbeth has murdered his wife and children.'

'And this gets us where, exactly?'

'Nowhere,' he said. 'Nowhere at all. But the mistaken identity thing, what was the evidence against him, do you know? Apart from the CCTV footage?'

'There was some DNA evidence but the defence brought in a forensics expert to question it. He'd sprayed tiny specks of saliva into the face of the bank cashier but it was quite degraded.'

'And the CCTV pictures, how good were they?'

'The guy was wearing a beanie pulled well down, and a scarf pulled up, so it wasn't conclusive, but he was picked out in an identity parade.'

'No fingerprints?'

'No. Gloves.'

'So it's possible that he didn't do it, but someone thought Karen knew where the money was. When she wouldn't say, he killed her.'

'And Lara? Why? It doesn't make sense to me. If there'd been signs that someone had tortured her ...'

'No. It doesn't make a lot of sense. But the chances are our killer is someone Brody knows."

'I'm not writing Jason Watts off,' she said. 'I want to check his alibi. He's a nasty piece of work and his girlfriend and children are scared stiff of him.'

'You pursue that. We need to talk to Karen's friends and fellow students as well, and go through Steve's list of Brody's criminal associates. Anything else you can think of?'

'There was an episode with the dog,' she said, 'but we can leave that for another day.'

7

Thursday 19th July

Counter Intelligence

When I go in to teach my wives on Thursday afternoon, I find a major international incident going on. I thought we had got past this sort of thing and arrived at a modus vivendi. In my pious, liberal, deluded mind, we had reached an East–West, Christian–Muslim–humanist fusion in which we acknowledged and respected difference and celebrated diversity et cetera, et cetera, et cetera. Apparently not. This afternoon, Athene is in full oratorical mode, thumping her fist on the table and looking rather magnificent. Juanita, sitting beside her, has her head down and her hands over her ears as Athene yells across her at Farah and Jamilleh, who are, I see, wrapped in their coats and headscarves once more. Our blundering intruder on Tuesday did his work thoroughly. Farah is scowling at what I see is today's edition of the *Marlbury Herald* and Jamilleh is glaring at Athene with tears in her eyes. Ning Wu has retreated to a corner at the back of the room and is busying herself with her iPad. No-one seems to notice my entrance.

'You are ridiculous!' Athene is shouting. 'Ri-di-cu-lous. Because it's murder it's a man's job? Why? He is more intelligent? Women are more stupid? No. You are stupid, yes, but all women? No!'

'Are you saying, Athene,' I ask, banging my books down on my desk to attract their attention, 'that it takes intelligence to be a murderer?'

She stares at me blankly. 'No!' she says. 'When did I say that?'

'For the policeman,' Jamilleh says, wiping the tears from her eyes. 'For the police must be intelligent. But I never said … I never said …' she gives a venomous look at Athene '… men more intelligent than women. And I am NOT stupid!'

I sit down. 'Well,' I say, in the bright, soothing tone I sometimes use to Freda, 'I'm a bit behind the curve here, but I'm sure Athene doesn't think you're stupid, Jamilleh, and in a bit when we've all calmed down, I'm sure she'll want to apologise.' I shoot Athene a warning glance as she gives a great huff of fury. 'Juanita,' I continue, 'I think it's safe to put your head over the parapet. No-one's going to shoot you. And Ning Wu, do please come and join us. I don't think there'll be any more fireworks.'

Why am I speaking in metaphors? *Parapet*? *Fireworks*? Normally I would write the words on the board and unpack the metaphors but I don't think this is the moment so I let it go. I turn to Farah. 'I take it,' I say, 'that you were talking about the murder case?'

Farah nods and passes the paper across to me. The deaths of Karen and Lara Brody are the front-page story. They have been reported in the national press, and from there I learned little more than I knew already, except that Karen Brody's common-law husband is in prison for armed robbery, but the *Herald* has breaking news in a *Stop Press* box, in bold. '*The Herald understands*,' I read out loud, '*that in the light of forensic evidence the police are treating the case as a double murder inquiry. Detective Chief Inspector David Scott has taken over the inquiry, replacing DS Paula Powell, who was leading it initially.*'

'Well!' I say, taking off my glasses and laying them on the

desk. And then, 'Would you excuse me for a moment?' I ask, and get my head down to rummage in my bag. This allows me some recovery time but I am also looking for my phone. *David Scott has taken over the inquiry.* When did that happen? How long has he been in Marlbury? When was he planning to tell me he was back? Is it just possible that he has been phoning or texting and I have missed his calls?

The answer to this last is *no*, as in my heart I knew. I put my phone away and turn the full beam of my attention back to my class.

'So,' I say, 'the subject of your heated debate was whether a man makes a better detective in a murder inquiry than a woman does. Is that right, Jamilleh?'

Colour rises in Jamilleh's face. 'I didn't say *better*,' she insists, with a glare at Athene, who, all passion spent, has reverted to looking bored. 'I said is more suitable for a man. Murder is not so nice for a woman.'

'Ah, *nice*! We talked about *nice* the other day. What did we say?'

Ning Wu comes to life. 'English people use a lot. It is safe word.' She executes an operation on her iPad. '*All-purpose word*,' she reads.

'Exactly. Brainstorm. What kinds of things can we describe as *nice*?'

They rouse themselves to their task.

'Nice weather!'

'Nice day!'

'Nice meal!'

'Nice holiday!'

'Nice view!'

'Nice person!'

'Good, yes.' I hold up a stalling hand. 'Nice person. So Jamilleh thinks Detective Sergeant Powell might be too nice to investigate a murder, but Chief Inspector Scott is maybe not

55

so nice, because he's a man.' If they have spotted my shameless piece of sophistry here no-one raises an objection. 'As a matter of fact,' I continue, 'I know Chief Inspector Scott and he is quite nice. If you met him you would think he was very nice, but maybe he's not as nice as he seems.'

I turn to Athene. 'Athene thinks he needs to be intelligent, and he certainly is that. But there are different kinds of intelligence, aren't there, Juanita?' Juanita gives a start as I intended that she should. She is unimpressed by my peroration and is sending a surreptitious text message. 'Emotional intelligence, Juanita. What do you think that means?'

'Maybe understanding how people feel?' she asks.

'Exactly. And at the risk of starting another row, I'd say that women are often better at that. Better at relationships altogether. Better at understanding, at trust and commitment. Men can be disappointing in that way.' I'm keeping my voice light and level, swallowing the curdle of venom in my throat, but I see a flicker of alarm in some eyes at the slightly startling turn this class is taking. 'And now,' I say, 'we'll do the grammar test I promised.' I distribute photocopied sheets. 'Question forms. Fill in the gaps with the right question. Mostly in class you answer questions. Now it's your chance to ask them.'

I have a meeting to finalise September resit papers immediately after the class, so I don't get back to my office till five thirty and only then do I have the opportunity to ring David. I decide not to call his mobile because on that he can pretend to be anywhere. Instead I call his direct line at the police station and he picks up.

'David Scott.' He sounds preoccupied and unwary.

'Really?' I ask.

'I'm sorry?'

'Can that really be David Scott? That same David Scott

who is at present in London, working with the Metropolitan Police, and cannot possibly have been teleported to Marlbury without bothering to inform the woman who has, possibly mistakenly, come to regard herself as his nearest and dearest.'

'Gina.'

'Yes, Gina. Remember me?'

'Gina —'

'When were you going to let me know you were back?'

'I —'

'When?'

There is a pause. I think I hear him sit down. I wait.

'How about,' he says eventually, '*Hello David. You must have had a hard day, taking over a double murder inquiry at a moment's notice, especially one involving a child, with all the distress that brings, not to mention the extra press interest. And then Paula must be pissed off having the case taken away from her so she can't be easy to work with, and you won't have enough officers on your team because of all the cuts, so I guess all in all you're having a pretty shitty time and I wonder what I can do to make you feel better?*'

Just for a moment I think my righteous anger might ooze away but I'm made of more obdurate stuff.

'Well,' I say, 'I don't think I will say that because you are, in fact, just doing your job and it's what you get paid for – handsomely. The deaths of a young woman and a child – that's horrible, but much worse for Paula, who actually saw the bodies, so don't forget that. However, I am prepared to concede that it's been a busy time and it is understandable that ringing me slipped down your list of priorities, but you could have rung me last night.'

'I didn't know last night.'

'But it said in the *Herald* —'

'The assistant commissioner rang me this morning.'

'So the press knew before you did. What a brilliant organisation the police force is.'

'I drove down from London first thing, and then drove to Wormwood Scrubs and back this afternoon to interview a prisoner, so I'm—'

'Yes, yes. Poor you. I would offer you a quiet supper at my house but there is no quiet there. The house is full of youf.'

'Full of what?'

'*Youf.* The young. Annie's friends. Staying in my house for an unspecified period, stripping my fridge and pantry with the effrontery of biblical locusts. If you want to see me, you're going to have to take me out to eat.'

'I was just going to pick up some fish and chips tonight. I'll give you a ring tomorrow.'

'I could come for fish and chips too. We could eat them in the car and then snog.'

'Fine.'

'I wasn't serious.'

'Shame.'

'I'll talk to you tomorrow. Did Paula tell you about the dog?'

'This dog keeps cropping up but I haven't had the full story.'

'I can tell you. I saw it. I was an eye witness.'

There is a lengthy pause.

'Of course you were,' he says, and he sounds very, very tired.

8

Saturday 21st July

Kitchen-Sink Drama and Apron Stage

I am not prepared to involve myself in the indolent Saturday morning habits of Annie and her posse. I don't want to be party to messy fry-ups and people eating in their pyjamas and getting bacon fat on my *Guardian*, so I'm up as soon as the paper arrives and off with it to The Pumpkin, the off-beat organic café that forms an integral part of my Saturday morning ritual. I used to meet my friend, Eve, here for morning coffee but she's living in Ireland now, blown west by a storm of scandal a couple of years ago, so now I usually go on my own. This morning, however, I text David before I leave the house. He has not been in touch since our conversation on Thursday afternoon – not even to follow up on my sighting of Karen and Lara on Tuesday – and I am still fairly annoyed with him but I decide to give him another chance. My text is breezy and cool: *Prepared to bet you have nothing in for breakfast. I will be in The Pumpkin from 9.30. Join me?*

Sitting in the café's front window, watching the town beginning to come to life, I order coffee with a jug of hot milk and a granola square that comes laden with nuts and dried fruit and is as big as the plate it sits on. David has not replied to my text but he soon appears, dressed not for weekend slouching but for work.

'Hi,' he says, sitting down opposite me without a greeting kiss. 'Paula will be here in a minute. She's just parking.'

'What?' I choke so hard on my granola square that I think I may need him to perform the Heimlich manoeuvre on me. *The closest we're likely to get to physical contact* I think grimly as I recover and swallow some soothing coffee.

'It's a work day, Gina,' he says in a tone one uses to an unreasonable child. 'We're talking to you as a witness.'

'Paula's heard it before.'

'And she's filled me in and we both want to ask you some questions.'

'Would you like some of this granola thing?' I ask. 'I can't possibly manage all of —'

'No thanks,' he says.

He summons the waitress. 'Poached eggs on toast for two,' he says, 'and more coffee.'

'I don't want poached eggs,' I protest.

'They're for Paula.'

'How do you know that's what she wants?'

'I asked her.'

'And she said, *I'll have whatever you're having.* How sweet.'

He doesn't reply and Paula soon appears, also crisply turned out in jacket and trousers for a work day. She sits down next to David so that the two of them are looking across the table at me in full interview mode.

'Hi,' she says to me, and then to David, 'Have you ordered?'

'Poached eggs.'

'Perfect.'

I think I may be going to be sick.

'So, Gina,' David says, 'you saw Karen and Lara Brody on Tuesday afternoon with their dog —'

'Billy,' I say

'What?'

'Billy. The dog was called Billy.'

'Right. Well, I think that's a detail we can do without. What time exactly did you see them?'

'Around four o'clock, I suppose.'

'The manager of the nursery confirmed that,' Paula tells David.

'Good thing you're here to check up on me,' I tell her. She ignores me.

'Did Karen look as though she had been drinking?' David asks.

I consider. 'It didn't cross my mind that she had,' I say. 'I'd never seen her before so I had nothing to compare with but she looked quite normal.'

'But she didn't attend the performance by the children that the rest of you were at?'

'She could hardly have taken the dog in, could she? Anyway, she was just picking up a child – Liam – who wasn't hers, I gather.' I give Paula a non-smile.

The eggs and coffee arrive and the interview is suspended. I pick at my granola square and watch them eat. I've never been a big fan of eggs, and this morning, as I look at the yolks running over the plates and being mopped up with toast, I find them truly revolting. I would take myself off to the loo but I know they'll talk about me while I'm gone, so I sip my coffee and look out of the window.

'So,' David says eventually, 'once the dog was back on its lead, what did the woman do then?'

'Which woman?'

'The woman in the burqa.'

'Technically, it wasn't a burqa,' I say. 'I explained to Paula. It was a niqab. The difference is that a niq—'

'I think we're sticking to burqa,' David says. 'Keeps things simple.'

'Simple's the word,' I mutter into my coffee.

'So what happened to her?'

'She hobbled off.'

'Hobbled?'

'Yes. It looked as though she had a bad leg – or hip.'

'So she wasn't young?'

'I don't think so. I thought she must be a grandmother.'

'And she was on her own?'

'As far as I could see. She certainly left on her own. One of my students went after her to try and help but she didn't seem to want help.'

'Who was the student?'

'Jamilleh Hamidi. She's Iranian.'

'I'd like to talk to her.'

'You'll need to be careful. Her husband won't like the police coming to talk to his wife. Remember that time with the Turkish wives?'

'It might be better if you talk to her, Paula,' David says. 'Maybe you could talk to her at the college, with Gina there to help?'

He turns from her to raise a questioning eyebrow at me. I turn back to the window. 'Maybe,' I say.

'And we need to track down the woman in the bur—niqab,' he says.

'The staff at the nursery didn't know who she was,' Paula puts in. 'They thought she must be someone's grandmother.'

'Does your Iranian student know her?' David asks me.

'No. From the niqab she thinks she might be Somali. She thinks she's a peasant, anyway.'

'But she must be related to someone who is studying at the university, or on the staff there?'

'She might have a very upwardly mobile son or daughter studying or working there. Anyway, anyone who works there can put their child in the nursery – cleaners, canteen staff, ground staff. Only it's expensive, so it's mostly academic staff who use it, or students, who get a discount.'

'Are there many Muslim children in the nursery?'

'I'm sure Paula has that information,' I say. 'She's the detective, after all.'

There is a silence. We all sip our coffee,

'Are you going to tell me,' I ask, 'how they died?'

'No.' David's reply is instant and brusque enough to make me want to hurl the mustard pot at him.

'Can I ask why not?'

'It's confidential.'

'And I am not in your confidence?'

'Not as far as this is concerned.'

Paula says, 'It helps to weed out the nutters. Any high-profile case you get nutters confessing to the crime. If we haven't given out details we can quickly establish that we don't need to waste time on them.'

'Well,' I say, gathering up my bags for my trip to the supermarket, 'you could at least tell me how the dog died.'

She glances at David. 'Throat cut in the kitchen sink,' she says. And then, 'Well, you did ask.'

We go our separate ways, David graciously picking up the tab. I cycle on to Sainsbury's, where I stock up on locust food and summon Annie to pick it up. When she arrives – in slippers and pyjamas, so I'm the one who has to hump everything onto the back seat – I ask if she and her friends have plans for the evening. 'Showing them Marlbury nightlife?' I ask, hopefully.

She looks shocked. 'It's *Strictly*!' she says. 'Can't be missed.'

'There are frozen pizzas in there,' I say, nodding to the food bags. 'You can cook those. I'm not watching *Strictly* and I'm not cooking.'

'Well you're a little ray of sunshine this morning,' she says, and slams her door closed. Then she winds the window down. 'The kitchen sink's blocked,' she says, and I have to close my eyes because the dog is there, bleeding in my sunny yellow kitchen. I take a deep breath.

'Soda crystals,' I say. 'You've cooked a fry-up – I can smell it on you – and you've poured a lot of fat down the drain. There are soda crystals at the back of the cupboard under the sink. Use them with boiling water. Do it properly. I don't want to have to deal with it when I get back.'

'*You are My Sunshine*' she sings as she winds up the window.

I'm not going home with her because I am still avoiding home and I have an excuse. This afternoon I have a rehearsal in the abbey gardens where, in ten days' time, the Marlbury University Staff Drama Group are to put on a production of *Much Ado About Nothing*. As ever, I have been tasked with doing the costumes, but I also have a role: I am playing Ursula, the unsexy one of a pair of waiting women. I do have one good scene, though, and I ought to be enjoying rehearsals more than I am.

The problem is the director. His name is Dominic and he is 'A Professional'. This means, I suspect, that amateur groups have occasionally paid him small sums, as we have done, to direct them. Dominic likes to remind us at every opportunity of his professional status. *What you're doing, dear*,' he said to our Beatrice at one rehearsal, '*is what we in the profession call upstaging*.' Is there anyone with only a passing interest in the theatre, who doesn't know what upstaging is? Let alone Alison, who is playing Beatrice and is a senior lecturer in theatre studies? What's more, the scene she was playing was her big scene in which she challenges Benedick to kill his best friend, so she's entitled to upstage him if she wants to, isn't she?

Dominic and I have had our run-ins but we have now reached a state of armed truce. He has felt the need to slap me down ever since the first rehearsal, when he gave us his spiel about the play with heavy emphasis on smutty stuff about the meaning of '*Nothing*' in the title. (*No thing* is a reference to the female sexual organs; we have no thing. Get it? Clever stuff from the boys, isn't it?) He is right, actually; Shakespeare uses it like that in the sonnets. However, there was no need for Dominic to use quite so many little-boy-showing-off four-letter words in his explanation and it is generally unwise to lecture a group of academics on their home ground. Mervyn Lewis, the professor of Renaissance literature, and I started up a counter-commentary on the lines of *nothing* being also *noting*. The play is full of people noting things – often incorrectly. In the first half of the play, people spy, overhear, misinterpret and misreport, heading for the climax, the super-misinterpretation in which Claudio, deceived by the villainous Don John, wrongly believes that he sees his fiancée invite another man into her bedchamber the night before their wedding. It's a much more interesting line than the *no thing* one and it also, as I unwisely pointed out, makes nonsense of performing the play in the open air. The play actually requires curtains and nooks and shadows and spy-holes.

Dominic has a sidekick, Terry, who is the technical director, and the two of them have very loud, jargon-ridden conversations designed to intimidate us and keep us in our amateur places. At the last rehearsal, however, we had sound effects for the first time and they were less than perfectly timed. When, finally, a flourish of sprightly dance music interrupted Leonato's distraught lamentations over his daughter's dishonour so that the actor stopped dead, I spoke into the silence more loudly than I had intended. 'And that,' I said, 'is what we in the profession call a balls-up.' Dominic, I think, would like to sack me but he needs my costumes.

I retrieve my bike from the bike blocks outside Sainsbury's and cycle round to The Burnt Cake, the health food shop just outside the back gates of the abbey. There I buy a wrap with hummus and red peppers in it for my lunch, and a selection of pots of salad for my supper tonight. If my sitting room is going to be full of overdressed and overexcited celebrities and my lover is blanking me out, then I shall go to bed. I shall read *Bring up the Bodies* and I shall eat my supper in bed. I shall feel hard done by and I shall get guacamole on the duvet cover. How's that for a risibly middle-class mishap?

I go into the abbey close and find myself a bench under a tree. I get my script out to go over my lines but I can't concentrate. I'm thoroughly pissed off with David, of course. I do understand that he has to get a grip on the murder inquiry and I want him to find the killer as much as anyone but I resent not even being acknowledged, being shut out and having bloody Paula waved in front of my face. And I want to know what happened. All I know is that I saw them, the three of them, a young mother, a little girl and a dog, just out on an ordinary summer afternoon, and they went home and they died. And I keep imagining what happened, and all the time, buzzing away underneath the teaching and the cooking and the shopping and the talking and the wondering where exactly David and I are, my mind goes round and round it, imagining. Who died first? The dog, I suppose, because he would have tried to protect them. And then? Did Karen have to watch her daughter die? Or Lara watch her mother? Was it quick? Now I know about the dog, I know there was a knife. Were all their throats cut? The terror is what I come back to, over and over again. And David could give me the answers to some of these questions but he doesn't trust me; he chooses to leave me in the dark with my wondering and I don't think I can forgive him for that.

I get out my wrap and munch away at it. It was a stupid choice, really, because the hummus squidges out of the sides and I drop bits of red pepper on my skirt. Halfway through I give up and donate the rest to the pigeons who have gathered round me, knowing in their scary, avian way, that I am the kind of person who will drop my food. Then I ring my mother.

I haven't rung her since the murders and Annie's invasion of my house. I'm never sure how important my phone calls are to her. She is eighty-nine, lives on her own and is in some pain from arthritis, I suspect, though she won't admit it. She was a GP and seems to think that illness is only for other people. She has friends and someone who does her shopping for her; she reads a lot, potters in her tiny garden, listens to the radio, watches documentaries on television, and goes out to concerts sometimes. When I ring, she always suggests that she is perfectly content and has no need of anything from me, but I continue to call twice a week and give news, in which she takes a moderate interest. Would she notice if I stopped ringing? I think she would but I'm not sure.

This afternoon, though, there is something odd about her. She asks after the girls and Freda and Nico, but I'm not sure that she's listening to the answers. When I ask what she has been doing she is vague – 'Not a lot, a quiet week' – and when I press for details she tells me snappily to stop interrogating her. In the end, although I know it will make her cross, I ask if she's all right. 'Of course,' she says, and rings off.

The rehearsal begins badly. I'm not in the mood for it and I have a major run-in with Dominic about costumes before we even get started. He sees a class war element in the play: the aristocrats – the Prince of Aragon, and Count Claudio – versus the middle-class family of Leonato, whose daughter is to marry Count Claudio. To this end, he wants Hero and Beatrice, daughter and niece of Leonato, to appear in aprons at every opportunity, suggesting that they personally are doing the catering for the crowd of army officers who have descended on the house.

'Dominic!' I protest. 'The very reason why all these aristocratic army officers are staying with Leonato is that he's the biggest man in Messina. He's the Governor of Messina, for heaven's sake. His womenfolk aren't kitchen maids. They're

Lady Beatrice and *Lady Hero*. Even their maids aren't kitchen maids, I would hazard. We're waiting gentlewomen, though if you want me to wrap myself in an apron I'm happy to do so. It's a costume I'm well used to.'

'So it's really a kitchen-sink drama we're in, I see,' Mervyn Lewis mutters sotto voce and I quip back, 'On an apron stage!' before the image of the dog can fell me again.

Dominic has gathered himself for what he clearly regards as his clinching argument. 'I suggest a little more attention to the text, my dear,' he drawls. 'When Beatrice comes to fetch Benedick into dinner, she says, '*Against my will I am sent to bid you come in to dinner.*' She has been *sent* on an errand, against her will. Doesn't that tell you something about her status in the household?'

'God, Dominic! Do you understand this play at all? *She* says she's been sent against her will because the scene isn't funny unless she's unequivocally unfriendly to him. He's been told that she's in love with him and then she comes in and is rude to him and he tells himself that *there's a double meaning in that*, when there can't possibly be. That's why it's funny!'

Silence has fallen. I know I'm being more vehement than the situation requires but I can't back down. 'Benedick, as men so often do, has let her down in the past. He won her heart from her with false dice – she tells us so. So she's armed against him. She's not going to give him a chance to let her down again. She—' I stop. Where am I going with this? I am being ridiculous; Dominic is smirking at me. 'Well, if you want sodding aprons you can have them,' I shout. 'I'll just go and order a hundred yards of calico, shall I?'

He opens his mouth but I'm done. I stomp off into the abbey cloisters and demand a cigarette from the young chap who is playing Claudio and is having a quick pre-rehearsal smoke. I have given up smoking, really I have, but there are times when a cigarette seems to be the only answer.

We limp through the rehearsal and we are none of us at our best. It is a sunless afternoon and a brisk little wind is blowing our voices all over the place. A few tourists watch us desultorily for a while but soon depart; Dominic is clearly bored and disappointed with us and at one point wanders off, leaving us to our own devices. Things fall apart quite quickly when we realise that he's not there; nothing exposes the oddness of performance as sharply as having no-one to perform to. Soon after this, he calls an early halt and we disperse with relief to the disparate pleasures of our Saturday evenings.

Pleasure features little in my evening. David does not ring to suggest dinner as I secretly hoped he would, the bump and grind of *Strictly* penetrates into my room enough to distract me from my book and my supper is disappointing, largely because it is an inappropriate meal to eat in bed. And, yes, I do get guacamole on the duvet cover.

9

Sunday 22ⁿᵈ July

No Confidence

I am, once again, a refugee from my home. When I go
downstairs in the morning, I am assailed by the high garlicky
reek of leftover pepperoni pizza, mingled with the gritty
undertones of unemptied ashtrays. I have a choice of fight or
flight: I can go and thunder on bedroom doors and demand
that they get their idle overprivileged arses out of bed and
downstairs to clear everything up or I can spend the day going
to see my mother in London and clear the whole lot up myself
if they haven't done it by the time I return. Choose the former,
and the friends will gaze at me in wounded disbelief at my
unkindness and Annie never speak to me again; choose the
latter and my mother will be annoyed and ungrateful but I
shall bask in my own virtue and self-restraint. The former
would be more fun but life can't be all fun and I am
determined on martyrdom.

Avoiding an encounter with the kitchen and its dubious
sink, I cycle off to the station without breakfast, allowing
myself the indulgence of a coffee and a Danish off the station
stall. I also find, at the tiny bookstall, among the John
Grishams, Jilly Coopers and Stephen Kings, a gardening book
which my mother might just like. I can't be sure, but it's better

than a bunch of station flowers, which she would certainly despise.

By the time the train has chugged its way to London with special Sunday slowness, stopping at every available station and a number of arbitrary spots in between, it's midday and I think I had better go into M&S Food at St Pancras and buy a couple of salads in case my mother has nothing in for lunch. I am beginning to tire of deli food; I need to get my kitchen back.

The tube journey to New Cross is pretty unsavoury and some of my fellow passengers look as though they haven't been to bed – and certainly haven't washed – since they were partying last night, so it's a relief to be out in the street, even though the air is hardly fresh and the sky is sullenly overcast. It is a twenty-minute walk to my mother's flat so I opt for a taxi and the driver is mercifully taciturn.

I ring my mother's doorbell and get no reply, so I find my key and let myself in. I can hear the radio in the sitting room but my mother is slumped in her chair with her eyes closed. For a moment I think she might be dead, but as I put down my bags she opens an eye.

'What?' she asks. 'Why?'

'A surprise visit,' I say, feeling foolish. Why didn't I ring to warn her? Because she would have told me not to come, and she probably would have meant it.

'What for?' she asks, rousing herself.

I would like to say, '*Because I was worried about you*', but she won't like that, so I say, 'Because Annie and her friends have invaded my house and I needed an outing.'

'Well,' she says, 'I don't know that there's any food.'

'I brought some salads. There's plenty. Would you like some?'

'Oh, I'm not hungry. I was going to make myself some toast.'

'I'll do it.' I hand her the gardening book. 'I thought you might like this. Amuse yourself while I get some lunch.'

The kitchen is immaculately tidy and aroma-free in a way that suggests that little cooking has been going on here. I find a fairly fresh loaf, though, and I put together a tray of toast and tea. As I'm looking for milk in the fridge, I notice a tub of anchovy paste. I put my head into the sitting room. 'Anchovy paste on your toast, I ask?'

'Yes,' she says. She is holding the book in her lap and looking at its front cover but I'm not sure that she has opened it.

I put the tray in front of her on the coffee table and settle myself opposite her with my salads. She eats her way dutifully through a slice of toast; I munch unenthusiastically at borlotti beans and coleslaw. I attempt conversation but she is no more forthcoming about what she has been doing than she was on the phone, so I end up prattling about my life: Annie and the Edinburgh play, Ellie, Freda and Nico, *Much Ado About Nothing*, the murders of Karen and Lara Brody.

This last stirs her slightly.

'Don't tell me,' she says, 'that you've got yourself involved in that.'

'Absolutely not,' I say. 'David has made it crystal clear that there is no place for me in his investigation.'

'Well, that must be a great relief to you,' she says, and just for a moment I see the glimmer of a smile, a hint of her usual self.

'He has a very able assistant in DS Paula Powell,' I say, packing up my plastic salad tubs with every appearance, I believe, of nonchalance. 'They seem to get on very well.'

I go out to the kitchen to throw them away and she calls after me, 'Don't underestimate him. He strikes me as a man of hidden depths.'

'Well, he's certainly keeping them hidden from me,' I call back. I return to take her tray. 'Of course, hidden shallows are more dangerous, aren't they? They're what you run aground on. I suspect Paula Powell of hidden shallows.'

She picks up her book and starts leafing through it; I go and wash up. After that, I do a few jobs: a curtain has come off its runner so I get up on a chair to fix it. 'While you're up there,' she says, 'that bulb needs changing.' So I do that too, and I notice that the handle on the sitting room door is loose so I go rummaging in a kitchen drawer where I'm fairly sure she has a screwdriver and I find a pile of unopened mail. The dates I'm able to read are all within the last two weeks, so this squirrelling has, at least, not been going on for long. I take the letters into the sitting room and brandish them.

'What are all these?' I ask. 'Why haven't you opened them?'

A look crosses her face, and it's a look I remember from childhood, a look so close to dislike that I tried very hard not to provoke it.

'Nothing to do with you,' she says shortly. 'Put them back where you found them.'

I was intending to ask her outright if she's not well but after this contretemps I can see that I shan't get anywhere. There seems to be little point now in hanging around, although I shall have a long wait at St Pancras for one of the infrequent trains home. I leave her with exhortations to eat and promises to return soon. As I'm closing the front door behind me, the door of the flat opposite opens and her neighbour, Margaret, comes out.

'Gina,' she says, 'I thought I heard you arrive. Have you got a moment?' I follow her into her flat, which is stuffed, as retirement flats inevitably are, with too much furniture. It is also very pink and floral, in contrast to the austerity of my mother's décor. Margaret is quite pink too, a large, comfortable woman, a former dental nurse, with a powerful Welsh accent, undimmed by forty years of living in Greenwich. She and her husband have lived in this flat for about ten years and she has been a godsend in keeping an eye on my mother.

'Cup of tea?' she asks, and I decline on the grounds that I've just had one with my mother.

'Well, at least she's drinking her tea,' she says darkly. 'That's something.'

'Is she not eating, Margaret?' I ask, sinking into the rosy depths of an armchair. 'It didn't look as though she was.'

'She hasn't said then?'

'Said what?'

'I wanted to ring you but she said not to. She'd tell you herself, she said. Of course, I should have known she wouldn't, knowing her like I do.'

'Tell me what, Margaret?'

She gets up and goes to the telephone. 'I wrote it down here,' she says, picking up the phone message pad. She squints at it. 'TIAs,' she says, 'transient ischaemic attacks. At least three of them she's had in the last three weeks. The first time I called the doctor, but she wouldn't let me after that. Said it was nothing to worry about, just her brain being short of blood for a bit. But they leave her confused, and she's lost all her go, if you know what I mean.'

'I do. Exactly. So when was the first one? Can you remember?'

'Yes, I can. Because it was our little grandson's birthday – our Sammy – and I called in after to see your mum and take her a piece of birthday cake. Well she didn't answer the door when I rang, so I used my key and I found her sitting there and she looked at me as if she didn't know me. I spoke to her but she didn't say anything, so I called Harold to come and have a look and he said, "Call the doctor, Margaret," so I did and then I waited with her till the doctor came. She'd come to a bit by the time he got here and told him it was all a fuss about nothing but he had a look at her and "You've had a TIA," he said to her. "I'd like to get you admitted for some tests," but she was having none of it. And she wouldn't have you told either.'

'And then there have been two more?'

'As far as I know. Once I knew what it was, I wasn't so alarmed, you know, but we looked up TIA on NHS Direct, you know, and I saw it's a kind of stroke.'

'I've heard of it,' I say. 'I know someone who's had one. They're quite scary, though you get over it afterwards. I think she's scared but she's not admitting it. And she's not opening her post.'

'Oh, I wondered,' she says. 'Couple of times I've gone in in the afternoon and the letters are still on the mat. "Can't be bothered with them," she says. "None of it's important." So I put them in the kitchen. Thought she'd find them when she went to make her supper – only I don't think she's cooking much these days.'

I return to my mother's front door, unlock it without ringing the bell and walk rapidly down the hall to the sitting room. I want to shout *'ischaemic attacks'* at her and shock her into confession but I can see that this might not be the best thing for an elderly woman in questionable health. I pause at the door, take a deep breath, slip in and sit down. Her eyes are closed but she knows I'm there.

'Haven't you gone?' she asks.

'Ischaemic attacks,' I say, quietly. 'What can you tell me about those, Dr Sidwell?'

She doesn't open her eyes. 'You've been talking to Margaret,' she says.

'I've been talking to Margaret, who seems to know a lot more about your recent medical history than I do.'

Her eyes snap open and she sits up straight. 'Ischaemic attacks are nothing to worry about,' she says. 'They're frightening for patients if they don't know what's happening but they're really nothing.'

'And for you?' I ask. 'How are they for you?'

'They are—' She stops and waves a hand dismissively. 'Margaret fusses,' she says.

'Of course she fusses. You're not yourself. Anyone can see that.'

'Of course I'm myself. I'm just my eighty-nine-year-old self, that's all.'

'I think you're giving up.'

She gives me a long, hard look but I won't look away. Then she hauls herself to her feet. 'Wait here,' she says and goes off into the bedroom. She comes back with an envelope and hands it to me. It has *Virginia Gray* written on it. 'To be opened when I'm dead,' she says, 'and not before. If you can't curb your curiosity – and you never could – please don't ask me to discuss it with you.' Then, quite unexpectedly, she leans forward to give me a kiss on the cheek. 'Go and catch your train,' she says.

Funnily enough, I'm not tempted to open my letter; I am quite content to sit on the train with it tucked into my bag because all the time it is unopened I can believe that my mother's last message to me is to tell me that she loves me and is proud of me. Opening it can only be a disappointment.

When my phone rings a short way out of St Pancras, I scrabble for it with the conviction that it is Margaret ringing to tell me that my mother has taken a turn for the worse, and this will of course be my fault. I am amazed to find that it is my colleague, Malcolm, calling. I didn't know that he even had my mobile number. 'Annie gave it to me,' he explains.

He sounds flustered and takes a while to get to the point. 'The conversation we had the other day,' he says, 'about the deaths on the Eastgate estate – Karen Brody and her daughter. Now they're saying Karen was murdered, there are some things I think the police ought to know, but I can't go to them directly. Samaritan confidentiality, you know. I wondered if I could talk to you about it and we might go through unofficial channels.'

'To David, you mean?'

'Well, yes.'

I am alight with curiosity, of course, but this is not the place for the conversation. 'I'm on a train, Malcolm,' I say. 'We need to talk face to face, don't we? I wasn't going to be on campus tomorrow but I'll come in first thing and we can have a proper talk.'

'All right,' he says, and I can tell that he's disappointed; he wanted to offload his awkward knowledge right away.

'Don't worry about it,' I say. 'I'm sure we can sort something out,' and I devote the rest of my journey to speculation.

10

23.07.12

TEAM MEETING

DC Darren Floyd lounged against a table at the back of the incident room. 'DC Arthur and I carried out a detailed examination of the delightful contents of the refuse bins in Windermere Road,' he drawled, 'and found nothing out of the ordinary, though I'm sure it was six hours of police time well spent.'

Scott felt the blood rise to his face. 'I make the judgements about how you spend your time, DC Floyd,' he said. 'Your opinions are the least of my concerns.'

'If I may say, boss,' Mike Arthur intervened, 'what we did notice was that she was a very neat housewife – Karen. All the kitchen refuse was in bags, tied up, and the recycling stuff in the other bin. The bins at the other houses were mostly a right old mess, but not hers. Proper middle class, if you know what I mean.'

Presumably what Jason Watts meant by *too up herself with no good reason*, Scott thought.

'Anything from the gardens or sheds?' he asked Mike Arthur.

'Nothing. Traces of blood on the front path at number thirteen stop at the pavement. He obviously got into a car.'

'Which nobody in the street saw?'

'So they say.'

Darren Floyd chipped in. 'Special Eastgate disability isn't it – blind, deaf and dumb? They get benefits for it.'

He was rewarded by a mild ripple of laughter.

'What about the Doug Brody angle, Steve?' Scott asked Steve Boxer, noticing as he did so that Steve was looking seedier these days. He had always had a nerdy look, but now he was grubby, with the weekend's growth of beard not shaved off that morning.

'Not promising,' Steve said. 'I followed up the known associates I got from the Liverpool end. Two of them are inside; one was admitted to the Royal Liverpool Hospital on Saturday 14th July after being knifed in a fight and wasn't released until last Friday; the other one they have a warrant out for, for armed robbery. They know he got away to Ireland and they're pretty sure he's not come back. There's a watch out at ports and airports.'

'OK.' Scott turned to the whiteboard, from which photos of Karen and Lara Brody gazed out at them. He tapped the photo of Karen. 'Sarah, how did you get on with Karen's friends?'

Sarah Shepherd got to her feet. 'I don't think she had what you would call real friends,' she said. 'She'd been back in Marlbury for a year or more but she doesn't seem to have caught up with school friends or anything. I got the names of some of them from her father – those he could remember – but none of them have seen her. The other students on her course all say they liked her: really nice, quiet, kept herself to herself. They can't believe anyone would have wanted to hurt her – the usual sort of thing – but I didn't get the impression that they really knew her. I talked to her personal tutor, though. He didn't seem to know her that well either, but he had a record of her assignment marks. She had very good marks through the year but the last assignment, which was a big one, carrying a lot of marks, was late in and pretty mediocre. He had been planning to have a word with her.'

'Her father said he thought she was worried about something,' Scott said, turning to Paula, 'didn't he?'

'And remember how Leanne reacted when we asked her if Karen was worried about anything?' Paula asked. 'I thought it was just because she knew she asked too much of Karen – ferrying Liam about, getting lumbered with the dog because she couldn't cope with it – but I wonder.'

Leanne Thomas Scott wrote on the board, next to Karen Brody's picture. 'Karen's sister. Also lives on Eastgate. We ought to have a picture of her up here.'

Darren Floyd stirred himself from his lounging posture. 'You can't think she's a suspect,' he said. 'This isn't a woman's crime, is it?'

Scott eyed him. 'I've known women do worse,' he said, 'but Leanne's a much smaller, lighter woman than Karen was so I can't see her forcing gin down her throat, but she was probably the last person, apart from the killer, to see Karen and Lara alive. They picked Liam up from the university nursery at the end of the afternoon and walked him back to Leanne's flat.'

'And,' Paula said, 'Leanne has at least three heavy-duty locks on her front door, so what is it she's worried about?'

'Which brings us back to the money,' Scott said, 'the haul from Doug Brody's petrol station raid. We're pretty sure that Doug didn't order the killings, so the next most likely motive is the money. Someone believed – rightly or wrongly – that Karen had the money, and killed her because she wouldn't – or couldn't – hand it over.'

'Except—' Sarah Shepherd spoke and then looked alarmed when all eyes turned to her. 'Except, I was there, you know. I was the first there when the neighbour called, and it was pretty nasty – a lot of blood – but I don't think the house had been searched – not ransacked.'

'Which would mean that she did tell them where it was but they killed her anyway.'

'And,' threw in Darren Floyd, 'it means that Leanne Thomas doesn't have all those locks on her front door because she's hiding Doug's loot in her flat.'

'We'll talk to her again,' Scott said. 'And Sarah, keep going with Karen's contacts, will you? Where are we with Jason Watts' alibi?'

'It checks out for what it's worth,' Steve Boxer said. 'He gave us names of people who saw him working at the Caz Bar and they say they did see him but they're none of them what you might call upright citizens.'

'And if Jason's got Doug's loot then he can afford to pay them generously. Let's put Jason Watts' ugly mug up there too.' He wrote the name on the board.

'You never know,' said Paula, 'we might get him for hitting his girlfriend at least.'

People started stirring, gathering up their coffee cups and reaching for jackets with the sense that the meeting was coming to an end.

'One more thing,' Scott said, raising a hand to stop them. 'There was an incident earlier in the afternoon on the day of the murders. It may or may not have any bearing on the case but I don't think we can dismiss it yet. Paula, would you like to talk about it?'

She gave him a long, questioning look and then shrugged. 'OK,' she said.

Woman in burqa she wrote on the board. There was a gust of laughter.

'Jesus,' Mike Arthur said, 'not an Islamic connection!'

'Not with Jesus, Mike!' someone quipped, and there was another laugh.

'When Karen and Lara went to pick up Liam from the nursery, they had their dog with them. While she was waiting in the garden for the boy to come out, the dog got away from her and attacked an elderly woman in the full Islamic garb. No big drama. Karen got the dog back under control and the woman left. It's probably got nothing to do with what happened later.'

'Where had the woman come from?' Mike Arthur asked.

'She'd been inside the nursery. The kids were doing some sort of show. We're assuming she was someone's granny or some such but we haven't tracked her down.'

'Probably a terrorist in disguise,' Darren Floyd called out. 'That's what they're doing now, isn't it? Putting on burqas?'

'We don't think so, DC Floyd,' Scott said, 'but we are trying to find her. How are you doing with that, Paula?'

'I'm going into the college tomorrow.' She turned to address the rest of the group. 'There was an Iranian woman who spoke to her as she was leaving. I'm going to talk to her tomorrow. She goes to English classes and we thought it would be better to talk to her there. These Iranian husbands can be difficult.'

'I'm thinking,' Sarah Shepherd said, 'it's odd, isn't it that she didn't have a child with her when she left? If she was a granny, wouldn't you expect her to be with her family?'

There was a silence, during which Scott realised that this was something that had bothered him about the story all along – the picture of the old woman hobbling off on her own, without the child she had come to watch. When did you ever see women in that garb on their own anyway? Didn't she always have a man with her?

'Maybe,' Mike Arthur said, 'she works at the college. Maybe she got an hour off to nip in and watch the show and then went back.'

'In which case,' Scott said, 'it shouldn't be difficult to find her.'

'And if we do,' Steve Boxer asked, 'what then? How would she fit in with the killings?'

Scott was reluctant to put into words the nightmare scenario that he feared. 'The woman was humiliated,' he said. 'Attacked in public by a dog – and dogs are unclean animals in Islamic culture – and laughed at. The girl, Lara, laughed, apparently. We have to ask if it's possible that someone felt honour-bound to avenge her shame.'

Silence. They exchanged glances. No-one spoke.

'OK,' he said. 'That's it.'

As they were dispersing, his phone rang. It was Gina. He had no time for negotiating his personal life now. He let it ring and a minute later saw *1 message* appear on his screen. He listened.

'David, my colleague Malcolm has some info for you that you'll want to hear. He's a Samaritan and he's pretty certain that he took a call from Karen Brody on the afternoon she died. You'll need to hear the story from him. He's reluctant to talk to you because of the Samaritan confidentiality ethic, so you'll have to handle it carefully. If you can find time in your busy schedule, I suggest you come here to the college and he can fill you in. No, no, no need to thank me. Always happy to help. Byee.'

He hesitated then snapped his phone shut and put it in his pocket. She could wait.

11

Tuesday 24ᵗʰ July. Morning

Inadmissible Evidence

Well, it's Tuesday again and time for another session with my wives. This afternoon, however, we are to be enlivened by the presence of DS Paula Powell, who is coming to interview my student, Jamilleh, about the mystery woman in the niqab. I have suggested that Paula comes at the end of the class because I don't want her fluttering my chicks at the start so that we can't get any work done, but I shall stay around to help with the interview if help is needed. That's this afternoon, though. This morning I am helping DCI Scott to interview my colleague, Malcolm, about his phone call from Karen Brody. *Helping the police with their inquiries*. I've always liked that phrase: so tactful and so far from the truth. *Help* is something willingly given, isn't it? Witnesses aren't said to be helping the police, nor members of the public who join in those hopeless searches for the missing, and yet that is exactly what they are doing – helping. Instead the phrase is reserved for those who are not feeling particularly helpful, those who have been transported or summoned to a police station, where the voluntariness of their help becomes uncertain at best, and so the use of the phrase is disingenuous, I would say, but also charmingly tactful. I particularly like reports that the police have applied for extra time to question someone who is helping them with their inquiries. I ask myself just how helpful a person can be.

Anyway, today I am not *helping the police* but being helpful to them. When David finally responded to my phone message yesterday evening, I set up a meeting between him and Malcolm for this morning, and now here we are in Malcolm's very neat office, sitting on hard chairs and nursing the very strong instant coffee which Malcolm has just proffered. I know what Malcolm has to tell, as he told me all about it yesterday, but I'm here to see fair play and make sure that Malcolm isn't bullied. David would like me to go away but Malcolm has insisted on my presence, so here I am, being helpful.

'The thing is,' Malcolm is saying, 'our director doesn't know I'm talking to you. I raised the matter with her but she doesn't feel our information is specific enough to be helpful and, of course, we do avoid giving information to the police, if we can, because it undermines potential callers' trust in our confidentiality.'

'The point is, David,' I chip in, 'can't this be off the record, this conversation, at least? Then if you think —'

'Gina,' he says, putting his coffee mug down on the floor, 'shall we establish some ground rules here? I am a police officer, Malcolm is a witness. This is an interview, not a conversation. We understand the Samaritans' position but if, when this case comes to trial, we feel that Malcolm's evidence needs to be heard in court then we will issue a court order requiring the director of Marlbury Samaritans to appear in court and it will not be up to her to decide whether the information is specific enough or not. In the meantime, I am going to ask Malcolm some questions, he is going to answer them and I am going to note anything that may be relevant to our inquiry. I respect Malcolm's wish to have you here but I'm asking you to keep quiet and to speak only if Malcolm or I ask you to.'

I can feel myself going scarlet and I have to bury my face in my mug and take a scalding gulp of coffee. How dare he speak to me like this, this man who is, occasionally, referred to by me as my beloved? And in front of Malcolm? There is a danger that tears of fury will rush into my eyes so I have to make a performance of choking and coughing in order that they can be attributed to the scalding coffee. 'God, Malcolm,' I gasp histrionically. 'Are these insulated mugs? I've taken the roof off my mouth!'

They both watch me in silence. 'Well, go on,' I say when I have given myself time to recover my aplomb, and I wave my coffee mug permissively. 'Get on with it. Don't just sit there.' I sit back with what I hope is a convincing air of amused insouciance and consider ways of punishing David.

I survey the range of options from keying his car to cutting up his best suit to (favourite at this moment) never speaking to him again, but none of these feel quite right – not exactly fitting for the crime. Humiliation is what I require. I would like some embarrassing photos that I could distribute among his colleagues – something to raise a snigger and demean him in their eyes – but they won't exist, I know. Look wherever you like, you won't find a photo of David Scott off his face, dancing with his shirt off or wearing antlers. Just at this moment I can't decide whether this is one of the reasons why I love him or why I hate him.

When I emerge from this reverie, Malcolm is speaking. 'I had spoken to her once before,' he says, 'and she told me her name was Karen.'

'What did she ring to talk about?' David asks.

Malcolm looks uncomfortable and I could intervene but I'm not risking another put-down, so I keep *schtum*.

'She's dead, Malcolm,' David says. 'Confidentiality hardly matters, does it?'

Malcolm compromises. 'She had worries,' he says. 'Single mother, husband in prison, isolated, short of money.'

Nothing you couldn't read in the paper, I think. *Good one, Malcolm!*

'You say you spoke to her once before her last call. Was that it? Once?'

'I think so.'

'But she may have spoken to other Samaritans as well?'

'I guess so.'

'And did she talk about suicide?'

'Not to me, but when I first heard about how she'd died I thought it was suicide and so, of course, I felt—'

'Did you ask her if she was suicidal?'

'We always ask.'

'What did she say?'

'She said—' He shoots a glance of appeal at me; I glance at David. 'She said she wasn't,' he continues.

'And the last call, when was that exactly?'

'I checked it in our log. On Tuesday 17th at 17.10 she called, and the call lasted about three minutes.'

I can feel David become instantly hyper-alert; it is as though he is suddenly emitting radar waves. 'You're sure of that, are you?' he asks in an even tone that belies his body language. He is writing stuff down for the first time.

'Yes. It's second nature to check the time when we take a call.'

'What did she say?'

'She said she had some information that the police ought to know about but she dared not go to them.'

David has become very still. 'Did she say what the information was about?' he asks quietly.

'No. I think – I think she was going to. She asked me if we could pass it to the police and I started explaining about confidentiality, but she said, "But you pass on bomb warnings to the police, don't you? This would be like a bomb warning."'

'She was thinking of the IRA days?'

87

'Yes.' Malcolm turns to me. 'Sometimes when the IRA wanted to give a bomb warning they would ring the Samaritans. Because they knew we were there twenty-four-seven. They used a particular form of words – a kind of password – so we would know if they were genuine, and then we would let the police know. It never happened in Marlbury, of course, but it did in some branches.'

'How did she know about that?' David asks. 'It wasn't common knowledge.'

'She must know someone who's a Samaritan.'

'Or have been one herself?' I mutter.

'What did you say to her?' David asks.

'I said the bomb warning procedure was an exception and we didn't pass other information to the police or to anyone else but I could see that she had a difficult decision to make and we would support her in making it.'

'What did she say?'

'She got quite emotional – said that was no good – and then she broke off the call.'

'Just put down the phone?'

'No. I could hear a dog start barking and then she said to someone, "Go upstairs, go on," and then she cut off.'

'Did you get a sense of who she was talking to?'

'I –' He gives a puff of frustration. 'I think she said *Lara*, but I can't be sure. I read in the paper that her daughter's name was Lara and I'm not sure whether I've invented that.'

'When you were talking to her, could you hear a TV in the background?'

Malcolm looks surprised but thinks about it, eyes closed. 'I don't think so.'

'OK.' David picks up his undrunk coffee, stands up and puts his mug on Malcolm's desk. 'Thank you,' he says. 'I will probably need to talk to you about this again.'

Malcolm takes off his glasses and rubs the bridge of his

nose. 'I take it,' he says, 'that I was the last person to talk to her before her killer did.'

'It seems likely.'

'Well,' Malcolm says, 'I thought for a while that I was the last person she talked to before she killed herself and the child, so this is better, I suppose.'

'Better for you,' David says. 'I'm not sure about her.' And he leaves.

It takes a while to talk Malcolm down from the state of agitation David has left him in. I don't like to leave him because he is a semi-recovered alcoholic and this is the kind of thing that could send him out for a bottle of vodka, so we go to the SCR for a proper cup of coffee and discuss some work issues before I go to my office to deal with emails. The only message of any substance is one from the vice-chancellor's secretary asking me if I will make an appointment to see the VC at my earliest convenience. This can only be bad news. I have had no trouble from him over the past year; ever since he interfered outrageously in a disciplinary case involving one of my students, succumbing, quite frankly, to bribery by her father, he has been at pains to avoid me. He actually runs away from me. Once he hid behind the drama studio. So, if he is summoning me to his presence it can only mean that I've given him a reason to shout at me or that he feels he has got one over on me and he wants to flaunt his triumph. (*Got one over on me* – isn't that a wonderful phrasal verb? It's a very sophisticated non-native speaker who can come up with that one.) I delve into my memory for anything I may have done in the past few weeks that would give him an excuse to yell and I come up empty-handed, so it's triumphing I have to expect, I suppose. I flag the message but do nothing about the appointment. He can wait.

12

Tuesday 24th July, Afternoon

Interrogatives

Unusually in this dreary summer the sun is shining and I decide to cycle into town, have lunch at The Pumpkin and buy a few treats for Freda and me to have this evening, since she is spending the night with me. Ellie and Ben are going out to supper with friends and taking Nico with them, so Freda and I can have a girls' night in. Annie and her posse have a technical rehearsal this afternoon, which is bound to drag on into the evening, so we shall have the house to ourselves. She will have to sleep in my bed since every other bed in the house will be occupied but she will like that. I worry a bit that I'm not really bonding with Nico. He's a lovely little boy – round-faced and cheerful, with melting brown eyes like chocolate buttons – but he's not Freda. And Freda, who has shown commendably few signs of jealousy as far as Ellie and Ben are concerned, does like to claim me as hers alone.

Fortified by quiche and salad, I return for my afternoon session with my wives. We are doing more work on questions. This follows on from the exercise they were doing on Friday but it doesn't escape me that there is an irony in spending an hour teaching them how to ask questions when Paula Powell is waiting in the wings ready to get them to answer hers.

Questions are a real problem for learners of English. They learn early on the simple survival questions of the *'Wh'* type: *Where is…? What is…? When is…?* but anything more complex is inclined to defeat them, and social questions are a minefield. Let's take my five students this afternoon: two Farsi speakers, one Spanish, one Greek and one Chinese. None of their languages has the equivalent of the *do/does/did* forms for asking questions and they are really difficult for learners to get their heads round. In Spanish and Greek, questions other than the *'Wh'* kind are asked largely by making statements with a questioning inflection: *You're going out? It's raining?* et cetera. Farsi speakers tend to do the same since there is no equivalent in English to the all-purpose question word that turns statements into questions in Farsi. We can do it in English, of course, the statement-question, but it doesn't work terribly well socially; it tends to sound abrupt and a bit challenging. Then there are question tags: *is/isn't it? does/doesn't it? have/haven't you?* and so on. We laugh at the all-purpose *innit* that peppers the street speech of the urban young but you can see how it arises because question tags are so various and complex in standard English, and other languages mostly have a simpler way of doing things (*n'est-ce-pas,* after all is only the French for *innit.*)

Failure to use English question tags properly doesn't make people incomprehensible but it does often make them sound rude. Farsi has the all-purpose tag, also used as an answer quite often – *chera?* – which translates into English as *Why not?* When questions like *It's time for our class, isn't it?* become *It's time for our class, why not?* they take on an unintentionally aggressive edge, so I am trying to eliminate them, but the speakers of European languages in the class tend to attach *yes?* or *no?* to questions, which can sound equally aggressive, so that has to be dealt with too.

This is a group of quite sophisticated young women so I

start this afternoon with the idea that questioning is an intrinsically impolite activity: it is intrusive and demanding and so it requires language strategies that minimise the impoliteness. This is why we use the cumbersome and grammatically complex forms, *Could you tell me…? Would you mind showing me…? I was wondering whether…?* and so on. These present problems in the answering as well as the asking. When the girls were small and I was working, we had an au pair for a year, a lovely Finnish girl whose English was really very good, but she could never cope with my polite *Would you mind…?* requests. *Would you mind getting the girls their lunch?* I would ask; *Yes*, she would say, and then stop in confusion. Native speakers find all kinds of ways to answer that sort of non-question question, just as we find answers to *Yorright?*. In the end Aliisa settled for *That's fine* as her all-purpose willing answer.

We have quite a lot of fun with the questions once I assure my students that they don't have to speak the truth in their answers – in fact, the wilder the better – and we are all laughing merrily when Paula Powell appears, bringing the unmistakeable aura of the authorities with her, and puts paid to the fun. As Juanita, Athene and Ning Wu leave, I explain to Farah and Jamilleh why Paula is here and the questioning starts in earnest.

Paula, of course, breaks all the rules that I have been laying down with such care. I need not have worried that she would fluster them with the *Would you mind answering a few questions?* approach; she is not bothered, it seems, by the intrinsic impoliteness of asking questions but plunges straight in.

'So you're Jamilleh?' she asks.

'Yes.'

'And you were at the Acorns day nursery on the afternoon of Tuesday last week – 17th?

'Yes.'

'Tell me what happened.'

If Jamilleh is surprised by the abruptness of Paula's questioning she doesn't show it. I guess, on the basis only of prejudice, that abruptness is the best you hope for from the Iranian police. She tells the story of the dog and the woman in the niqab quite coherently despite her struggle with the language. Paula turns to Farah. 'You can confirm this?' she asks.

Oh for heaven's sake, Paula, give up on the statement-questions and use some proper interrogatives.

'Yes.'

'And after the young woman got the dog on the lead what happened?'

'The woman wearing niqab left.'

'On her own?'

'Yes.'

'Were you surprised at that?'

Farah glances at Jamilleh. 'Why I would be surprised?' she asks.

Oh, Farah, has this afternoon been completely wasted?

'Well—' Paula hesitates. She doesn't want to make a crass remark about *those sort of women* generally being accompanied by a man. 'Didn't you expect her to be with one of the children?' she asks.

'She sat on her own at the concert,' Farah says. 'No family.'

'Had you ever seen her before?'

Farah shrugs. 'It is hard knowing,' she says.

'Because she was all covered up?'

'We never saw her before,' Jamilleh says. 'I know.'

Paula turns her attention to her. 'How can you be so sure?'

'I spoke to her.'

'And?'

'And?' Jamilleh queries.

'What did she say?'

93

'Nothing. She said nothing.'

She is beginning to look uncomfortable and Paula has noticed. 'You're quite sure?' she demands.

'Yes.'

'What did you say to her?'

'I asked, "Are you all right?"'

'In English?'

'First I try Arabic but she seemed not understanding. She was just walking, with back to me. Then I said in English and I took her arm, but she turned round and pushed me, like—' She makes quite a violent pushing movement with her right arm.

'You say she had her back to you but you also said you were sure you hadn't seen her before. How can you be sure if you didn't see her face?'

Jamilleh twines her fingers together in her lap and looks at them. Then she looks at Farah, and at me. Finally, she looks Paula in the face. 'When she pushed,' she says, 'I know how it feel when woman pushes. It was—' She stops and takes a deep breath. 'I think,' she says, 'she was man.'

After that, Paula's questions come thick and fast, and I get interrogated too. I feel stupid because as soon as Jamilleh drops her bombshell I know that she is right. When I visualise the figure now, as it limped away from us, I can see that, even under the black robe, it was too square, too broad in the shoulders to be female.

'You couldn't tell from the way she walked?' Paula asks accusingly, and I explain about the limp but it sounds a pretty feeble excuse now.

'Bloody Darren may have been right after all,' I hear Paula mutter under her breath, but I don't get the reference and don't feel that now is the time to enquire.

She looks back at Jamilleh. 'Did you tell anyone that you thought she was a man?' she demands.

'No. Only to Farah.'

'Why no-one else?'

Jamilleh drops her head and says nothing.

'Why, Jamilleh?' Paula presses.

Without raising her head, Jamilleh says quietly, 'Because if it was man, then is man's business.'

'Tell me, Jamilleh,' I ask. 'Is that what you said to Farah? When you came back from talking to the "woman", you said something in Farsi. I thought it was something like *peasant* because of what you'd said about the kind of women who wear niqab.'

Farah looks at Jamilleh. 'She said me "Wolf in sheep's wool,"' she says, 'like in old story.'

This makes me think of Red Riding Hood and the wolf sitting up in bed wearing her granny's clothes. How can we bear to terrify children with such an idea? I am reminded too of an urban myth that was told to me in all seriousness a few years ago by a woman I knew only slightly. We had been at a meeting and she asked me if I would walk back to her car with her because she had been told a story that had made her nervous. The story involved a friend of a friend, as these urban myths generally do, and I hadn't heard it before, though I have heard it, with variations, several times since. The friend's friend, she told me, had parked her car in a multistorey car park one winter afternoon and returned to it, as it was growing dark, to find a nun sitting in the front passenger seat. The nun was terribly apologetic and explained that she was feeling ill and needed to get to a hospital. Could the woman drive her there? The woman agreed, feeling that she had no other option. She got into the driving seat and started the car, but as she was pulling out of her parking space, she noticed the nun's hands, lying on her lap. Broad, strong and hairy, they were unmistakeably a man's hands. Quick-thinking, the woman said she was having trouble manoeuvring out of the space and asked if the nun could get out and guide her. Once the nun was out of the car, she revved off as fast as she could go and drove straight to the nearest police station. When the police examined her car they found a number of things in its boot. What they were varies in different versions of the tale but they usually include a length of rope and a meat cleaver.

It's a daft tale, as cheesy and full of holes as a piece of Emmental. Why didn't the woman wonder what a poorly nun was doing wandering round a multistorey car park? How had the 'nun' got into her car and why didn't the owner wonder how? Why wasn't the 'nun' suspicious about being asked to get out of the car? That doesn't matter, though. The story was effective enough to rattle a sensible professional woman because it tapped into a deep fear of the disguised other, the threatening male masquerading as the harmless female. Confronted with this, we are as fearful as a child who wonders if her granny just might be something else altogether.

And now we have a new version of the myth, a new and specific fear. Why didn't Jamilleh tell anyone else about her suspicion? Well, maybe because the thought was so scary that she wanted to put it in a box and forget it, but more likely because she knew that this was a story we were all waiting for, the story that plays to our terror of the masked and the disguised, the story that justifies our paranoia, that tells us that under any burqa, niqab, chador or hijab may lurk not an oppressed woman but a young man in a suicide vest.

Paula perhaps understands some of this. She doesn't press the point anyway. She thanks Jamilleh, says she may need to talk to her again, and leaves. If I thought she might let them go and stay behind to discuss things with me I was deluding myself. No-one is going to let me in on this case however helpful I make myself.

I spend a bit of time with Jamilleh and Farah, telling them that they did well, reassuring them that they have done nothing wrong and reminding them that Paula is a police officer and that her interrogative style is not one to be imitated in more relaxed social situations. Then they leave, I gather up my files and walk out of the classroom straight into the arms of the vice-chancellor. Well, not into his arms exactly – I think his arms remain resolutely at his sides. I just bounce off the mound of his substantial belly, really, and drop my files on the floor.

He stands watching me as I grovel around picking them up, and doesn't speak until I'm back on my feet again.

'Mrs Gray,' he says. 'I was hoping I might bump into you.'

Is this a joke? *Mrs Gray* doesn't suggest that he is in a joking mood – I'm *Gina* when he's feeling genial. I decide to be upbeat anyway.

'Well, you have your wish,' I say, dusting myself down. 'That was quite a bump.'

He doesn't smile. 'If you're going back to your office,' he says, 'I'll walk with you.'

I can do nothing but trot along beside him, clutching my slipping files and thinking furiously. Was he actually waiting for me outside my classroom door? I think he must have been. He must have got Janet to find out where I was and then came over and hovered around. Hovered for quite a long time, actually, if he arrived at the end of the lesson. The vice-chancellor hovering outside a classroom door; what is going on? Was he listening in to Paula's interrogation? Did he know about that? If so, how? Was that why I got the email summons? What is so urgent that he has felt compelled to seek me out?

He waits until we are upstairs and I am fumbling for my office key before he starts talking.

'Since you haven't had the courtesy to respond to my request to see you,' he begins, raising a peremptory hand to stop me as I open my mouth to start with the excuses, 'I'm doing you the courtesy of coming to see you.'

I have the door open now, we step inside and I offer him a chair, which he disdains. Not a cosy chat, then. We stay on our feet. I look at him. He is a choleric man, given to ill-temper and sudden rages. He used to have an alarmingly high colour that spoke of high blood pressure as well as choler, but this has subsided in recent months, dashing the expectations of the many who hoped to see him felled by a stroke at any moment. Mrs vice-chancellor, the lovely Lynette, has taken him in hand, we assume, and though the belly shows no sign of diminishing, he is either off the booze or on beta-blockers. So it is disconcerting to look into his face and to find it unnaturally pale. All the fury is there but no pulse throbs dangerously at his temples. I stand beside my desk and I wait.

'You'll get official notification in due course,' he says, digging his hands into his pockets to give himself an appearance of relaxation and ease, a ploy at which he fails signally. 'We've been considering ways of rationalising – restructuring – making ourselves a slimmer, sharper operation. We have a number of plans, one of which is to amalgamate the English Language Unit with Student Learning Support.'

I have to work hard to stop my mouth from dropping open in inane astonishment. 'But—' I manage before he cuts me off.

'You cover much of the same ground. You're both giving weaker students extra help with writing essays and so on. It really makes no sense to hive off the foreign students into a separate unit just because they're foreigners. I'm not sure, in fact ...' he adds, as though this is a clever thought that has only just occurred to him, '... I wouldn't be surprised if it counted as discrimination.'

I allow myself a single hoot of derisive laughter. 'They are taught in the English Language Unit,' I say, 'because they need help with the English language. They're not there because they're foreigners but because they're not native English speakers. The USLS is for students with poor study skills.

Many of our overseas students have excellent study skills – they're very bright.'

'Splitting hairs,' he says. 'You both help them with writing essays, don't you?'

'Among many other things.'

'Well then.' He starts to move towards the door.

'You can't make staff economies, you know,' I say. 'Teaching English as a foreign language and supporting dyslexic students, for example, are two completely different areas of expertise.'

He shrugs. 'We'll see,' he says.

'And what about assessment?' I ask. 'We teach units on a lot of degree courses. USLS doesn't do any assessed work.'

'A detail for you and Margaret Jones to sort out, I would have thought.'

He's on the move again, his hand reaching for the door knob.

'The job of running this new, amalgamated ... thing,' I say. 'Presumably that will be advertised as a new post?'

He turns. 'I've obviously not made myself clear. This isn't so much an amalgamation as the ELU being subsumed into the USLS. We're obliged to advertise it as a new post, of course, but Margaret is the obvious candidate to take on the wider responsibility.'

'And in that case, what happens to me?'

'There will still be teaching to be done. I'm sure Margaret will keep you busy.'

'But I shall have no administrative responsibility?'

'Won't be necessary.'

'As director of the ELU, I have senior lecturer status. I shall need to do something to earn that, shan't I?'

Now he allows himself a sharky smile. 'That's an area,' he says, 'where we're looking to make efficiency savings.'

'What about assessments ... exams? Margaret has no

experience of running assessed courses. That's a huge amount of work, which I shall need to continue with.'

'We can all learn, Mrs Gray,' he says as he pulls open the door. 'We can all learn.'

I stand rooted for a moment as he disappears. Then I run to the door and shout at his retreating back, 'Do you know what the students call the USLS? *The Useless Unit!* No-one ever calls the ELU useless!'

He doesn't falter or turn. I watch him till he is out of sight.

After that, I sit down because my legs are feeling odd and I try to make sense of the idiocy I have just witnessed. This amalgamation makes no sense on any strategic level. The ELU is a major money-spinner; thousands of students take our courses, pay inflated overseas students' fees and leave with qualifications moderated by us. The USLS – useless or not – makes no money; it is a branch of pastoral care, really, offering one-to-one or small group help to students who feel that they are drowning. I don't actually think it's useless – I'm sure it saves some students from going under – but the staff there can't possibly do what we do. The overseas student market is a highly competitive one; any university that doesn't employ highly qualified, specialist English teachers will soon lose out, and the VC must know this. So if there is no prospect of saving on staff – apart, possibly, from the pittance gained from docking my salary – what is this really for? At the moment, the only answer I can come up with is so absurdly egotistical that I blush to acknowledge it. I can only conclude that the VC is proposing this ridiculous piece of restructuring as a ploy to get rid of me.

Well, maybe later I can come up with something more sensible by way of an explanation but for the moment I'm going with this one and its very absurdity gives me hope. I shall apply for the new job and I shall get it. It's not in the VC's gift, after all. There will be a proper appointment panel and I can't have made so many enemies on the campus that the panel can be stacked with them, can I? Prejudice aside, I am plainly a better candidate than Margaret. We are the far bigger outfit and the money-spinners; my relentless schmoozing of Far Eastern universities has given us a healthy stream of postgraduate students to swell the coffers; I know how to handle the International Office, Student Accommodation and the Border Agency. I have put sweat, smiles and sleight of hand into all this and Margaret Jones will never manage it. Her clothes alone are enough to doom her: flat brown sandals and lumpy pleated skirts worn winter and summer. Who could possibly take her seriously?

I'm all right now. I see a fight ahead and I'm ready for it. And Freda is coming for the night. The thing about spending time with a four-year-old is that it's impossible to think about anything else. At times, obviously, this is quite annoying but this evening I welcome it as an alternative to obsessive brooding.

Ellie drops Freda off at about six, and we make pizzas for supper, starting from scratch with Delia's scone pizza dough and distributing flour and tomato juice liberally across the kitchen table. After supper, we retire to the sitting room, where we eat strawberries and macaroons and watch a wildlife programme. This wouldn't be my first choice – I have a preference for human interaction – but Freda likes it. We both have to cover our eyes when a gazelle gets eaten by a cheetah, though. This is supposed to be entertainment? And before the watershed? We shall be bringing back public hangings next.

When the wildlife is finished we play dominoes. Freda has discovered them in the old toy cupboard in Annie's room and is delighted with them largely, I think, because – unlike most of her own toys – they involve no screen, no battery and no moving parts. The great thing about dominoes is that it lends itself to match-fixing. Freda is satisfied with a three–nil whitewash and we go upstairs. Here I am put in my place. When I go to help her undress she pushes me away. 'I'm starting big school soon, Granny,' she says. 'I don't need you to help.'

I am unreasonably put out by this. Usually I welcome and encourage these signs of independence but not today. 'Well,' I say more snappily than I intended, 'are you going to read your own bedtime story too?'

She considers me judiciously. 'You can do it today,' she says, 'but soon I shall do it myself.' She returns her attention to unbuttoning her cardigan.

So that's me then: already redundant as David's significant other, I am now redundant as director of the English Language Unit and will soon be redundant as a grandmother. Useless.

Freda goes off to sleep instantly; I watch *Silent Witness* and then start an elaborate process of sedation designed to secure me a night's sleep. I take a long bath, scented with something that claims to soothe and relax; I drink warm milk laced with brandy; I creep into bed beside Freda in the dark and plug myself into my MP3 player so Martin Jarvis can read PG Wodehouse to me. And I stay wide awake all night, lying rigid in my concern not to disturb Freda, compulsively composing job applications, convening possible interview panels and interviewing myself into gibbering irrelevance. When Freda prods me and demands breakfast, I am delighted.

13

Outside Sources

'So, if the niqab woman was actually a man, all my probing at the university and upsetting the people in HR was pointless, wasn't it?' Paula Powell said, getting up from her chair in David Scott's office. 'This "woman" doesn't work at the university and she isn't anyone's grandmother. So where do we go from here?'

'We've got two lines, haven't we?' Scott said. 'If this witness, Jamilleh Hamidi, is right about it being a man – and we've only got her word for it – then there is the possibility that he's the killer. I doubted whether the dog incident was related to our case at all, and it's still a long shot, but now it seems more likely. So we need to pursue that angle. Your work at the university isn't necessarily wasted. The guy had to get the niqab from somewhere. We still need to look for households where the niqab is worn and there's no Islamic community in Marlbury other than that associated with the university, is there?'

'HR say they have no-one on the staff who wears a niqab and Student Records said they couldn't give me names of Muslim students.'

'Couldn't or wouldn't?'

'Said they didn't categorise students by religion.'

'Which is fair enough, I suppose. I think I'll approach the chaplaincy.'

'The chaplaincy? How's that going to help?'

'It isn't just dog collars. They've got a multifaith centre there. Someone must look after the Muslim students. Anyone with access to a niqab must be pretty devout, surely?'

'I suppose.'

'Traditional, anyway. It's a start. Unless you've got a better idea?'

She shook her head. 'No.'

'OK. So, I'm taking you off Islamic duties for the moment and sending you to tread on some other sensitive toes.'

'You're too kind. Whose?'

'The Samaritans. You know what Malcolm Burns told me. Go and find out who else talked to Karen Brody. I've asked Steve to get dates and times of her other calls to the Samaritans from her phone record. Find out, if you can, what was said. Check them all in their log – the call to Malcolm included. Find out if they make notes about the calls they get. If so, ask for them.'

'And if they refuse?'

'Use sweet reason. Point out that Karen is dead, so any secrets that may be revealed can do her no harm. Try to keep Malcolm's name out of it if you can. I don't want to get him sacked if we can help it. They'll pass your request on up to the director, I'm sure. If she's difficult, threaten her with a search warrant and a possible subpoena. I have every respect for the work the Samaritans do but this is a case where being obstructive is just pointless.'

On the university's crowded campus, he was directed, at the third time of asking, to the multifaith centre and found it to be a small and characterless room tucked away behind a room with blackened windows from which the beat, thump and shuffle of a vigorous dance routine could be heard. Distracting for the faithful, he thought, imagining those sweaty, half-naked bodies just next door. The room, he realised, was characterless precisely because of the multiplicity of faiths it was designed to accommodate. No artwork, no emblems, no fixtures, no books, even, could be guaranteed offence-free, so there was nothing. This wasn't a room designed for the meeting of faiths but for keeping them apart. Scott found this vaguely depressing.

More depressing for him was the notice on the wall which gave the times of different services but said that the chaplains were to be found in the chaplaincy office, room 135b in the registry. Cursing, he got back into his car, threaded his way across campus, picked up signs to the registry, parked in a space labelled *Reserved for the Deputy Vice-Chancellor* and went inside to enquire for room 135b. As he made his way up to the first floor, Scott reflected that there was no shortage of character here. The architect had let his imagination roam free, designing a fancifully round building of mildly oriental appearance, a building that nonchalantly denied the dullness of the bureaucratic workings within.

Room 135b had obviously been carved out of room 135, a slice taken just big enough to accommodate two desks. A youngish man sat at each of them, both wearing jackets and ties, both looking up with professionally welcoming smiles. Scott addressed the older and swarthier of the two. 'I'm looking for the Muslim chaplain,' he said.

'And you've found him.' The man stood up and offered his hand. 'Rashid Malik,' he said.

'David Scott.' He fished in his pocket with his free hand. 'Marlbury CID.'

If Rashid Malik was taken aback he didn't show it. 'Have a seat,' he said. 'How can I help you?' His accent was educated and slightly patrician, his manner relaxed. A man who could be comfortable almost anywhere. Scott revised his approach; he would need to be more open with this man than he had intended to be.

'It's a delicate matter, I'm afraid,' he said, glancing at Malik's colleague. 'Maybe we should —'

'Don't worry about me. I can make myself scarce.' The younger man stood up. 'Things to do, you know,' he said, gathering up papers.

'Thank you, Michael,' Malik said as he left.

'I'm sorry if I've inconvenienced him,' Scott said.

'Don't worry. It's a regular routine. We often have students in here wanting to discuss personal matters, as you can imagine. The shared office isn't ideal.'

'How many chaplains are there?'

'Six.' He looked round the little room. 'We box and cox.'

'My issue,' Scott said, 'is this. We have had a report of someone in full Islamic dress – the niqab specifically – on the premises of the university day nursery, unaccompanied by any family members and not apparently connected to any of the children.' Malik was about to speak but Scott continued, 'In itself this is not a police matter, of course, but one witness at least believes that the person was a man.'

Scott saw the muscles tense in Malik's face but his voice was quiet and his tone even as he said, 'These stories go around, you know. One actual incident begets a hundred rumours.'

'I know. But the witness concerned is a Muslim woman, if that makes any difference.'

Malik nodded. 'Does she think she knows the man?'

'No.'

'How do you think I can help?'

'We have to take this seriously because of children being involved. I'm sure you understand that.'

'Yes.'

'The other thing is …' Scott hesitated. He had not intended to talk about the murders but this man's calm gaze changed his mind. 'You will know about the murders – the mother and child – last week. The person in the niqab was attacked by their dog in the garden of the day nursery shortly before they were killed. The dog was killed too.'

This time Malik did look shaken. He pressed his hands to his face for a moment and closed his eyes. 'The newspapers have said nothing of this,' he said.

'It's information we're not releasing.'

'No. Well, I'm glad of that, of course.' He looked into Scott's face. 'What do you want me to do?'

'We need to identify men who have access to a niqab. Is there any way that you could identify such people?'

'There are people I can talk to. I shall need to go carefully.'

'But not too slowly.'

'No. Have you thought that a man might have purchased the niqab?'

'Could a man do that? It wouldn't seem odd?'

'Not at all.' He allowed himself a smile. 'It's not a fashion item, you know.'

'No.'

'In a family where the women wear full niqab it is quite common for the men to do all the shopping.'

'But you can't buy a niqab in Marlbury, can you?'

'No. London would be the nearest place. Or they can be bought online. I can give you the names of some online sites.'

'Thank you.' This world, Scott thought, was odder than he could have imagined.

In Butchery Lane, trapped in the maze of crooked, narrow streets behind the abbey, Paula, with Sarah Shepherd beside her, drove slowly, scanning the crowded terrace of house fronts for the discreet sign that read *The Samaritans*. There was nowhere to park and she wondered how the volunteers managed. She parked round the corner on double yellow lines, then they walked back and rang the doorbell. An elderly woman opened the door, looked flustered when Paula waved her ID, said she would have to talk to the director and closed the door on them. After some time she returned, allowed them into the tiny hallway and directed them up the narrow stairs.

'Right up the top here,' a voice sang out as they reached the first landing, and they climbed an even narrower flight to a sloping-roofed eyrie with a single window and a startlingly close view of the abbey tower. The woman who stood up to greet them confounded Paula's expectations. She wasn't sure what she had been expecting, but it wasn't this. The woman was tall, blonde and manicured, slightly blowsy but expensively dressed, vaguely theatrical. Her voice had a smoker's rasp to it and a half-smoked cigarette burned in an ashtray on the desk. She stubbed it out before moving out from behind the desk.

'Filthy habit,' she said. 'Estelle Campion. I'm the director.'

'DS Paula Powell and DC Sarah Shepherd,' Paula offered, shaking hands.

'Lovely.' She beamed at them. 'Would you like coffee? I'm sure one of the volunteers downstairs would bring us some.'

'Well, I don't want to interrupt—'

'Oh, it's an easy gig, the morning slot. We're rarely busy at this time.'

She moved to the phone on her desk. 'Milk, sugar?'

'Both milk, no sugar, thanks.'

'Fred, my darling,' she purred into the phone, 'if you're not busy, could you bring us three coffees, two with milk, mine the usual? Brilliant!'

Paula and Sarah seated themselves on a small sofa under the window, while Estelle Campion pulled a handsome leather swivel chair from behind her desk and sat down facing them.

'Orthopaedic,' she said, by way of explanation of the chair. 'Bad back.'

'I'm afraid,' Paula said, 'that I really don't know much about the Samaritans. I know what you do, of course, but ... is this a full-time job, being director?'

Estelle Campion gave a hoot of laughter. 'If only!' she said. 'I'm just a volunteer like everyone else. I do this for three years and then return to the corps de ballet.

'So how much time do you spend here?' Sarah ventured.

'Oh, I'm here most days. It's how I choose to do the job. Some directors have full-time jobs, of course, and can't give the time, but I'm fortunate in having a husband who can keep me in the manner I enjoy being accustomed to, so I can give this my full-time attention. I want to make a difference. It's mainly fundraising, if I'm honest. We have to raise money all the time just to keep going. This is my latest project.' She gestured at the room. 'It was a storeroom full of junk up till six months ago, and now *voilà*! Of course, it helps that my husband is in business locally. I have connections.'

Feeling that she was getting more information than she needed but unwilling to start on the substantive business until the coffee arrived, Paula said, 'Lovely view.'

'Yes,' Estelle Campion said, frowning slightly. 'The bloody bells can get you down, though.'

The clinking of china signalled the arrival of coffee and a small, neat, silver-haired man arrived with a tray.

'My favourite man,' Estelle murmured, patting his arm as she took her coffee. Black, Paula noticed, and with quite a bit of sugar in it to judge from the way she stirred it. A woman who liked to be wired, then.

'So,' Estelle asked as Fred disappeared, her eyes suddenly sharp, 'what is it I can do for you?'

'You'll have read about the murders of Karen and Lara

Brody,' Paula said, putting her coffee down to cool. 'We are aware that Karen made several calls to the Samaritans in the week before she died, the last of them very shortly before she was killed.'

'And who gave you that information?' The geniality had quite disappeared from her voice.

'We have Karen's phone records,' Paula said. 'The calls are there.'

Estelle Campion sipped her coffee. 'So, you know about them. What more do you expect me to tell you?'

'I would like to know what she said. We believe it's information that will help us to find her killer.'

'Ha! You really don't know much about us, do you, if you think that I'm going to tell you what a caller said to us in confidence?'

'I know that you can be subpoenaed to give that information in evidence in court. And you know that too.'

'And I know that there is no court case in the offing.'

Paula sighed. 'Karen Brody is dead,' she said. 'I think your duty of confidentiality ends with death, doesn't it? Don't you have a duty now to help us find her killer?'

'Our duty of confidentiality doesn't end with death. Sadly, we lose some of our callers – some do kill themselves – but what they said to us remains confidential.'

'So you won't help us to find a murderer?'

'No.'

Sarah stood up and moved towards the door. 'You keep notes on your callers, don't you?' she asked.

'Who told you that?'

'When I was at school. We had a talk. Two people from the Samaritans came and talked to us. Someone asked if they kept notes and they said yes.'

Estelle looked her in the eye. 'We have no notes on Karen,' she said. 'I destroyed them when we heard that she'd died.'

'How could you be sure that it was the same woman who had talked to you?' Paula asked. 'Was there anything she said that made you think she was in danger?'

'The names. She told us her name was Karen and her daughter was Lara.'

'Just that?'

'Just that.'

They stared at each other.

'I'm just going to pop downstairs now, Mrs Campion,' Sarah said suddenly. 'I'm going to take a look at your records. You can give us access or you can wait for us to come back with a search warrant. If we do that, you'll have a couple of marked police cars sitting outside for several hours and I'm not sure what that will do for your public image.'

Go Sarah! Paula thought as she heard her start down the stairs. It was a card she hadn't intended to play just yet but it was obviously going to work. Estelle Campion picked up her phone. 'There's a policewoman coming down to look through the log, Fred,' she said. 'You know the procedure, don't you?'

Paula heard the emphasis on *log* and *procedure*. Fred was being given instructions to hide everything except the log. On the other hand, she was prepared to believe that notes on Karen had been destroyed. What would be the point of keeping notes on a dead woman? She stood up.

'Did you ever talk to Karen yourself?' she asked.

'No.'

'But you knew about her? You discussed her with other volunteers?'

Estelle gave a slight nod.

'Did you think she was in danger?'

'No.'

'Why not?'

'She wasn't suicidal.'

'And not in danger from anyone else?'

'No.'

'So why was she calling?'

Estelle gave a sigh. 'You've only got to read the papers to know why. Husband serving a long prison sentence, young child, no money, lonely. Who wouldn't be depressed?'

'But she had been in that situation for months, and she was finding her way out of it, getting a qualification. Why did she suddenly start calling?'

'She had something she was trying to sort out. A problem. She was cagey about it. Said it was about divided loyalties – something like that.'

'And that was it?'

'That was it.'

She stood up and took a raincoat off a hook on the back of the door. 'And now I'll just see you off the premises before I go. I'm due out at Hartfield Hall. They're very kindly putting on a fundraiser for us – a strawberries and champagne tea.'

Paula found Sarah in a small, messy room with four telephones. She was completing her check of the log. 'The dates and times tally,' she said, 'and this *Y/N* column here is for suicidal or not. She's always an *N*.' Under her breath, she murmured, 'No sign of any other records. They've spirited them away somewhere.'

Paula turned to Estelle Campion, who was standing in the doorway with her raincoat on. 'Thank you,' she said. 'If you think of anything else, I'm sure you'll let me know.'

Outside, at the car, she said to Sarah, 'You did well in there. Quite changed the weather.'

Sarah flushed scarlet. 'Was that all right? I was worried I was out of order.'

'Just don't try it too often,' Paula said. 'OK?'

Her phone rang.

'David?'

'Paula. Are you finished at the Samaritans?'

'Yes, Not much joy. She—'

'Can you get up to the hospital right away?'

'Yes. Why?'

'Jamilleh Hamidi has just been taken in. We don't have much detail yet. She was found semi-conscious on the university campus. Someone appears to have tried to strangle her.'

'Will she be all right?'

'They don't know yet. She tried to say something, apparently, according to our guys who responded to the 999 call.'

'This has to be to do with her talking to me yesterday, doesn't it, David?'

'It's … possible.'

'And it links her assailant – Karen and Lara's killer – to the university.'

'I think that's moving too fast. There are a lot of unknowns.'

She was in the car now, with Sarah driving. 'David, it doesn't have to be the killer who attacked her, does it? What she told me made it more likely that Karen and Lara were killed by a Muslim man. If Jamilleh told anyone – her husband, for instance – what she told me, do you think she could have been punished for directing us towards the Muslim community?'

'Paula, we don't know and we can't know yet. We need to hear from her, which is why I need you and Sarah at the hospital.'

'Have you got a guard on her there, or are we it?'

'Mike Arthur's there. He was on the 999 call and I've told him to stay.'

'OK.' Just about to ring off, she had a sudden thought. 'What about Jamilleh's friend – Farah? She was there that afternoon and there yesterday when Jamilleh talked to me. If it was the killer who attacked Jamilleh, Farah could be in danger too.'

There was silence on the other end. Then he said, 'For that matter, Gina would be in danger too.'

'So? What do we do?'

'We can't offer protection – we haven't the resources. But they should be made aware.'

'Do you want me to do that?'

There was a silence.

'No,' he said. 'I'll do it.'

14

Wednesday 25th July

Safety Catch

Although Freda and I get off to an early start, I am slow-moving from lack of sleep and it takes us an age to be ready to leave the house. For a start, there is a fair bit of clearing up to be done in the kitchen. I heard Annie's troupe return and crash about last night, and the evidence is here in the form of malodorous burger wrappings, bloody ketchup smears and a small puddle of beer. Then we make eggy bread for breakfast, which necessitates further clearing up; I require a second cup of coffee and take longer than my allotted ten minutes to do the quick crossword; Freda gets bored and goes to find some morning rubbish on the television, from which she has to be prised away. In the end, it is after nine before I get her strapped into my bike's child seat and we set off for the campus. I am dropping Freda at Acorns. Although term has finished, there are children's holiday activities going on in venues around the campus, and activities for the under-fives happen at Acorns. This morning, Freda is looking forward to dance and percussion sessions – less messy than yesterday's potato prints.

I drop her off and as I'm wheeling my bike through the car park I spot a familiar figure unloading a toddler from a shiny green four-by-four. It is Lavender, my ex-husband's newish wife, looking as fragrant as ever, despite having produced two sons in quick succession. This morning she is wearing tailored cream trousers, a crisp tan-and-cream-striped shirt, a tan bow tying back her discreetly streaked blonde hair and pearl earrings. Earrings, even? For the nursery run?

I have nothing against Lavender, actually. She is a sweet, if not very bright young woman and Andrew and I were long divorced before he met her. If anything I feel a bit guilty towards her; I feel I should have warned her what hopeless husband material Andrew is. She looks cheerful enough, though. It all depends on what you want, I suppose. I am surprised to see her here; I assumed she was going for total immersion motherhood.

'Good morning,' I call as I approach. 'Is Arthur a regular Acorns attender these days?' I flash an obligatory smile at the solemn infant.

She leans in to *mwah mwah* me. 'I'm getting him used to it,' she says, blushing slightly. 'I'm starting a course next term – just part time – Art Appreciation.'

'Lovely,' I say.

'Well ...' the blush deepens '... I thought I should have something to talk to Andrew about in the evenings. Don't want to be a drudgy wife who can only talk about nappies, you know.'

'Absolutely,' I say, not adding that in my experience Andrew prefers talking to being talked to. 'Well, good luck with that!' and off I go.

As I'm wheeling my bike past the Student Union towards the English Language block, my eye is caught by activity over to my right, near the dance studio. There are flashing lights. An ambulance and a police car. I swerve round and steer in that direction, trying not to look like an obvious rubbernecker, keeping my eyes to the ground as though deep in thought.

When I'm close enough, though, I look up, just in time to see someone being loaded into the ambulance. She is being carried feet first, so I see first the folds of a grey chador, and then her face.

I am so shocked that I let my bike fall to the ground and the clatter alerts one of the policemen, who comes bustling towards me, waving me away.

'This is a possible crime scene,' he calls. 'No nearer, please.'

'But I know her,' I call, moving closer. 'I'm her teacher.'

'Well, good for you,' he says. 'We still don't need you all over the crime scene.'

'I can identify her,' I say. 'I know who she is.'

'We know who she is, madam. She had ID on her. Now if you wouldn't mind —'

'Of course,' I say. 'Sorry.' But I linger as I pick up my bike, until he turns back and scowls at me and I am forced to wheel it away.

Jamilleh. A crime scene. What the hell is going on?

There is one person who could definitely tell me and he is the very person I have sworn not to contact. I have decided, since yesterday's meeting in Malcolm's office, that I am not speaking to David any more, and that it – whatever *it* was – is over between us. I am not being unreasonable. David has been back from London for almost a week now and he has not contacted me once. All attempts at communication have come from me and the only ones he has responded to have been those relating to the murders. Otherwise, he has not answered his phone, he has ignored my texts and has sent automatic out of office replies to my emails. I didn't expect the *affair*, *relationship, folie à deux* or whatever else you like to call it between us to end like this. I fully expected it to end some time, but by mutual agreement between two mature adults. I didn't envisage one of us dumping the other as though we were a pair of hormone-crazed teenagers. When I think about it, though, David has played this cleverly. He wants to be rid of me but hasn't the guts to dump me, so he is ignoring me, knowing full well that I won't be able to stand that and so will be the one to dump him. He walks away feeling virtuous – even hard done by – and I have no-one to shout at.

I am pondering this, and probably snarling a bit, as I round the corner of the English Language building and come face to face with Margaret Jones, current head of the USLS and putative director of the new, amalgamated unit. This is a situation which is beyond even my social aplomb, and it is certainly way out of her league. We stand and stare at each other until she ducks her head, performs an odd little scamper and heads off in the direction of the registry. I watch her go. Those sandals! As I walk upstairs to my office, I'm reminded of a scene I had with Annie when she was fourteen and insisted on giving up GCSE Physics. 'Miss Proctor's shoes,' she said. 'I cannot spend another year looking at those shoes. There is a distinct possibility that one day I shall throw up.' I rebuked her, of course, and told her how immature it was to let such trivia get in the way of her education, but today I'm with Annie all the way.

In my office I can't settle to anything. I need to know what happened to Jamilleh. Would Paula tell me? Unlikely, I know, but there's no harm in trying. I don't have her mobile number, so I ring the police station, to be told, brusquely, that DS Powell is out of the station and they can't say when she will be back. So where is she? At the hospital? Well, I can ring the hospital, can't I? I ring reception and I explain, in my most authoritative tone, that I am the director of the English Language Unit at the university (*for how much longer?* an insidious little voice in my head asks me). 'I have been informed,' I say, 'that a student of ours, a Mrs Jamilleh Hamidi, has met with an accident and has been taken to A&E. I wanted to enquire about her condition and the circumstances of the accident as I may need to inform her family.'

'Just a minute,' the receptionist says, and the line goes quiet. I wait. She returns. Her tone is unfriendly. 'Mrs Hamidi is still being assessed,' she says. 'We are giving out no information about her at this time.'

'So, if I ring back later?'

'You're not family, are you?'

'No, but as I said —'

'Her family will be kept informed.' She snaps, and cuts me off.

So that's that. I'm not done yet, though. In a while, I'll ring Monica in the International Office and see if she can find anything out. And I'll try Paula again. In the meantime, I turn to my emails, where I find an application form for the post of Director of the Unit for Specialist English Language and Enhanced Skills Support. Look at it! See what they've done? It is, quite literally now, USELESS.

I print off the form, nonetheless, and I track down my CV document with a view to updating and enhancing it. In the pursuit of this, I find my end-of-year report, just submitted, which reveals, among other things, that the unit had over 2,000 students through its doors in the course of the last academic year – some of them, admittedly, for only one class a week – and that our stand-alone courses raised over two million in overseas student fees. *And how much did USLS make, you arseholes?* I mutter, as I insert this information into my CV.

I make myself some coffee, though I know I've already had more than enough this morning, and I start to read through the application form. I can't fill it in. I suppose it's the combination of the coffee and the sleepless night, but I am seized with an overwhelming urge to scrawl all over it, like spoiling a ballot paper. *MY JOB, DICKHEADS* is what I seem to want to write, but I don't. I am distracted by a call on my mobile, which is sitting on my desk. The call is from David and I am not going to answer it. Whatever he may have to tell me,

I have vowed not to speak to him and I will keep my word. So, I sit and watch as my phone glows and buzzes and jumps about, pleading eagerly for my reply. When it stops, I pick it up and put it in my bag, and a minute later I hear a message buzz. Well, I haven't sworn off reading his messages, so I take a look. *Jamilleh Hamidi attacked on university campus,* it reads. *Possible connection with yesterday's interview. You and Farah should be aware. David.*

I stuff the phone back in my bag and pace the room, fuming. *Thank you, David, for your care and concern. Be aware? Is that the best you can do? And Farah? Have you told her or am I supposed to pass the message on? I didn't ask to be there at Paula's interview yesterday, did I? You can't claim this time that I've been sticking my nose in and have only myself to blame. You asked me to be there, remember? So if it has put me in danger and all you can manage is Be Aware, I call that dereliction of duty, quite apart from being a totally heartless and inadequate response to the possible peril of a woman you claimed, until quite recently, to love.*

It is a good thing I don't say any of this out loud because the walls of these offices are scarcely more than hardboard and I would, undoubtedly, have shouted. As an alternative to shouting or breaking things, I decide to leave. I shove the application form into my in-tray, put my copy of *Bring up the Bodies* into my bag, get on my bike and cycle round to the abbey, picking up a sturdy-looking cheese and coleslaw roll from the The Burnt Cake on my way. It is not really the weather for alfresco reading and eating but it's not actually raining and I have a windproof jacket and my rage to keep me warm. We have a run-through in costume of *Much Ado* starting at one o'clock and it is already half past eleven, so I'm unlikely to succumb to hypothermia in the interim. I succumb to the book instead, to Mantel's lyrical, haunting, spiky, witty, addictive prose.

An hour or so of this, helped by my cheese roll, restores me enough to face the irritations of a rehearsal in costume. People are so incompetent. They have all had the chance to try on their costumes but the women still turn up without the right bras to go under the wide square necks of their dresses, and I know I shouldn't make gender assumptions but I do think any woman should be able to do the odd running repair – a bit of hem come down or a seam coming apart – rather than handing the damned thing to me. As for the men: they can't seem to master the idea of keeping all the bits of their costume together, so they end up fighting over ruffs and people are wearing odd shoes. I almost experience a wince of fellow feeling with our *we-in-the-profession* director as I mutter *so bloody amateur* under my breath.

As Ursula, I'm on and off throughout the play but I do get a chance to watch quite a lot and I think it's going to be all right. It's difficult to wreck it completely if you have a decent Beatrice and Benedick, and our B & B are doing a good job. They are well cast – young enough to have a life ahead of them but old enough to know this is probably their last chance. They are both wary and warm in equal measure and you hope the audience will cheer, or at least sigh with satisfaction, at the final kiss. There was a time when I liked to think of David and me as a Benedick and Beatrice couple, our spiky exchanges masking an attraction we were too wary to acknowledge. In recent months, though, when David has been working in London, our weekends together have been more Elyot and Amanda in *Private Lives*, our rows, I freely admit, generally started by me. There was too much pressure of expectation about those weekends, too much drinking on Friday nights for quick relaxation, too much hung-over disappointment and ill-temper, too many apologies and regrets. It's a good thing, really, that David has decided to call it a day; if we had stayed together much longer we would have morphed into *Who's Afraid of Virginia Woolf.*

When the run-through is over and I have restored some order to the men's dressing room, I go back to the campus to pick up Freda. Nico's ear infection is not clearing up and Ellie has an appointment for him at the doctor's. In the car park at Acorns I encounter, of all people, Andrew, the man I was once married to. He has come, he says, to pick up Arthur because the news has got round about the attack on Jamilleh and he doesn't want Lavender on the campus while there's some maniac on the loose. This is, you will have to agree, a whole order of magnitude more caring than *Be aware*. I consider Andrew, taking in the details. He has just jumped out of the green Range Rover I saw Lavender in this morning. This will not be Andrew's usual car; he will always be driving something zingier, more sporty. But you can't get a baby seat into one of those, can you? I see from Andrew's clothes – lightweight silver-grey suit, gleaming with a hint of silk, and polished Italian shoes – that he has been at work today, so he must have left his law chambers, driven to his gracious Georgian home in Marlbury's rural hinterland, exchanged whatever the latest sports model is for the Range Rover and returned to pick up his son

Would Andrew ever have gone to these lengths for me? Been this protective? Not a chance. Lavender is young, of course, and a more obvious candidate for protection than I ever was. It would be a pleasure to look after Lavender, wouldn't it? She would be so grateful, blush so prettily. And me? Tough as old boots, that Gina. Woe betide any man who tries to look after her.

I seek around for something unkind to say to Andrew, and I find it.

'Well,' I say, 'what a model father you've become, Andrew. Quite hands-on. Don't forget that you've got a couple of daughters too, though, will you? You are going to see Annie's play at the Aphra Behn, I assume?'

'Ah,' he says, feebly, 'babysitters, you know, with the two boys. Tricky.'

'Well, you don't have to drag Lavender along. I'm going to the matinée on Saturday. Why don't you join me? Annie's boyfriend's coming too. Jon. Remember him from Elsinore?'

'Ah,' he says again, and I see a faint blush rise under his permatan. 'Weekends – family time, you know.'

'Absolutely,' I say, smiling sweetly. 'It just depends which family you're talking about, doesn't it?'

'Annie's a grown woman,' he protests, summoning up his adversarial skills. 'The boys need me.'

'Of course,' I say. 'But Freda's not a grown woman, is she? Remember Freda? Your granddaughter? She's four now, five soon. Come into Acorns now and I'll introduce her to you. You've probably forgotten what she looks like. They change so fast at that age, don't they?'

I tuck my arm into his and start to propel him towards the entrance. There are a number of other parents around and he can hardly resist without making a scene. 'Of course,' I say conversationally, 'it's rather ageing being a grandparent, as I know, especially if the image you're aiming for is groovy, ever-youthful, second-time-around dad, but it has it's rewards, I can assure you, and Freda is a delightful child when you get to know her.'

'I know her,' he growls. 'Don't talk as if I never see her.'

His protestations are belied by Freda herself, however, who comes hurtling towards me, brandishing sheaves of yesterday's potato print designs, now dry enough to be taken home. She stops when she sees Andrew, says, 'Oh, hello' with perfect coolness and then tugs me by the hand. 'These are for Mummy and Nico,' she says, 'and we have to take them home very carefully so they don't get crumpled.'

We walk away and leave Andrew to collect his boy.

When I've dropped Freda and her artwork and enquired after Nico, who has been prescribed a second round of antibiotics but raises a cheerful smile, I cycle home with the troubles of the morning crowding in on me once again. Jamilleh, David, the job. Where to start? With a glass of wine, I decide, but the phone is ringing as I walk into the house so I dump my bag and run to it, forgetting to consider that it might be David. It's not David. In fact, it appears to be nobody and I'm about to put it down, assuming that it's one of those automated phantom calls, when I hear my mother's voice, fainter than usual, but still with its crisp edge.

'Virginia?'

'Mother. Are you all right?'

'Of course.'

'It's just ...' how should I put it? *It's just that you never ring me.*

'I just wondered,' she says, 'if you were in need of refuge again.'

'In need of refuge?' I ask, bewildered.

'Yes.' She sounds irritated. 'Last time I saw you, you were taking refuge from Annie and her friends.'

I remember now, Sunday's white lie. 'Oh yes, I say. They're all still with me.'

'So, I thought you might like to come here at the weekend.'

She wants to see me. The invitation is not for my benefit but for hers. My white lie has become her face-saver, because heaven forbid that she should say *I'd like to see you.* Why do our dealings have to be so complicated?

'On Saturday,' I say, 'I'm going to see their play in the afternoon, and then we've got a dress rehearsal for this production of *Much Ado About Nothing* that I told you about, but on Sunday Annie and the others will be packing up to leave for Edinburgh and the house will be chaos. How would Sunday suit you?'

'Fine.'

'Shall I bring food?'

'Food?'

'Yes. Lunch. Or will you —'

'Yes, better bring something,' she says, and rings off.

15

27.07.12: 09.00

Team Meeting

Jamilleh Hamidi's passport photo was now up on the whiteboard alongside the pictures of Karen and Lara Brody. Scott pointed at it. 'Paula has the latest on her,' Scott said, and stood aside to let Paula take the floor.

'You all know,' she said, 'that early on Wednesday morning, Jamilleh was attacked on the university campus. We've now pieced together her movements before the attack. She had left her child at the day nursery and was walking across the campus to the multifaith centre, where a Muslim women's meeting of some sort was taking place. She took a route along a path behind the drama studio and someone attacked her. Tried to strangle her. It was a serious attack. No sexual assault. It looks as though someone was trying to kill her. Her larynx and windpipe were badly damaged and she was unconscious when the paramedics got to her.'

'Who raised the alarm?' Darren Floyd asked.

'A guy working in the dance studio next to the drama studio. Justin Smyth. He had the windows open to get rid of the previous day's sweat. Heard the scuffle, looked out and shouted, and the attacker ran off.'

'Any description?'

'Not much. Thickset, youngish man, he thought, wearing a hoodie. He only saw a back view.'

'Anything from Jamilleh?'

'A bit. She regained consciousness quite quickly but she can barely speak and we were allowed only a few minutes with her yesterday. She recognised me, though, and she must have remembered our conversation. When I asked about her attacker, she said, "His eyes were the same." I asked if she meant the same as the "woman" in the niqab, and she said yes.'

This was new information to everyone except Scott. She waited for the buzz to die down. 'One other piece of information. Jamilleh was talking on her mobile when she was attacked. She was talking to her husband, who was working in one of the physics labs. He heard her gasp and drop the phone and then nothing more. When he tried to phone her back and her phone was dead, he went over to the multifaith centre to check that she was all right and got there in time to see the ambulance arrive. The area of the attack was searched and no phone was found. We have to assume that the attacker took it with him.'

She turned to look at Scott. 'That's about it.'

'Thanks, Paula.' He looked round the room. 'Any comments or questions?'

Sarah Shepherd raised a hand and Scott wondered, not for the first time, how she always managed to look like an overgrown schoolgirl.

'Yes, Sarah?

'I know it's probably just coincidence but did anyone else think it was odd that both Jamilleh and Karen were attacked while they were on the phone?'

'It's a good point. In both cases we think the women were attacked because of something they knew. Seeing them on the phone would have emphasised the need to silence them.'

127

'Do we think they both had the same information?' Mike Arthur asked.

'Possibly, but probably not. All Jamilleh said was that her attacker was the same man as she had seen wearing the niqab. If he was Karen's killer, it's a reasonable hypothesis that he killed her because of something she knew about him. We know she had some information that worried her – worried her enough to call the Samaritans.'

'And her father said she seemed worried about something,' Paula put in, 'and he doesn't seem like the most observant person in the world.'

'So we need to find out what it was Karen knew. Paula, do you think there's more information to be got from the Samaritans? With what we've got now, I'm prepared to go in for a search.'

'The director claimed that she had destroyed the notes on Karen when they knew she was dead, but that may not be true. Someone spirited the notes away before we got down to the call room. And anyway, we can insist on talking to the volunteers who spoke to her, can't we?'

'That's a grey area. We'll go for the search first. I can get a warrant this morning. And I'll talk to Malcolm Burns again – the volunteer she was speaking to when she was attacked, we believe. I'll get him …' he glanced at Paula '… on his own this time, and see what I can squeeze out of him. I'm not pussyfooting around this any more.'

'I think we can get in without a warrant,' Paula said. 'Sarah did a great job last time we were there. Search warrants mean screaming police cars and flashing lights – bad PR for a confidential service. If we can take them by surprise before they've got time to hide anything, I think we're in.'

'OK. We'll apply for the warrant as back-up then. We'll also have another go at Doug Brody. He didn't want to talk before, but he was still in shock. Let's see how he's feeling now. Sarah, get onto The Scrubs, will you? Find out when Karen last visited Brody, and find out if they keep a record of phone calls the inmates make. They'll be allowed a fixed number of calls per week from a payphone and you'd expect the prison authorities to want to know who they're phoning.'

'Yes,' Sarah said. 'I've got a question, though. Whoever killed Karen, if he did it because of something she knew, why did he kill Lara and the dog as well?'

Scott looked round the room. 'Any suggestions?'

'Panic?' Steve proposed.

'Are we losing sight,' Paula asked, 'of the possibility that the attacker was after the loot from the petrol station raid? We put that on the back burner because the house hadn't been ransacked, but suppose he believed that it was hidden somewhere else? Suppose he wasn't wanting to shut Karen up but to make her talk? He starts by killing the dog but she won't tell him what he wants. Then he threatens Lara, and carries out the threat when she still doesn't tell. Can't tell, we assume, because she doesn't know. Because she would have told rather than let her daughter be killed, wouldn't she?'

'And then he disposes of her,' Sarah said, 'because he knows she can't tell him anything. We didn't think of that when we said the killer couldn't have been after information because he didn't torture Karen. He would know, wouldn't he, that if she hadn't talked to save Lara then it was because she couldn't. She didn't know?'

'Except,' Steve said, 'the autopsy on Karen showed no real signs of a struggle – no defence wounds, did it? I mean, I'm not a parent, so I don't know, but wouldn't she have fought tooth and nail to save Lara? And there were no signs that she'd been tied up, were there?'

'So we put that back on the back burner, I think, Paula,' Scott said, 'though we don't rule it out.'

'I had one more thought,' Sarah offered.

'Red hot today, our DC Shepherd,' Darren Floyd murmured to Mike Arthur in a perfectly audible aside. Paula shot him a warning glance. Sarah pressed on.

'We think Jamilleh was attacked because she told us that the person in the niqab was a man, but he must have thought she knew more than that, mustn't he? Because just knowing he was a man was no good to us. He must have thought that she actually recognised him.'

'She said she didn't,' Paula put in. 'She was sure it was a man but she didn't know him.'

'But maybe he didn't know that. And if he thought she'd recognised him just from his eyes, then he must be someone she sees regularly, a friend or neighbour.'

'Well, we've always assumed that he comes from the Muslim community,' Scott said. 'How else would he have got hold of a niqab? But that doesn't get us far, and we certainly can't start interviewing people on the grounds that they're Muslim men. We need to narrow it down.'

'And we need to think about the kind of life Jamilleh leads,' Paula said. 'She'll spend most of her time with other women and with children, won't she? So this man would need to be a relative or a neighbour.'

'The place she goes to regularly is the day nursery, isn't it?' Darren Floyd said. 'Suppose this guy is a paedo and she's seen him hanging around there before? She hasn't put him together with the man she saw in the niqab thing, but she might at any time.'

'What, hanging about in different disguises, Darren? That's stretching it a bit, isn't it?' Paula asked.

'No, in fact, it's not, DS Powell. Maybe he was legit – had a child in the nursery, who's now at school, but he still needs his fix, so he's finding ways to hang around.'

'It's possible,' Steve conceded reluctantly, 'And maybe that's what Karen knew too. She'd spotted him and he knew it, and he suspected that Lara might tell someone too. Remember there was something in Gina Gray's statement about Lara laughing when the dog attacked? That always seemed odd but it wouldn't if Karen had warned Lara that he was a nasty piece of work.'

'It's a nice, neat solution,' Scott said, 'but I'm not sure it'll wash. If Karen thought there was a paedophile hanging around the nursery, why didn't other people see him? The staff, too? And why was it such a problem for her to inform us? What kind of moral dilemma could she have had?'

'If he was a relative or a close friend's husband, or a boyfriend even?'

'None of which Karen seems to have had. No brothers, no close friends, no boyfriends.'

'Suppose he threatened her – or threatened Lara? That could have been why she wanted the Samaritans to pass on the information to us, couldn't it?' Paula suggested.

Scott considered. 'You're right. It's not impossible. We need to find out whether the staff at the nursery have been aware of children being approached by a man. If this guy did no more than hang about you wouldn't expect him to start killing people who noticed him.'

'Except,' said Darren Floyd, 'you know how people are around paedos. Chances are this guy lives on Eastgate. If we'd even spoken to him it would have gone round like the clap. Next thing they'd be stringing him up.'

'Which reminds me,' Scott said, 'talking of things going round. How did Jamilleh's attacker know about her suspicions? The incident with the dog was more than a week ago. He didn't take action immediately. He took action after she spoke to Paula. He could assume that she hadn't identified him to Paula because he wasn't questioned, but he decided she had to be silenced before she said any more. How did he know that she had talked to us? Paula interviewed her at the university and reported to us on Tuesday evening. The other people present at the interview were her friend, Farah, and Gina Gray who sat in to help out if Jamilleh's grasp of English caused problems. Jamilleh and Farah had managed to keep it quiet until they spoke to Paula, so it seems unlikely that they went home and started blabbing. I would very much like to know whose tongue has been wagging and how far the information has gone.'

The room had gone very still. David allowed the silence to stretch out before he said, 'Well, if anyone wants to talk to me they know where to find me. Paula, as soon as we get the warrant, you take Mike with you and go back to the Samaritans. I'm going to talk again to Malcolm Burns and I'll chase up Rashid Malik on possible sources for this guy's niqab. Sarah, you're getting onto The Scrubs about Karen's visits to Doug Brody and his phone calls. I'll go and talk to him again tomorrow. You can come with me to The Scrubs, Darren.' When Darren Floyd looked about to protest, Scott asked, 'You weren't expecting the weekend off, were you? When we've got a double murder and a serious assault on our hands?' Without waiting for a reply, he went on, 'Steve, check out Jamilleh Hamidi's address and check out her neighbours for anyone known to us. Nothing new on Doug Brody's associates, I suppose? No? Well keep on it. Sarah, go back to the hospital. See if Jamilleh has anything more to say. Darren, go along to Acorns and find out if they've had any concerns about a man hanging around there. And mind your language. Cut out the *paedo* references. And everyone, the attack on Jamilleh has brought the media down on us again, as you'll have seen. I made a statement yesterday and now they'll have to wait until there are further developments. You don't talk to anyone. Right? And bring me the developments.'

As they filtered out of the room, Scott looked at his phone. He had had no reply to his text to Gina the previous day. He considered ringing her to make sure that she was all right. He was somewhat ashamed of that text, really: ashamed of the relief he had felt when his call went unanswered, and ashamed of the impersonal tone of the text itself. She was entitled to better than that, of course she was, but this case called for his full attention and he couldn't be distracted by the need to mend things with her. Mending would need to be done, he knew that, but it would have to wait until they had caught their killer. He couldn't afford the expenditure of energy that any negotiation with Gina involved. In good form, he relished the duel, the lightning flick of the wrist, the feints, the nifty footwork that was called for, but this case was demanding everything from him. The media were snapping at his heels, hungry for every detail, and would soon turn against him if progress seemed to stall. At the same time, his team was laughably underpowered for this sort of case – and they were distressed by it. They might joke around or play blasé, but he could feel their tension and their frustration at not making faster progress. As for Paula, she was wound up tight enough to break. This was her case, after all; she had seen the bodies; he could see how personal this felt to her. He was doing his best to be tactful and not to sideline her but it was his case now, his failure if they didn't find the killer soon. They had all been shaken by the attack on Jamilleh Hamidi; another attack like that would be his responsibility.

It was always too much to hope, of course, that a murder could happen in Marlbury without Gina finding some connection with it, and he had to admit that she had been useful in putting him onto Malcolm Burns and the Iranian women, but the trouble with her was that she had no respect for police work, really. She was quick with her insights, of course, and dogged in her way, when she got her teeth into a case, but she despised the painstaking slog that was ninety-five per cent of police work. And she underestimated the skills of good police officers: intelligence, observation and empathy; the ability to see patterns and cut through the irrelevant; thinking both linear and lateral. The fractious weekends they had spent over the past weeks, when he had been working with the Met, had not been altogether her fault, but they owed a lot to her insistence on regarding his secondment as a sort of sabbatical, as though he was just swanning around New Scotland Yard playing at policing. In fact it had been demanding, stressful and often demoralising. The Met officers he was working with regarded him as a provincial who could not possibly understand the complexity and seriousness of global crime. At any opportunity they would make him feel like a slow-minded rustic, so he had to be twice as well-prepared and twice as focussed as everyone else just to stay in the game. This, combined with a lot of eating out alone in unfriendly London and miserable evenings spent in a B&B, meant that what he wanted at weekends was some peace and quiet and, quite frankly, some TLC. But TLC was not Gina's strong point, and what she wanted from their weekends, he knew, was fun. The trouble was that Gina's concept of fun inevitably involved an element of verbal combat and that had too often turned into linguistic sumo wrestling.

It could be mended, and it would be, once this case was done. In the meantime, he was pretty sure that it was her tongue that had wagged over Paula's interview with Jamilleh and that annoyed him, as well as making him unwilling to talk to her. She would only prise more information out of him, which she would then feed into the rumour mill. If she couldn't keep her mouth shut, then she couldn't blame him for keeping his distance. He put his phone away.

16

Friday 27th July

Relative Values

Annie is in a foul mood this morning. She comes down early, before any of the others are stirring, and sits and glowers at me while I'm drinking my morning coffee. I know better than to ask outright what the matter is; she will simply yell at me for not having the sensitivity to intuit the nature of her pain. Instead, I pretend obliviousness and try to involve her in the crossword. The glower darkens; torrents threaten. I give in.

'Is there anything particular the matter?' I venture.

She slams her mobile across the table at me. 'Only being woken at seven thirty in the morning by a crap text message,' she growls.

'Oh, crap text messages,' I say. 'I know all about them.' But she is not interested in my problems.

'Well, look at it,' she storms.

I pick up the phone, afraid that this will be her charming, sweet-natured and altogether desirable medical student boyfriend, Jon, finally deciding that she is too much like hard work and declaring his intention to move on, but the message is from Andrew. He is sorry that he can't get to the play. Family stuff. He is sure she will understand. I immediately feel guilty. This has been prompted by my reminder to Andrew. He had obviously forgotten all about the play. If I'd said nothing, he would have said nothing and Annie might not even have noticed that he hadn't been to the play. Yes, she would. Of course she would. That he takes an interest in her matters to her and I could kill him for that. The girls got used to Andrew's lack of interest in them even before I divorced him. We were a contented little trio during their teenage years. We screamed at each other quite a bit, but that didn't matter; we knew we could rely on each other, and Andrew hardly impinged at all. He had rights, of course; he was supposed to see them every other weekend, but he's an international lawyer and he was often away, and the girls increasingly had weekend activities – dance and drama classes, hockey matches and birthday sleepovers. The weekend visits dwindled from sporadic to blue moon frequency and no-one, it seemed to me, minded. Then Annie involved Andrew in her plan to study law, he encouraged her to try for his old college at Oxford, she got in and there was a very irritating love-in between the two of them for a few months, until baby Arthur stopped mewling and puking, hauled himself to his feet and became a delightful toddler, followed briskly by baby Hubert, who will, no doubt, be equally delightful soon. Andrew has sons; they are the pride of his heart and Annie has been dumped.

I push the phone back to Annie. She takes it and rereads the message. Is this to fuel her rage or in the hope of a crumb of comfort? I need to deflect her. I know from experience how this will go otherwise. She will start offloading, beginning with Andrew but then allowing the whirlpool of her discontent to suck in all the other annoyances and injustices of her life while I attempt helpful comments and suggestions, only to find that at the dark, swirling core of this whirlpool one person is to blame for everything, and that, it turns out, is me. I have been there before and I am anxious not to go there again.

'I'm reading *Bring up the Bodies*,' I say. 'I'll lend it to you

136

when I've finished. It explains a lot about fathers and sons.'

She says, 'Pa isn't the King of England. The fate of the country doesn't depend on his having a son and heir.'

'I know. I'm just saying there's a thing about men and sons. I don't think I realised it. I couldn't see any reason why Andrew shouldn't be delighted to have you and Ellie, but he wasn't. I thought he just didn't like children, but now I think if you and Ellie had been boys we might still be married.'

'Well, I'm sorry if we screwed up your life for you.'

'Not at all. You revealed him in his true colours and I have never regretted divorcing him.' I drain my nearly cold coffee. 'If Lavender had produced another couple of girls, I don't think she'd have lasted long,' I say.

'He'd have had her beheaded, would he?' she asks, with the morning's first glimmer of a smile.

'More or less.'

'And this aperçu of yours is supposed to help me how?'

'It's supposed to tell you that it's not personal. It's not a judgement on you. Pa just likes the boys because they're boys. If anything, I'm the one who should feel it personally. Lavender is so much the opposite of me in every way, I can't help feeling that *definitively-not-Gina* was what Andrew was looking for second time around.'

'Well she is fragrant, of course, dear Lavender.' She fetches a mug and pours herself some coffee.

'She is sweet and soft and fragrant and pliable. And rich, of course.'

'You make her sound like a cake.'

'So she is. She is like a particularly delicious little cake with pink icing on the top and little sugar flowers. One that you have to handle with care or it will crumble to pieces in your hand.'

'And what are you?' She is watching me over the rim of her mug and I think she's smiling.

'Oh, I'm one of those thick, solid slabs of flapjack – terribly worthy, full of fibre and likely to break your teeth if you're not careful.'

She lets out a hoot of laughter. 'You actually are quite a funny woman, you know, Ma.' She swirls her coffee round. 'Men, you know – well boys, really – they make jokes all the time. It's the way they come on to you. Trouble is, they're mostly not as funny as you.'

With this, she gets up and leaves, saying as she goes, 'You know Jon's arriving this evening, don't you? I shall be at the theatre. Can you give him some supper?'

'Well, no,' I call after her. 'I've got the tech for *Much Ado*. I shan't be here.'

'Oh well, just leave him something, then. He's not fussy.'

Her voice floats down airily from the stairs.

'How's he going to get in, Annie?' I ask, going to the foot of the stairs.

'I'll tell him about the key in the shed,' she says over her shoulder, and disappears into her room.

The key in the shed. We have always kept a key in the shed, under an old bird bath which turned rusty but never made it to the tip. We have had it there for years and I have never worried about the insecurity of the arrangement until now, when I've been told to *be aware*. That seemed to be a perfectly useless injunction and I couldn't see what practical action I could take, but now I see that not having a key to my house available to anyone who takes the trouble to go through the side gate (bolt broken) and look in a few childishly obvious places in my shed might be the sort of thing David had in mind.

It seems suddenly urgent that I retrieve the key and I run out to the shed – pyjamas, bare feet and all – and lift up the bird bath to find nothing there. I stare stupidly at the empty space, then get down on my knees, regardless of the filthy floor, and grope around helplessly for the key which I feel must be here. I run back indoors and bang on Annie's bedroom door. She opens it and peers out at me, looking irritated. I can hear music from inside. The other girls are sleeping in her room too, on an old studio couch with broken springs.

'Someone's taken the key,' I say. 'I just went to check.'

'Well, it wasn't me. I haven't used it for years. I don't live here, remember?'

You could have fooled me.

'And it wasn't me. That's the point. I always have my key with me. It's on the same ring as my office key and the one to my bike padlock. That's what I mean. Someone's stolen it.'

She looks at me in puzzlement. 'So Ellie's got it,' she says.

'Ellie hasn't lived here for eighteen months. Why would she have it?'

'So the last person who used it forgot to put it back and nobody has needed it for ages so we didn't notice it was gone. Doesn't matter. I'll leave my key for Jon.'

'No!' My voice comes out very sharp and startles her. I take a breath. 'We've had a few break-ins in the road,' I say. 'I think we ought to be a bit careful. Why don't you tell Jon to go to Ellie's house and get her key?' '

She opens her mouth to argue but I think the agitation she's picking up from me stops her. She shrugs. 'OK,' she says and retreats into the room, closing the door on me.

I go and shower, taking care with my dirty feet, and dress for a day which involves a morning with Freda, an afternoon with my wives and an evening in the abbey gardens (where I shall, of course, be wearing a farthingale). I offered yesterday to take Freda out this morning because she has had her allotted quota of holiday activities, Nico was still fretful and Ellie was looking fraught. This afternoon I shall go in to teach the wives but I'm not sure how many will be there. I have managed to get news of Jamilleh by the simple expedient of finding her husband's university email address and contacting him. I got a reply – brief and guarded – yesterday evening, telling me that Jamilleh was improving but would be in hospital until next week. I doubt that Farah will be there, if she has had the *be aware* warning, and it may be that the others are steering clear of the campus too, if Andrew's anxiety for Lavender is anything to go by.

I cycle round to Ellie's and inspect Nico, who is looking much better. I tell Ellie about the missing key. She looks vague and says she doesn't think she's got it, but she supposes she might. She looks helplessly round her chaotic kitchen and I can see that there is no point in pursuing this. Ellie was once the orderly member of our trio but motherhood seems to have put paid to that.

'But you have got your own key to my house?' I ask. 'The one you've always had?'

'Yes,' she says doubtfully, 'I'm sure I have.'

'Well, find it. Jon's going to need it this evening.'

'Why?'

'Because Annie and I will both be on stage.'

'Oh, yes. I don't think I'm going to be able to get to Annie's play. With Nico and everything.'

'It would do you good to get out. Have you even been out of the house this week?'

'I had a nice trip to the doctor's.'

'Seriously. Get Ben to look after the kids and come with me tomorrow afternoon.'

'I don't know. I'm not sure he can manage both of them.'

'Ellie! Don't do this. Don't assume that he's useless. It's what I did and look what happened to me. Nico's looking better, isn't he? He'll be fine with Ben.'

'I'll see.'

She looks so exhausted that I'm thinking of offering to take Nico out as well as Freda. 'I could—' I start, eying Nico, but

140

Freda's sharp eye has noted my wobble and she takes command.

'Come on, Granny,' she orders, taking my hand firmly in hers and dragging me towards the door. 'We really must be off.' And that is that.

The plan is to visit the playground, where Freda intends to attempt the black run of the big slide, to move on to The Pumpkin for elevenses and then to pass the rest of the morning browsing in the children's sections of Marlbury's two bookshops, where I shall spend far more money than I meant to because buying books is virtuous, isn't it?

The playground goes well. Freda baulks, in the end, at the dizzy height of the big slide and is disappointed with herself, but my definition of a successful playground outing is that it is one in which no blood gets spilt, so I am quite happy and try to console Freda with my philosophy of *refusing the arbitrary challenge*. 'You don't have to do things, you know,' I say, 'just because they're there.' She looks doubtful but I persevere as I push my bike into town with her strapped into her seat on the back. I need to go carefully: recently she has become resistant to my teacher's instinct to extend the range of her understanding. *I don't get it*, she will say dismissively, and shut the lid on me.

'You wanted to be brave,' I say, 'but slides are supposed to be fun. If it's not fun for you, then why do it?'

'Because it's good to be brave,' she protests.

'Yes, it is, but it's good to be brave when you need to be. Like when you had an injection at the doctor's and you didn't cry. That's brave.'

'You were brave with the spider,' she says, 'in the bath.'

'I was. You have to learn to be brave with spiders because you're bound to meet them from time to time, but you can take or leave slides. I'm not brave with slides.'

I have stopped wheeling and I turn to look at her. She is

141

grinning. She is picturing the absurd sight of her grandmother hurtling down a slide, but she is too polite to say so.

At The Pumpkin, she is thrown into an agony of indecision as she presses her nose to the glass display cabinet to view her cake choices. She gets her choice down to a shortlist of three and dithers for a long time between a chocolate éclair, an iced gingerbread man and a fancy cupcake. In the end, the cupcake wins and we order it, together with a bambinoccino for Freda, a latte for me and the éclair for me too, in case the cupcake proves disappointing and she wants to swap.

We claim the best table, in the window, and watch the street outside as we wait for our order. A dog with a squashed-looking face is led by and I am reminded of the dog, Billy, and the impostor in the niqab and the boy with the angelic voice. 'Has Liam been coming to the holiday activities?' I ask Freda.

'Yes,' she says, watching the dog, 'but he was sad.'

'Why was he sad?'

She gives a disconcertingly grown-up shrug, which must be copied from someone. 'Someone murdered his dog, didn't they?' she says.

I restrain myself from telling her that only people can be murdered and ask, 'When did that happen?'

She turns to look at me, surprised at my stupidity. 'Everyone knows about that, Granny,' she says. 'Someone murdered his auntie and his cousin and his dog.'

'I didn't know that was his dog.'

'His mummy gave his dog to his auntie because she was too much trouble.'

'His auntie was too much trouble?'

She sighs in exasperation. 'No, the dog. She was too much trouble.' She says, and gives another of her grown-up shrugs. 'His mummy's got depression,' she adds.

So the dog wasn't called Billy but Billie, I think, *as in Holiday.* I have several other questions for Freda but our order has arrived and demands her full attention. Freda likes to dismantle food, to arrange it in its component parts. Give her a pizza and she will carefully remove the slices of mushroom, bits of ham, chunks of pepper and whatever else and put them in neat piles round the edge of her plate. She will then eat the base and follow up with the toppings. She does a similar job with her cupcake, which has a mound of pale pink butter cream on it, and two deep pink spun sugar roses, with leaves, perched on top. It is, in fact, very like the kind of cake to which I compared Lavender earlier this morning, but Freda is a little young for metaphor so I don't tell her that she is, in effect, eating her step-grandmother.

We linger over our repast but after that things have to speed up a bit if I'm to be on campus to teach the wives at two o'clock. To accelerate matters, I spend freely in the bookshop, then deliver Freda and her pile of loot to her home and head for my office, skipping lunch to make up for the éclair. I notice, as I check my emails, that the job application form is still sitting on the top of my in-tray. *Later. Later.*

Only Ning Wu turns up for the class. She has no information to offer about the others, is disinclined to chat and wants to take the opportunity of the one-to-one to sort out some specifically Chinese problems. These are mainly with pronunciation. Ning Wu has been here for a whole academic year; she has attended classes religiously, done all her homework and made lists of new vocabulary on her iPad. What she has not done at all, I suspect, is speak English socially outside the classroom. Her husband is one of a group of Chinese graduate students studying in the Business School and he and Ning Wu socialise entirely in that group. Her sons, one at Acorns and one at infant school, are completely fluent of course, and she is frustrated by her lack of progress. She has tried to socialise more widely but people find her so hard to understand that she gives up and retreats into her Chinese

143

world. It's a bind many overseas students find themselves in.

Her main difficulty – and it's a very common difficulty with both Chinese and Japanese speakers – is consonant clusters. Chinese has a much higher vowel to consonant ratio than English does, so Chinese speakers tend to put vowels in between consonants. Thus, *spread*, for example, will become something like *sapared* and is likely to be heard as *separate* by a native English speaker. Of course, our consonant clusters don't seem like a problem to us but consider the word *strength*: seven consonants to one vowel. What a nightmare for anyone more accustomed to a one-to-one ratio. A word that is one syllable for us can extend to four syllables on a Chinese or Japanese tongue. Or *crisps*: think about that. What chance of getting what you want when you ask for a packet of *cirisipis*?

For pronunciation work you need to be uninhibited and to have a sense of humour, because it involves a lot of facial contortion, aspirating and spitting. Ning Wu is solemn and dignified, so I am the clown, twisting my face about making exaggerated efforts with lips and tongue. Ning Wu follows my instructions politely but she is just too ladylike. After three-quarters of an hour, I give up and ask if there's anything else she would like to work on. *He, she* and *it*, she tells me. And my heart sinks because there is no answer to this. *You just have to remember* I want to say. *How hard is that?* Bizarrely to us, in spoken Chinese, the same sound stands for *he* and *she* and *it*. It's not that they don't make gender distinctions – they do in writing – but in speaking they all sound the same. I draw a clumsy picture on the board: a man, a woman and a dog – what else? She practises sentences about these three and I go home with pronouns ringing in my ears.

I arrive home just in time to see Annie and co heading off for their evening at the Aphra Behn in the flat-tyred Volvo and a cloud of noxious exhaust. I remember that I'm supposed to be leaving supper for Jon and I curse Annie when I find that all the convenient food I stocked up on has been demolished and not replaced. I'm quite hungry myself, having skipped lunch, and I know the evening ahead will be long and trying, so I throw together a large macaroni cheese with bits of mushroom and tomato in it and eat a third of it, leaving the rest for Jon to heat up. I find a bag of salad leaves and instead of my usual random sloshing of oil, lemon and salt, I make a proper vinaigrette, which I hope will compensate for the leaves being two days past their *Best Before* date. I write a note to Jon, introducing him to his supper and inviting him to help himself to beer (in the fridge) or wine (in the bottle just opened and partly consumed by me), and to fruit and ice cream. I think of leaving him instructions about reheating the macaroni cheese but decide that this would be patronising. He is, after all, nearly a doctor; he must have done harder things than this, mustn't he?

I am, by now, tired and grumpy. My supper may sustain me later but at the moment it's weighing me down, and my glass and a half of wine has taken me straight to the sleepy stage, bypassing the cheerful lift I was hoping for. I climb onto my bike and pedal on leaden legs down to the abbey. My only comfort, as I turn the wheels, is that everyone else will be feeling as grumpy as I am. The technical rehearsal is the nadir of the rehearsal period as far as amateur actors are concerned. You are tired at this point as rehearsals have become more frequent and combining them with the day job has become hard work – though nothing to the week ahead, when you will be performing every night. On top of that you are terrified because first night is forty-eight hours away. What you want is to get on stage and rehearse, to reassure yourself that you do know what you're doing and you can remember the lines, but instead you are tantalised by being required to go on stage but not to act. You are in the hands of the technical crew, who move you about the stage and shine lights on you as though

145

you were no more than a piece of scenery. It is at this point that you realise, if you didn't know it before, that the techies regard the actors simply as a nuisance, an irritatingly unpredictable intrusion on the perfection of their staging. A friend of mine, a great lighting man and much in demand for amateur productions, once complained to me that he was lighting a production of *The Importance of Being Earnest*. 'What a terrible play that is,' he said. When I said that I supposed it might seem a bit heavy-handed these days but ... he interrupted me. 'Oh it's not that,' he said. 'It's the hats. All those bloody great hats the women wear. Impossible to light their faces. Four hats in the final scene and will they wear them on the backs of their heads? No! What am I supposed to do?'

In theory, I straddle the two worlds of cast and crew this evening since I need to scrutinise the costumes under the lights as well as doing my bit as an actor, and because of that I do grudgingly appreciate what a difficult job it is to light an open-air production, where you constantly have to adjust to the fading of the natural light. In fact, I think as we proceed and the unfriendly evening chill starts to seep into me, everything is more difficult in an open-air production: actors have to project twice as hard – and then some, if an ambulance goes screaming by or a low-flying plane amuses itself up above – in damp, cold conditions which are disastrous to the vocal cords; costumes need constant restoration – muddy hems, ruffs that detach themselves in a brisk breeze, torn sleeves from attacks by tree branches, sodden velvet crushed by a sudden squall. And then there's the audience: the cold, the wet, the inaudibility, the hard chairs. Yes, we have all of us been to the one magical open-air performance on a still, balmy night, when no extraneous sound could be heard but the gentle song of a nightingale and the light faded exquisitely until, in the velvet darkness, the magical final scene was played in a golden pool of light and a pin could be heard dropping in the breathless silence. But haven't we paid for it, that one rapturous, remembered moment? In trying to recapture it, how much cold, misery and boredom have we suffered? As evidence of the triumph of hope over experience it trumps second marriages every time.

With my costumier's eye in, I can't say I'm very happy with my costumes. I hired them from the Aphra Behn and I took trouble with colours and have altered things to fit, but the effect is not what I hoped for and I decide that the actors are to blame. They are just not wearing them right. They have had several opportunities to wear them for rehearsal but they have mainly only worn bits of them – a skirt or a cloak or a hat. Now they are in full fig they look awkward. The men have no swagger and the women no grace, I think gloomily. Several of the men have little, short cloaks which are meant to swirl dashingly from one shoulder, but they all look as though they're auditioning for Richard III. And the women stride about in their skirts as though they were in jeans and trainers (some of them, I suspect, are indeed wearing jeans under their skirts to keep warm, and I do sympathise but there will be none of that in performance). Conversely, Michael Da Souza, who is playing Friar Francis, is mincing about in his cassock, holding it up in front of him like a pantomime dame.

'Michael,' I say, 'you won't trip over it. I've made sure it's the right length. You can stride about. Go into the abbey and watch the priests in there. They stride about and their cassocks billow about nicely round their feet.'

'Yes,' he says dutifully, but he doesn't move.

'Well, go on then,' I say, sounding very much like a hearty PE teacher, 'let's see you stride.'

He turns and I see his hands go to lift up his skirts. 'Hands by your sides,' I order, now moving into RSM mode. He drops his hands and walks on. I watch to see if his cassock billows out nicely round his feet and I am assailed by the memory of the niqab person and the dog running at his/her feet and I know that there is something wrong with the picture but I can't work out what it is. One thing I do see now, in my mind's eye – and I should have thought about it before – is that the 'woman' was wearing trainers. They were black trainers, admittedly, but definitely trainers, all the same, and I think, now, that that was what the child, Lara, might have been laughing at. Now I feel bad because I think that if I had been paying attention the trainers would have told me that this was an impostor of some kind and I could have told Paula or David, and Jamilleh need not have been involved and would not, now, be lying half-strangled in hospital.

There is something else, though. Something else is wrong with my picture and I can't work out what it is. It hovers there, on the edge of my consciousness, like a word you can't quite find, and just as I think I'm going to reach out and touch it, Michael's plaintive voice comes breaking in. 'You're not even watching me!' he protests, like an aggrieved child, as he comes marching back towards me, and I realise that I have been standing with my eyes closed as I try to recover the picture and its soundtrack.

'Sorry, Michael. That's great,' I say and then, without even knowing that I've made a decision, I turn and head for the dressing room. I need to think and I can't do it here. It is already nearly ten o'clock and we have just reached the beginning of act four. We could be here for hours yet and there is no chance that I can find my inspiration while I stand around getting cold and cross. The dressing room is empty because everyone is needed for the big scene of Hero's and Claudio's aborted wedding. *Focus, focus,* I tell myself as I change out of my costume. *Don't think about anything else.*

I pick up my bag, take a look round the room, promise

myself that I will come in in the morning and clear up the chaos that will be left, and slip out. The quickest way to make my escape would be through the darkness of the cloisters but I have been told to *be aware* and I have had a bad experience once before in these cloisters so, instead, I set off the other way, through the school courtyard where, rounding a shadowy corner, I bump straight into our director, the loathsome Dominic. Caught, I try going on the offensive. 'Skiving off, Dominic?' I ask. 'Leaving it all to the techies?'

It doesn't work. 'And you? Some sort of emergency?' he asks.

I could invent an emergency but I don't feel like it. Instead I say breezily, 'Something like that,' and make to sashay past him. He grabs hold of my arm, though. 'Where the hell do you think you're going?' he asks, his face close enough for me to get the benefit of the gin and cigarettes that have been sustaining him. He has a cigarette in the hand that isn't holding me, and I wouldn't put it past him to stub it out on any bit of bare flesh he can find on me. I go still. We stare at each other. He seems to realise that he is overacting. He releases my arm. 'Well?' he asks, more mildly, dropping his cigarette and grinding it under his foot.

I decide to try the truth. 'The fact is, Dominic, I have something on my mind and I have to go away and think about it. If I stand around here any longer I shall lose it and it could actually be a matter of life and death.'

He looks at me, and even in the murky light of the tasteful 'antique' lamps that light the courtyard, I can see an expression of such dislike on his face that I am slightly taken aback. 'You really think you're something, don't you?' he asks, but because it's obviously not really a question I don't try to reply. 'You walk out of here,' he says, 'and you don't come back.'

I stare at him. 'And who plays Ursula?' I ask. 'Who gets the costumes sorted and back to the Aphra Behn?'

He turns away and starts to walk back towards the stage area. 'You are eminently dispensable,' he calls. 'Eminently.'

Exit stage left.

Well, I really don't care about being out of the play; the prospect of a week not spent shivering in a farthingale feels like a release, actually. Which leads me to wonder why I got into it in the first place. Another case of hope over experience, I suppose. Dominic has unsettled me, though. I think, as I pedal home, that he did, at least, say *dispensable* and not *disposable* but I can't shake off the sense that there seems to be a threat there, all the same. And, infuriatingly, the altercation with Dominic has blown away that fragile thought that I was trying to hold on to. As I approach home I see lights on, which calms my paranoia about the missing key, though it still occurs to me, as I unlock the door, that a really clever assassin would lull me by switching lights on, wouldn't he?

Inside, I call out a greeting and get no reply. I go cautiously into the kitchen, where I find macaroni and salad eaten and everything scrupulously washed up and put away. Jon has eaten and gone to meet Annie, presumably. The message light is flashing on the phone. David? I pour myself a glass of wine and press *play*. At first all I hear is heavy breathing and I am seized with fright. Then a voice emerges, thick with tears. *Oh Gina, I'm so sorry. It's your mum. She passed away, Gina. I'm so sorry.* There is some wordless weeping and then, *It's Margaret here, Gina, I should have said. It was a stroke. Very quick, the doctor said. I found her. Just in her chair. Quite peaceful, bless her. You take care of yourself, Gina. Bye now.* And that was it.

Why does shock attack the knees? The first thing I feel is that I must sit down. Then I take a gulp of wine. Then I think that I don't believe it. Oh, I believe that she is dead. I've felt that coming for a while now, and so did she, I'm sure. It's *very quick* and *quite peaceful* that I don't believe. *Killed instantly,* wasn't that what the families of soldiers killed in the First World War were always told? Even if they had hung, screaming, on the wire in no-man's-land for three days? How long was it before Margaret went in and found her? How long did she lie, helpless? Did she want me? She wanted me yesterday, didn't she? And I said I'd see her in three days' time. Why didn't she say *come now*? Because. Because of who she was. Because of who I am.

I look at the clock on the cooker. It's nearly eleven. Too late to ring Margaret now. I stand up and go to the phone to play her message again and I freeze as I hear the sound of a key turning in the front door. I don't know if I scream but I certainly let my glass fall from my hand, so that when Jon opens the kitchen door he finds me standing on a battlefield of red wine and glass.

'Are you all right?' he asks and all I can say is, 'My mother's dead,' before the tears come.

He is, of course, wonderful. He sits me down, makes me a cup of tea (*better for shock than wine*) and clears up the bloody mess on the floor with quiet efficiency.

I don't weep for long. Weeping isn't really my thing and these tears came from shock and fright more than from grief. Grief I shall have to think about later. I realise, as my tears subside, that I am hugely relieved that Annie isn't here.

'Did you see Annie?' I ask.

'Oh yes. Thank you for supper, by the way. Delicious, and just what I needed. I saw her after the show but they were all going out for a drink and I didn't think I could match the post-performance euphoria after the day I've had.'

'Annie should have come back with you.' *Why doesn't she look after him better?*

'She needed her wind-down. It was a good audience tonight, apparently.'

'So you came back for some peace and quiet and found a hysterical woman.'

'Very mild, as hysterics go.'

'I'm sorry about your bad day. Do you want to talk about it?'

'No. People die, you know, when you don't expect it, and too young. I'm learning to get used to it.'

'Is that a way of reminding me that my mother had had her time? Well, I know that. The tears aren't grief, you know. Shock. And guilt a bit. She rang me and asked me to go and see her – well, as close to asking as she ever got – and I said I'd see her on Sunday. And now she's dead and I wonder if I'd gone right away …' I stop. 'I don't know.'

'You don't think you could have stopped her dying, do you?'

'No.' I drink my tea while I think about how to phrase my question to him. 'I've always suspected, without any evidence really, that doctors have a sort of freemasonry and help one another out at the end – something painless, an extra shot of morphine and something bland on the death certificate. Does that happen? Have you heard of it?'

'I'm only a student. If it does happen, I'm not in the freemasonry yet.'

'No. But I can't get it out of my mind. I knew my mother was expecting to die soon but now I wonder if she was planning it.'

'And asking to see you was what?'

'A test, I suppose. If I'd gone right away, maybe she would have said something to me. As it was, she went ahead without me.'

'What do you think she would have said?'

'I have no idea. We never understood one another. But she gave me a letter the last time I saw her, to be opened after her death. Very nineteenth-century novel, though she wasn't like that at all, in fact. Well, you know. You met her, didn't you?'

'Several times. I liked her very much.'

'Most people did.'

'Are you worried about opening the letter?'

'I'm not rushing. I know it'll be disappointing. I have to prepare myself.'

'Yes.'

I look at the clock. 'Could you do something for me, Jon?'

'Of course.'

'Could you tell Annie when she comes in? I'd really like to have a bath and go to bed. I'll ring Ellie in the morning.'

I take myself upstairs. I feel the kind of exhaustion that is actually quite pleasurable when you know you have a good night's sleep in front of you, but I'm afraid I shan't sleep, even drugged by a hot bath and some more Wodehouse. I go through the motions, though, soaking in soporific bubbles, and then, when I'm in bed, I put paid to any hope of sleep by opening the bedside drawer and taking out my mother's letter. Giving myself no time to change my mind, I rip it open and scan it rapidly. It is dated 1st July 2012 and it is short but not quite to the point – at least not to any point that I understand. The writing, I notice, is fainter but no less precise than my mother's usual hand (she had no truck with stereotypically illegible 'doctor's writing' and her prescription forms were renowned for their clarity).

Her letter reads as follows:

My dear Virginia,

My solicitors, Hart and Lyman, have my will. The arrangements for my burial will come as a surprise to you, I realise. We buried Christopher in the churchyard because I wanted to be able to go and talk to him. Your father wanted to be cremated, but his ashes are there too. I prefer burial. Earth to earth seems right to me. The churchyard plot may mean that a church funeral is obligatory. I don't mind that if you don't. It's a good service and I am sure you will appreciate the words.

We did not intend to keep secrets from you. It was too painful at first, and anyway you were too young. Then time went by and there seemed no point. There was no conspiracy,
  With love,
  Mummy

It's the *Mummy* that gets me first, though that is hardly the most striking thing about this letter. When did I stop calling her *Mummy*? At fourteen or fifteen, I suppose, when I decided that *Mother* was more grown-up. It always seemed right to me, appropriate for the adult detachment of our relationship, but did she always think of herself as *Mummy*?

But this is not really the point. Thinking about this is just a displacement activity to avoid thinking about the other stuff, which is making me dizzy. My mind moves cautiously from the outside in. A church funeral; let's start with that. I have thought about her funeral from time to time, knowing that I would, eventually, be the person who would have to organise it. I assumed a nice, rational, secular affair for my atheist mother, in the crematorium. I anticipated a big crowd, of course, because she was admired and respected, and even loved, I suppose. She had cured and comforted and saved the lives of generations of her patients. My main concern was how we were going to fit everyone in. But now it's to be in a church – large or small, I don't know – and I shall have to choose hymns and bible readings, shan't I? And negotiate with the vicar and not be difficult or make it obvious that I think it's all nonsense.

Then there's the burial. I had assumed cremation. It's what I choose for myself and I know my choice is based on a rather childish horror of decay, of blowflies and worms, fluids and corruption. Cremation has its horrors too, of course, the coffin sliding away behind that prim little curtain always turns my stomach. I was twelve when my father died and I remember that moment when the coffin started to move. My mother had explained to me what would happen but at that moment I was seized with the irrational fear that he was not actually dead and would be burned alive. My mother must have sensed my agitation because she put a hand on my arm. 'He really is dead,' she said. At the time I was angry with her for the matter-of-fact way she said it; now I think it was remarkable that she read my mind.

But now we come to it, the centre of all this. She must have a church funeral because she must be buried in a churchyard, and she must be buried in a particular churchyard because that is where Christopher is. *Christopher.* It means nothing to me. I never heard the name pass between my parents, not even in a muttered aside. It was *too painful*; I was *too young*; there was *no point*; there was *no conspiracy*. Off the top of my head, I have three theories about Christopher. One, the least painful, is that he was my mother's beloved brother, dead tragically young and mourned ever after. I don't believe this, however, because my mother talked often about her childhood and her sister, Alice. Wouldn't Christopher's name have slipped out at least once?

Option two, then, which owes a good deal to a certain kind of romantic novel. Suppose that Christopher was my mother's lover and my real father? He died, leaving my mother pregnant or alone with a small child, until decent, kindly Harold Sidwell came along to give her respectability and a father for her child. The problem with this is that my mother was thirty-eight when I was born, and a respected professional woman. My birth out of wedlock could hardly be a matter of such shame that it could never be spoken of, could it?

Option three, then – the only viable one, I know, and have known ever since I read the letter. The other options were just further displacement exercises. Christopher was my brother, wasn't he? And since I don't remember him I assume he was born and died before I existed, and I came along eventually as a poor substitute. This would be the real reason why my parents never mentioned him, wouldn't it? Because they couldn't have done so without revealing the depth of their disappointment in me. There is an even worse version of this option, one that also has its inspiration in fiction – this time the genre of psychological thriller. Suppose he was not born before but after me? Suppose the reason why he couldn't be mentioned is that I was somehow responsible for his death? Were we twins, and did I – greedy and demanding even then – get the lion's share of nutrition *in utero* so that he was born too fragile to live? Or did I kill him? Did I smother him, drop him, drown him? Did I suppress the trauma and did my parents decide that the best thing was to do the same? *No conspiracy*? How can two people, living with a third, impose a complete embargo on the mention of a fourth member of the family without conspiring to do it? My mother's sometimes brutal truthfulness has caused me pain and rage over the years, but they were nothing – nothing – to what I feel about this mealy-mouthed apology for a letter.

17

27.07.12: 09.25

A Morning's Work

'Paula, you take Mike with you and go back to the Samaritans. I'm going to talk again to Malcolm Burns and I'll chase up Rashid Malik on possible sources for the guy's niqab. Sarah, you're getting onto The Scrubs about Karen's visits to Doug Brody, and his phone calls. I'll go and talk to him again tomorrow. You can come with me, Darren. You weren't expecting the weekend off, were you? When we've got a double murder and a serious assault on our hands? Steve, check out Jamilleh Hamidi's address and check out her neighbours for anyone known to us. Nothing new on Doug Brody's associates, I suppose? No? Well keep on it. Sarah, go back to the hospital. See if Jamilleh Hamidi has anything more to say. Darren, go along to Acorns and find out if they've had any concerns about a man hanging around there. And mind your language. Cut out the paedo references. And everyone, the attack on Jamilleh has brought the media down on us again, as you'll have seen. I made a statement yesterday and now they'll have to wait until there are further developments. You don't talk to anyone. Right? And bring me the developments.'

At 09.25, so instructed, the team dispersed. Sarah Shepherd

went straight to the nearest phone and called Wormwood Scrubs prison. She was surprised at how quickly she was put through to a senior officer; calling from CID, she realised, gave her clout she had never had as a family liaison officer.

'Douglas Brody,' she said, striving for an authoritative tone. 'His wife and child were murdered ten days ago. We're anxious to establish what contact he had with his wife in the days before the murders – visits and phone calls, if possible.'

There was a silence and Sarah waited for the brush-off. The reply, when it came, though, was perfectly courteous.

'I can get that information for you. We do monitor phone calls and keep a record of numbers called. I shall need to put you through to the wing officer. It is a busy time but I'm sure he can help you.' There was another pause. 'I'm just looking to see ...' he said, with the unmistakeable tone of someone who is scanning a screen, '... ah, yes. You know, I assume, that he was in the infirmary following an attack on an officer. He is back on the wing now, but we have him on suicide watch. He has taken the deaths very badly.'

'It's hardly a thing you could take well, is it?' Sarah commented, and then regretted it. That was family liaison talk, wasn't it, not CID? The response on the other end of the phone was brisk.

'No. I'm putting you through to the wing if that's all?'

'Yes, thank you.'

The wing officer sounded harassed but not unhelpful. 'Yes, DC Shepherd. You're interested in Doug Brody, I gather?'

'Yes. How is he?'

'Quiet. The medics sedated him after he got violent. He's off the medication now but he's still quiet. Like a zombie. We've got him on a twenty-minute suicide watch.'

'We'd like to know if his wife visited him in the days before her death. Between 1st and 16th July. And phone calls. How many he made and who he made them to.'

'Visits are easy. She came regularly every two weeks. Never missed. Sometimes brought the little girl. He'd requested a transfer from Liverpool to be nearer for visiting.'

'So what would the dates of those visits have been?'

'I'm just looking now. Yes, Sundays. 1st July and 15th July.'

'Did she bring the little girl to either of those?'

'We don't keep a record of that.'

'How did he seem after the visits? Can you remember?'

'Visits always shake people up.'

'He didn't seem more upset than usual?'

'I don't think so.'

'And phone calls? What about them?'

'He's allowed two calls a week.'

'Can you tell me who he called?'

'I can but it'll take a bit of time. I'll need to call you back later.'

Sarah, with *That'll be fine* trembling on her lips, took a deep breath. 'Actually,' she said, 'we're conducting a double murder inquiry and I'm afraid *later* won't do. I'll wait while you find the information.'

She got no reply and thought, at first, that he had put the phone down on her, but faint noises of activity told her otherwise and she waited, uncertain whether he would leave her hanging there, come back with the information or summon someone senior to bawl her out. She looked at her watch. She would give it ten minutes before giving up. After five, the wing officer was back, grudging but with the data. Doug Brody had called Karen on the Monday and Thursday evenings that were his allotted times. His last call was a fifteen-minute call on Monday 16th July at 20.45.

'When you say you monitor calls,' Sarah asked, 'does that mean you listen in to them?'

'We monitor the numbers. Calls are allowed only to approved numbers. We have the facility to listen in to calls and we do it if we suspect criminal activity. We had no concerns on that score about Brody.'

'Right. Well, thank you.'

'Just one thing, though. Monday 16th, Brody tried to make a call to an unregistered mobile. We automatically block those, for obvious reasons.'

'Was that before or after his call to his wife?'

'Before.'

'Thank you,' she said, and then added. 'I'm sorry if I hassled you.'

'Just doing your job, love,' he said.

Paula would have had something to say about the *love*, she knew, but she let it go.

By 09.40, David Scott had a warrant application to search the Samaritans' office ready to go to the magistrate. At 09.45 he phoned the university, asked for the chaplaincy and spoke to Rashid Malik.

'I'm so sorry,' Malik said, 'but I really have very little to tell you. I'm aware of no family where the woman wears niqab and my wife confirms my belief that it is necessary to go to London to buy any kind of hijab. Or order online, of course.'

'Would she be able to give me the names of online outlets?'

'I imagine so.'

'Can you email those to me today?'

'If you like.'

Was it his imagination, Scott wondered, or did Malik sound cooler today, more defensive? If Paula's enquiries in HR about niqab-wearing staff had caused resentment, no doubt that had been fed back to him. The university's Muslim community would be closing ranks, if not putting up barricades. He thanked Malik for his help and rang off.

By 10.15, he had driven to the university, found a parking place and was tapping quietly on the door of Malcolm Burns' office. The office was uncomfortably close to Gina's and he had slipped past her door with care. *Furtive*, was what she would have called him; she would have been right and he was ashamed of it, but he needed to get Malcolm without the benefit of her beady-eyed protection. He tapped again.

'Come,' a voice called indistinctly, and he walked in to find Malcolm Burns with his head deep into a filing cabinet.

'Something slipped down the back,' he explained as he emerged red-faced. Then he registered Scott and laughed uneasily. 'David! Back so soon?'

'Records, Malcolm,' Scott said, settling himself in the room's one easy chair and opening his arms expansively. 'Tell me everything you know about record-keeping in your branch of the Samaritans.'

Burns looked nervously at the door and then glanced at the window, for all the world, Scott thought, as if he expected Gina to come flying, caped and masked, to his rescue.

'We don't,' he said, clearing his throat and moving to the protection of a seat behind his desk, 'keep *records* as such. Some branches keep no notes of any kind but we do keep brief, very brief ...' he ran an anxious hand over his thinning, pale hair. 'We don't like it to get about – the fact that we keep notes. It could deter people from calling us.'

'So why keep notes?'

'People who are in trouble often ring several times and each time they speak to a different volunteer. They'll tell different people different things. Once we realise that someone is calling regularly, we set up an index card. The cards help us to have a complete picture and decide how best to help the callers.'

'So you don't just listen to what people tell you?'

'Yes. That is what we do.' His voice rose in agitation. 'Active listening is what we do, but we can do that better if we know what we're dealing with. And then there are the hysterics.'

'Hysterics?'

'People don't always tell us the truth. There are people who ring with a different tragedy each time: cancer, rape, multiple bereavements, near-fatal car accident, all in one week. The cards help us to spot that. We still listen to them, of course – they obviously need to talk – but knowing what they're doing helps to save the volunteers from getting too distressed.'

'Where do you keep these cards?'

'In the phone room.'

'In what?'

'I'm sorry?'

'What do you keep the cards in?'

'Well, boxes.'

'And what do you keep the boxes in?'

'I don't see why –'

'You don't? You don't see why I need to know where the boxes are kept? When last time my officers visited they had been somehow spirited away?'

'It's a matter of confidentiality.'

'For a dead woman?'

Burns sat back in his chair. 'They're kept on a trolley,' he said, 'so they can be moved from one phone station to another.'

'And so they can be wheeled away as soon as the police get anywhere near. Where do they get wheeled to, Malcolm?'

'The kitchen. There's a walk-in pantry in there.'

'Thank you. Now, next question. Presumably you cull the cards from time to time. What's the system?'

'Once a year. We go through them. If someone hasn't rung for a year we take the card out.'

'And destroy it?'

Burns squirmed uncomfortably. 'We used to but Estelle likes to keep everything.'

'Why?'

'It's just how she is, I think.'

'So where do those cards go?'

'They're archived.'

'Come on, Malcolm, don't make me drag it out of you. Where are the archives kept?'

He sighed. 'In Estelle's office.'

'And a card for someone who has died, that would be archived too, I assume.'

'We can hardly ever be sure that someone has died; even if people tell us they've taken an overdose, we can't be sure, so—'

'But you do know that Karen Brody is dead. Has her card been removed?'

Burns lifted his head and looked straight at Scott for the first time. 'I really don't know,' he said. 'I haven't looked.'

At 10.30, Paula Powell parked again on a double yellow line round the corner from the Samaritans, walked with Mike Arthur to the front door and rang the doorbell. This time a young woman with piercings and pink hair opened the door.

'Who are you?' Paula asked.

'I'm Greta,' she said, startled.

'Well, I'm Detective Sergeant Paula Powell,' Paula said, waving her ID and breezing past her, heading straight for the phone room.

'What the fuck?' Greta protested. 'You can't just barge in there. There are confidential calls happening. It's—'

'—absolutely quiet,' Paula said. 'It's a doddle, isn't it, the morning slot? Your director told us so.'

'I'm ringing Estelle,' Greta said. 'I'm not letting you in there without her say-so.'

'That's quite all right,' Mike Arthur said. 'These are what we're looking for.' He took hold of the metal trolley that stood in the middle of the room and started to wheel it out into the small room that appeared to be a sort of rest room for volunteers, leading off from the phone room. 'If we just take these in here then we can have a look at them without disturbing anyone and we'll be out of your hair in no time.'

Greta grabbed hold of the trolley. 'I'm not letting you take them,' she growled. 'Estelle will be furious. I've gotta have her permission.'

She looked really scared, Paula thought, but she hardened her heart. 'We have already talked to your director about this,' she said. 'We explained when we came in on Wednesday. My chief inspector has got a search warrant for these premises but a search warrant comes along with two or three police cars, a lot of sirens and police officers with big feet swarming all over the building, taking it apart. Really, taking it apart. You have no idea what a place looks like when that sort of search has happened.'

'But if you agree to let us take a quick look through these,' Mike Arthur put in, 'then we'll be in and out in no time. No problem.'

'I can understand that you're scared of Estelle,' Paula said. 'She's a scary lady, I imagine, but you'll be in more trouble if she finds we've ripped the place apart, won't you?'

'Why can't you just wait till I ring?' Greta asked plaintively.

'Because this is a double murder inquiry we're engaged in, Greta, and we haven't got time to mess about.'

Greta looked at them, undecided. She didn't ask what murder inquiry or look surprised, Paula noticed. The volunteers knew about Karen and they knew the police had already been in, she guessed. No doubt instructions were to ring Estelle if the police turned up again.

'I don't believe Estelle let you look before.'

'She did,' Paula said. 'Only we didn't find what we were looking for.'

'What were you looking for?'

'A card for Karen Brody.'

Greta looked at the cards on the trolley. 'You better look, then,' she said. 'I'm calling Estelle.'

'Estelle will be down here like a shot,' Paula said to Mike as Greta left. 'Which is just what we want. We're not going to find Karen's card here, are we? But they know more than they're telling.'

Mike pulled the trolley towards him. 'They're alphabetical,' he said. 'So I'll take A to F and look for Brody, and you can take G to L.'

After a minute, he said. 'Not here. They don't seem to use surnames anyway.'

'And not here either, I think.' Paula lifted out a few cards and fanned through them. 'Katherine, Katy, Ken, Kirsty. No.'

'So what now?'

'We take a gentle look round while we wait for Estelle Campion to arrive and then put the fear of God into her.'

At that moment her phone rang.

'David?'

'How are you doing?'

'Nothing in the card index on show here. We're about to start a search. Estelle Campion's been summoned. We'll see what more we can squeeze out of her. Anything helpful from Gina's friend?

'Malcolm Burns? Yes. They hide records in the kitchen – in the pantry, apparently – when they don't want them seen. And there's an archive of past – and passed – callers, if you get my meaning.'

'Any information that will save us time?'

'The director's office.'

'Naturally.'

'And she doesn't throw anything away.'

'OK.'

'Keep me posted.'

He rang off.

In the kitchen, the pantry held only odd items of clothing: lost property or emergency hand-outs, Paula wondered. The other cupboards held mugs, coffee, biscuits and an extensive array of herb and fruit teas. On the first floor, they found a small room obviously designed for interviews, a bathroom and an office with a photocopier and an unlocked filing cabinet containing printer paper, ink cartridges and publicity leaflets of various kinds. Which left the director's office, and this was, of course, locked.

Mike Arthur went back downstairs and heard Greta in the phone room talking to another woman who seemed to be in a fluster of apologies. *Just blocked solid,* he heard, *all the way to the roundabout,* and Greta's grudging reply, *Can't be helped but I could really have done with someone else here with those two just swanning in.* He put his head round the door and smiled cheerily.

'Key to that room up at the top?' he asked. 'We'll just take a quick look in there and then we can leave you in peace.'

Greta turned to glare at him. 'That's the director's office. We don't have a key.'

'Then we shall have to trouble her to bring it in,' he said.

The two women exchanged a look. 'She's coming in,' Greta said.

'Now?'

'She lives out at Lower Shepton. She'll be fifteen minutes. I suppose you can wait that long before you break the door down?'

'Probably,' he said, and gave her another smile.

Estelle Campion arrived ten minutes later and climbed, slightly breathless, to the second floor, where Paula and Mike were waiting outside the locked door. She was less perfectly groomed and less composed than on the previous day, Paula noted, though just as expensively dressed, in cream trousers and a blue jacket with a silk shirt under it.

'So, you again,' she said, with a tight little smile at Paula. 'But without your sidekick.' She coughed. 'Too many fags,' she said.

'This is DC Mike Arthur,' Paula said.

Estelle Campion gave him a brief, appraising glance and turned back to Paula.

'And how can we help you today?'

'We'd like to take a look in your office.'

'What for?'

'Information relating to Karen Brody.'

'I don't keep that sort of information up here. If you're looking for the caller information —'

'We found the cards, thank you, but nothing on Karen there.'

'I told you, we destroyed it.'

Yes, you did. But there's an archive, isn't there? And it's in your office and we'd like to see it.'

Estelle Campion's face flushed under its screen of creamy foundation. 'How do you know —'

'We're CID, Mrs Campion. We know all sorts of things.' Paula allowed an edge to sour the sweet reasonableness of her tone. 'And lying to the police is a criminal offence for anyone, Samaritan or not.'

'I resent that, DS Powell.'

'Just open the door, Mrs Campion.'

Estelle Campion made a theatrical gesture that was almost a flounce and took a bunch of keys from her pocket. She unlocked the door and flung it open, standing aside to let them in. 'Be my guests,' she said, 'and if you don't find anything I shall expect an apology. I didn't want to mention it but my husband knows the chief constable.' She turned to go. 'I'm going downstairs for a coffee,' she said.

'A cigarette more like,' Mike Arthur muttered as he closed the door and removed the keys she had left in the lock. Then a thought struck him. 'Do you think she could be double-crossing us and destroying something downstairs?' he asked.

'David's info is that the archive is up here. He got that from Malcolm Burns. We'll go with that.'

They looked round the room. It had been built into the attic of the little house and had a steeply sloping roof under which sat a large, untidy desk. Under the window was the sofa Paula and Sarah had sat on during their previous visit, with a coffee table in front of it, and against one wall was a tall filing cabinet. In the opposite wall were two doors. Paula walked across and opened them. One led to a cupboard, empty except for a couple of cardigans hanging on a rail and a pair of velvet slippers. 'Comfort clothes for when she's not on show,' she commented. The other door opened to a flash of gleaming ceramic walls. 'And her own executive bathroom,' she reported.

Mike Arthur was at the drawers of the filing cabinet, trying the keys on the key ring. He opened the bottom one first, to reveal a bottle of single malt whisky and four heavy, cut-glass tumblers. 'Who do you think these are for?' he asked.

'For cosy chats with favoured volunteers?' Paula suggested. 'She strikes me as a woman who might play favourites.'

'Or she drinks on her own and the other glasses are there so she can kid herself that she doesn't really drink on her own.'

'How cynical you are, DC Arthur.'

'Just a student of human nature, ma'am.'

'You can mock me with *ma'am*. Just you wait till I'm a DCI.'

'Is that what you want?'

'It is.'

She had pulled out the drawer above the bottom one and was running through the hanging files in it. 'This seems to be all fundraising,' she said. 'Details of donors, copies of receipts, copies of letters of thanks, and some newspaper clippings, all relating to fundraising, I think.'

'Being a DCI doesn't seem to make our DCI Scott particularly happy,' Mike Arthur commented as she pushed the drawer back in.

'That's because he's got the wrong woman.'

'This seems to be stuff about the volunteers,' he said, scanning the contents of the next drawer. 'What's wrong with his woman?'

'She doesn't understand about police work.'

He turned to look at her. 'And you do,' he said.

'I do,' she said.

'Is there — ?' he asked.

'Might be,' she said. 'Are you sure it's only volunteer stuff in that drawer?'

'I think so.' He opened the top drawer. 'Ah. Here's the archive.'

They looked into the contents of the drawer together. It contained neat stacks of cards, held together with rubber bands, each labelled with a year. Paula flicked through one or two.

'There aren't any for this year,' Mike Arthur said.

'There wouldn't be, would there, if they go through the cards at the end of the year to decide which ones to archive?'

'Then why isn't Karen's card still there downstairs. Because she died?'

'Let's get all of these out. Maybe there's a separate group of dead ones.'

They carried the bundles in armfuls over to the coffee table by the sofa and spread them out in date order.

'Realistically,' Mike Arthur said, 'how often do they know that someone who called them has actually gone ahead and killed themselves? '

'Some suicides get reported in the *Herald*.'

'I guess.'

Paula flicked through a set of cards, pulled one out and passed it to him. 'Look at this one. Someone has written *believed deceased* on it. So the cards of callers who've died do go in with the others. So where is Karen's?'

'It ought still to be downstairs with the others, until the end of the year.'

'It ought.' She looked round the room. 'Bring those keys over, Mike.' She went to the desk and pulled open the left-hand drawer, which contained the usual litter of desk drawers – pens, staples, paper clips, a spare printer cartridge, a pack of tissues, a half-eaten Kit Kat, a couple of postcards, some paracetamols, a lipstick and a map of the Marlbury district. The other drawer was locked and none of the keys on the ring fitted. Paula and Mike Arthur looked at each other. 'OK,' she said.

He reached into his pocket; she moved away and headed for the door to the bathroom. 'I'm going to the toilet,' she said. 'I never saw you.'

When she returned, he had the drawer open and was running a gloved hand round its interior. He picked up a card from the desk. 'Archived all by itself,' he said, and waved it at her.

'Karen's?' she asked.

'Yup.'

'Anything else in the drawer?

'Just these.' He indicated half a dozen packs of cigarettes piled on the desk. 'The card was hidden underneath.'

She pulled gloves out of her pocket and picked up the card. 'Have you read this?'

'Only glanced.'

She took the card over to the window to scrutinise it. In the top right-hand corner someone had written *KAREN*. Beneath that were five entries, dated between July 9th and July 17th. The entries were written in different hands, each signed, and the first four entries all said the same thing: *Asked to speak to the director*. Only Malcolm's, the final entry on July 17th, gave any indication of what she had wanted to talk about: *Initially asked for director (not available). Said she had info for the police. Has promised not to go to police herself but fears for her and her daughter's safety. Asked if we would pass info to police. Sounded desperate. Call broken off.*

She handed the card to Mike Arthur. 'Why has no-one written anything else? You see all these cards – people write the sort of thing Malcolm wrote. Why nothing here?'

'Could it be they wouldn't pass her on to the director so she didn't talk?'

'No. Because we've got her phone records and she was on for between five and fifteen minutes each time.'

'So they did pass her on to the director and she didn't fill in the card?'

'Looks like it. Why? And why is the card hidden here?'

'We'd better ask her,' he said, moving towards the door.

'Hold on a minute.' She took the card back from him and sat down with it. 'Let's see if there's an innocent explanation – if only because that's what she'll come up with and we need to be ready for it.'

'OK.' He came and sat down beside her.

'Suppose,' she said, 'that they did pass Karen on to Estelle Campion every time. Karen was desperate: she had this secret and it scared her. She was frightened for herself and for Lara, and she was sure that it could all be solved if Estelle would just pass her information to the police, but Estelle wouldn't do it. So they had these conversations and no doubt Estelle would have been doing the right thing in refusing – it's not what the Samaritans are about – but she felt bad about it. Did Karen tell her what the secret was? Who knows, but she wasn't going to write on the card for all the volunteers to see, was she? And apart from that, some of the volunteers would have thought that she ought to help Karen, wouldn't they? It might be against the rules but these are people who give up their time to help. They would think she ought to help.'

'So she writes nothing on the card and then, when Karen dies, she feels bad and she hides the card. Why didn't she destroy it like she said she had?'

'People are funny about destroying evidence. They know that the cover-up is often worse than the offence – look at all the phone-hacking stuff.'

'OK. So that's the innocent explanation. What's the guilty one?'

'I don't know.'

'Let's go and find out.' She took an evidence bag out of her pocket and slipped the card into it.

Estelle Campion went for a third way: denial. Fortified during their search by caffeine, nicotine and the application of more lipstick, she sat opposite them in the small interview room on the first floor and faced them wide-eyed and smiling in astonishment at the forensic precautions of gloves and evidence bag. She had hidden the card because she knew it would upset her volunteers to come across it; it was a very emotional business, the murder of a young woman and a child, and initially she had thought that Karen might have done it herself. No, she had never spoken to Karen; it was an absolute rule that callers could not pick or choose who they spoke to. Whoever picked up the phone was their Samaritan for that moment; that was the way it worked.

'So why, then,' Paula asked, 'did none of the people who spoke to her write anything on the card? I've seen how the other cards are filled in. This one is odd, isn't it?'

Estelle reached out a hand for the card but Paula held it

back. 'We can't contaminate the evidence,' she said, and held it for her to read.

'You get patterns set up on these cards,' Estelle said with an air of professional detachment. 'The first person records in a particular way and everyone follows suit. Especially if they're inexperienced.' She squinted at the card. 'These are all quite new volunteers.'

'But the last entry – Malcolm's – that's different.'

'Ah, Malcolm's an old hand.'

'But one of the other entries is Malcolm's too, isn't it?'

She glanced again at the card. 'Oh, yes,' she said casually.

'And it's just coincidence that on that last occasion you were *unavailable*?'

'Just coincidence.'

'And you never spoke to Karen?'

'Never.'

'You're quite sure?'

'Quite sure.'

'Well, of course we shall need to talk to the volunteers who did speak to her.'

'You try to do that,' she said, leaning forward so that her face was very close, 'and I shall speak to the chief constable.'

Paula leaned forward too. 'You do that,' she said.

She got up to leave, but Mike Arthur, getting to his feet, asked, as he took the card from her, 'As a matter of interest, Mrs Campion, were you in the building when Karen made those calls and asked for you?'

'Probably,' she said. 'They were daytime calls. I'm usually here.'

'But you were unavailable at ten past five on 17th July, shortly before Karen was killed?'

'Yes.'

'Where were you, Mrs Campion?'

'You don't really think she could have killed Karen, do you, Mike?' Paula asked as they walked back to the car.

'Well, it's a funny coincidence and she's hiding something. I thought it would do no harm to rattle her cage a bit.'

'Attending a reception for representatives of the voluntary sector at the town hall is a pretty decent alibi, though.'

'So you think she couldn't have slipped out and done it?'

She laughed. 'Not without getting a lot of blood on some very expensive clothes.'

Her phone rang.

By 11.00 Scott was back from the university and heading to the canteen for a cup of coffee when he heard feet pounding behind him. Steve Boxer, in uncharacteristically animated mode, was pursuing him.

'Have you got a moment?' he panted.

'Yes. Have you got something?'

'I might have. Two things, actually.'

'Tell me.'

He turned and followed Steve back to the incident room.

'You asked me to find Jamilleh Hamidi's address,' Boxer said, sitting down at his computer. 'She lives in Keswick Rise,' he said, pointing to the screen.

'And that sounds like Eastgate estate – whatever possessed the town planners to call those streets after Lake District beauty spots?'

'A sense of humour? Anyway, Keswick Rise is a bit different. It's on the edge of the estate, backing on to that bit of copse that runs between the estate and the university campus. The university owns several of those houses. Not many people took up 'Right to Buy' on Eastgate, but people in Keswick Rise did, and the university has bought them up as they've come on the market.'

'OK. But it's the other end of the estate from Karen Brody's house in Windermere Road, isn't it?'

'Yes, but it's just round the corner from Leanne Thomas's flat in Kendal Way. A stone's throw.'

'Is it indeed?'

'So, if the killer thought that both Karen and Jamilleh might recognise him, isn't it likely that he lives somewhere nearby?'

'Or regularly visits somewhere nearby. First thing is to talk to Leanne again. We were pretty sure she knew more than she was telling.'

'She may be scared too.'

'So we'll need to make her scared of us. You said you had two things?'

'Yes. The other one is pretty random and it may be just coincidence.'

'Try me.'

'Well, when I'd found this link between Jamilleh and Leanne I thought I'd just play around and see what I got, so I got the names of everyone we've interviewed so far in this case and I got all their addresses. What I found was that Estelle Campion, the Samaritan director, used to live next door to the Thomas family – Karen and Leanne and their parents – in Albert Road.'

'That doesn't fit Paula's account of her. Dripping money, Paula said.'

'That's recent. She was Estelle Hodge in those days. She lived there first with her husband, Keith Hodge, and then after they got divorced, she lived there alone. She lived there from 1995 to 2008, and then in 2008 she married Bruce Campion and went up in the world, to The Gables, Lower Shepton.'

'This is good stuff, Steve.' Scott leaned over his shoulder to look at the screen. 'So she was the Thomas family's neighbour from the time Karen was eight until she left home. Does she have any children?'

'No.'

'So she could have been quite close to the girls – babysat

for them, maybe. I wonder how long she's been a Samaritan. No – no point in doing a search on that – that you won't find on any database you have access to. I bet, though, that it was she who told Karen about the Samaritans passing on bomb warnings. Good work, Steve. Inspired.'

Steve bridled with pleasure at the commendation, like a small boy getting teacher approval. 'What now?' he asked.

'Keep digging.'

He went to his office and phoned Paula. 'Are you still at the Samaritans?'

'We've just left,' she said.

'OK. Never mind. It can keep.'

'What can?'

'I'll tell you in a bit. I need you to come with me to Leanne Thomas. Can you come back to the station?'

'OK.'

She seemed to be waiting for something.

'Did you get anything?' he asked.

'Karen's index card.'

'Good. Useful?'

'I'll tell you in a bit,' she said.

At 11.35, Darren Floyd passed Scott and Paula as he drove to the university. An interview with nursery staff, he thought, was hardly his style, but one or two of them might be fit. He would see what he could make of it. The nursery staff, however, having experience of small boys rather too big for their boots, proved more than a match for him. Caroline, thirty-something and attractively maternal, looked at him with pitying amusement.

'Do you really think, DC Floyd, that there are any circumstances under which we would not have reported to the police immediately any suspicion we had about a loiterer?'

'People don't always. You'd be surprised.'

'But we're not just *people*, are we? We're childcare professionals, and the safety of the children is an absolute priority, above everything else. Hence the high fences, the locked gate, the safety bars, the soft flooring, the sand under the swings and the climbing frame, and so on and so on.'

She sat back and smiled patiently at him, reducing him to child size.

He got up and squared his shoulders. He'd left his jacket somewhere, he realised, the leather one. No wonder he had failed to impress this irritating woman. He felt a surge of spite.

'Fences are all very well,' he drawled, 'but I suppose you realise that you let a man into your cosy little nest, disguised in a burqa.'

'What?' She stood up too.

'Yes. The one who got attacked by a dog in your garden. Seems the dog was better at spotting a predator than you *professionals* were.'

He swaggered out, and it was only as he was getting into his shiny new car that it hit him that his gibe had been confidential information and he had probably set himself up for serious trouble.

．

At 11.45 Sarah Shepherd arrived at Marlbury Hospital and found her way to Jamilleh Hamidi's room. She had been told, when she phoned, that Jamilleh would be *going down for assessment* that morning, and would not be back in her room until twelve, but she found a uniformed officer guarding her door who told her that she was in there.

It was not a good time, though, she realised. The nurse who was settling her back into bed looked disapproving. 'She's very tired,' she said. 'She's been having tests. She really needs to sleep. Can't you come back?'

Sarah hesitated. It was a perfectly reasonable request but it felt weak to give up on a job she had been sent to do. She gave the nurse a smile. 'Just two minutes?' she asked. 'And then you can throw me out.'

'Is that all right with you, Jamilleh?' the nurse asked. 'Just two minutes?'

Jamilleh nodded and Sarah seated herself by the bed. 'I just wondered,' she said quietly, 'whether you have remembered anything more about the man who attacked you.'

Jamilleh's head went from side to side on the pillow, 'I didn't see,' she said.

'But his eyes. You saw his eyes?'

Jamilleh's eyes clouded. 'No,' she said. 'No eyes.'

'You didn't see his eyes?'

'No.'

'But you said —'

'Nothing. I saw nothing.'

She was trying to shake her head again and the nurse laid a restraining hand on her. 'You need to keep your head still,' she said, and glared at Sarah.

'The person in the niqab, though,' Sarah persisted. 'You saw his eyes, didn't you?'

'No. I see nothing. Nothing.' Tears seeped out from under her long, dark lashes.

'Right. That's enough,' the nurse said. 'You're upsetting her. Enough.' She ushered Sarah to the door.

'We are actually trying to find out who attacked her,' Sarah said as she was hustled out. 'I'm not just doing this for fun.'

'And we're trying to make her better. Which do you think matters more?'

At 11.35, Scott picked Paula up from the station. As they drove through steady drizzle to Leanne Thomas's block in Kendal Way, Paula asked, 'So what have you got?'

'It turns out Jamilleh lives in Keswick Rise, which is, as you might guess, just round the corner from Kendal Way.'

'Which means we have a possible link between Jamilleh and Karen – other than the nursery.'

'And if Jamilleh's attacker thought she might recognise him then there's a chance that he lives round there.'

'So, are we doing a house-to-house?'

'A job for you for this afternoon. For the moment we're going to see what Leanne says about the coincidence and if she'd like to tell us more about what was worrying Karen.'

'Not to mention all the security on her front door.'

'Right.' He paused and glanced at her. 'What about you?'

'I ... we ... got Karen's card.'

'So you said.'

'Well, first of all, we found it on its own in a locked drawer in the director's desk. Second, there's what's on it. They're like file cards, these things. The Samaritan who takes the call writes the date and a brief sentence or two about the caller's problem, and then signs it. Karen's card has five entries. The last one is Malcolm's but the other four just say *Asked to speak to the director.*'

'And what does she say?'

'That she never spoke to Karen.'

'So, here's my other piece of news. Estelle Campion was Karen and Leanne's neighbour all the time they were growing up.'

'No! I wouldn't have put her in Albert Road.'

'She married up a few years ago.'

'Did Steve get all this?'

'Yes.'

'Bless his heart.'

'So do we think Karen knew Estelle was the director when she asked to speak to her?'

'Yeah. She's high profile, Estelle – all that fundraising. Karen would have known.'

'But she says she never spoke to Karen. Did she give a reason for hiding the card?'

'Didn't want to upset the volunteers.'

'Where's the card now?'

'Back at the station.'

'Good. This afternoon we tackle Estelle Campion again and talk about fingerprinting her volunteers.'

'She threatened me with the chief constable if I tried to even talk to her volunteers.'

'Hah!'

'Her husband knows him.'

'We'll take the risk.'

The light from the sullen sky did the flats in Kendal Way no favours, Paula thought, taking in the concrete's adornment of rusty streaks from blocked gutters before they pushed through the outer door into the scabby lobby.

Leanne Thomas took a long time to open the door, possibly because the belting music playing in the flat drowned out their hammering on the door, possibly because she was getting dressed. If the latter, she had made no more effort, Paula thought, than the last time she had seen her. Her unbrushed hair was scraped into a scrunchie, old mascara gave her pale face panda eyes, her feet were bare and she was wearing a T-shirt and shorts that might have been pyjamas. The sitting room, when they were eventually admitted to it, was much less tidy than when Paula had seen it previously – verging on the chaotic, in fact. Was this the effect of doing without Karen's support, Paula wondered?

'Is Liam at home, Leanne?' she asked.

'I thought you were police,' Leanne muttered. 'You social workers too, are you?'

'Just taking an interest, Leanne,' Paula said breezily, and stood watching her, eyebrows raised, waiting for a reply.

'Well, he's at nursery if you must know.' She flung herself down on the sofa as though exhausted by a day's work. 'My … friend took him,' she added as if feeling a need to explain in view of the bare feet and unbrushed hair.

Scott stood looking out of the window. 'Do you know the Hamidi family?' he asked.

'You what?'

'Jamilleh Hamidi. Young mother, four-year-old son. Lives just over there in Keswick Rise.'

'The Arabs, you mean?'

'She's not Arabic, in fact. She's from Iran,' Paula put in.

'Same difference.'

'She'd tell you otherwise.'

'Wears one of them *burqa* things, doesn't she?'

Scott froze. 'There's a woman living over there who wears a burqa?' he asked quietly. 'What's it like?'

'What d'you mean?'

'This *burqa*. What colour is it? What's the face part like?' Paula asked.

Leanne eyed her contemptuously. 'There's nothing over her face,' she said. 'It's one of those headscarves, and the dressing gown thing.'

'What colour?'

'I dunno. Grey, I suppose.'

'That'll be Jamilleh,' Scott said. 'Have you spoken to her?'

'Dah! I can't speak Arab, can I?'

'She speaks English.'

'Huh!'

Scott walked over and stood looming over her. She shrank back into the sofa. *Scared of men for all the bravado,* Paula thought. She watched as Scott moved some clothes from the sofa and sat down beside her. He spoke quietly.

'Did you hear that she got attacked – over at the university? She'd just dropped her little boy off at the nursery.'

She looked at him sideways but didn't meet his eye. 'I heard someone got attacked. I didn't know it was her.'

'The thing is,' Scott said, 'we think the same person may have attacked her as killed Karen and Lara.'

Her head came round and she stared at him. 'What?'

'We think Karen and Jamilleh both knew this guy and we need to find out who he is.'

Leanne turned away and Paula took a breath to speak but he gave her a warning look. 'We know Karen was worried about something in the days before she was killed, Leanne. We think she had some information – knew something that worried and frightened her. She was your sister. You saw her most days. I think you know what frightened her. I think what frightened her is the reason why you have all those locks on your door.'

She looked at him, her face white and startled with its black-ringed eyes. Then she gave a wobbly little puff of ridicule. 'Bollocks,' she said. 'That's all bollocks.'

In the afternoon the investigation proceeded as follows:

Paula Powell and Sarah Shepherd went house-to-house up and down Kendal Way and Keswick Rise. *Have you noticed any strangers lurking around?* was their question, but they were picking up as much information as they could about youngish men living at these addresses. The responses they met at the door ranged from guarded to garrulous. They were all unhelpful.

Steve Boxer continued to trawl for connections but found that his luck had run out.

Darren Floyd picked up his jacket from his girlfriend's flat, put it on, regained his swagger and took a circuitous route back to the station in order to give his brand new Audi TT Roadster a spin.

Steve Boxer learned that the Garda in Kilkenny had picked up an associate of Doug Brody's, wanted by the Merseyside force, and were returning him to them.

David Scott paid a visit to Estelle Campion at her home, where she confessed, charmingly, to knowing Karen Brody and withholding that information from DS Powell. Under polite but relentless pressure, she admitted to having spoken to her on four occasions as a Samaritan caller but insisted that Karen had refused to divulge details of the information she wanted to have relayed to the police *for her own safety*. On the whole, Scott was inclined to believe her.

Sarah Shepherd reported to Scott Jamilleh Hamidi's retreat into unhelpfulness and was puzzled at being told that this was actually very helpful, confirming as it did the view of this case that he had now arrived at.

18

Saturday 28th July

Mourning's Work

My mother's letter has me chasing thoughts round my head like a coked-up hamster on a wheel, but I do eventually doze off into semi-sleep for a couple of hours, before waking, dry-mouthed and panicky, just after five. I decide to make a virtue of the early start and catch the first train to London, thus avoiding Annie and whatever emotional extravagance she may produce at the news of her grandmother's death.

I shower and conscientiously eat a bowl of cornflakes; I drink tea rather than my usual coffee, sensing that a caffeine rush might just undo me. Then I dither lengthily and ridiculously over what to wear. It has been hard enough finding the right clothes during this unsummery summer, but factor in some concession to mourning wear, a visit to an unknown solicitor and the likelihood of a tramp round a muddy graveyard and the problem seems, to my befuddled mind, insoluble. I somehow get hooked on the idea that a skirt is called for but I need flat shoes for the graveyard and the skirt/flat shoes combo looks frumpy in the extreme. And, besides, it has settled in to rain again and I would end up spending the day with folds of wet cloth flapping round my legs. So trousers it is, which means sewing up the hem of my black linen ones, but once that's done, and I've got my grey jacket on, I decide that will do. My outfit lacks the éclat I usually go for, with varying degrees of success, but dreariness is, perhaps, what is called for now. I depart, leaving the chaos of discarded clothes for later.

I cycle to the station, stopping for cash at the bank cashpoint in the high street, and get myself onto a seven fifteen train. I am outraged to find that this hour on a Saturday doesn't qualify as off-peak but I have no heart for making a scene. I buy myself a *Guardian* but can't concentrate, even on the crossword. I wish I'd bought a cup of coffee to take on the train with me.

I lean back and close my eyes and remember suddenly that yesterday evening I had a theory about the murders of Karen and Lara Brody. Well, *theory* is too strong a word; I had a glimmer, a thought lurking in the outer shadows of my mind that I was reaching for and I had to go home to think clearly and pin it down, but home turned out to be no place for thought, clear or otherwise. For this, the absconding from rehearsal, the dereliction of duty, I was sacked, wasn't I? I had completely forgotten all this. I am on a train to London on the day of the dress rehearsal without even thinking that my sacking has turned out to be timely, leaving me free for whatever weirdness I'm about to encounter today. I am shaken. This is not the woman I am. I don't forget things. I seem to have lost myself and I want myself back.

In pursuit of finding myself, I decide to text David. I have not forgotten my vow not to communicate but since I'm not going to catch hold of yesterday's elusive thought any time soon, I had better pass it on to him and see what he can do with it.

Had a thought about the murders, I type, *but lost it due to circumstances beyond my control. Involves shoes, pronouns and*

idiolect, with something about Odysseus, I think. Will try to think further. Meanwhile, find out the name of Karen's sister's boyfriend.
G

At St Pancras, I buy a modest latte and an apricot croissant and sit watching people as they come off their suburban and provincial trains ready for a day of excitement in the capital. Do I look as though I'm one of them? I rather hope so. I hope, at least, that I don't look as bewildered and disoriented and, frankly, crazy as I feel.

When I get out of the tube at New Cross, I ring Margaret, awarding myself a small nod of approbation for having her number stored in my phone. She sounds a bit bleary and I realise that it is still quite early, so I decide to walk the twenty minutes to the flats and give her some time. She opens the door to enfold me in a plump, spongy hug. 'Such a lovely lady, she was,' she says. 'Such a lovely lady.' I hug her back, envying her uncomplicated grief.

She gives me a cup of coffee – 'Decaffeinated all right?' – and goes through the events of the previous afternoon, such as they are. 'Just sitting in her chair, she was. Quite peaceful. So like her, isn't it? No bother. Bless her.' I ask the question I have to ask but feel absurd asking.

'So, where is she now, Margaret?'

'Oh, not over there, bless you,' she says. 'The ambulance took her.'

'So she'll be at the hospital?'

'I suppose so, love.'

'Which one?'

'Well, Queen Elizabeth, I suppose.'

'Right.' I feel more helpless than I remember feeling ever.

She is looking at me, head on one side, as though she has only just really noticed me. 'You'll need an undertaker, Gina,' she says gently.

'Yes. Yes, I will. And then there's the solicitor – I hope he's there on a Saturday – and the funeral. A church funeral, would you believe? And letting everyone know. And then the plot in the churchyard and – did you know about that?'

'About what, dear?'

'About Christopher?'

'Christopher?'

Relief of a sort; not a secret kept just from me then.

'It's nothing,' I say. 'Doesn't matter.'

She gives me that examining look again. 'I don't want to butt in,' she says, 'but would you like me to find an undertaker for you? Once you get that settled, you know, they'll do a lot of the work for you.'

'Would you?' Gratitude brings tears to my eyes. What is the matter with me? I'm a woman who is equal to anything, aren't I? How come organising a funeral seems such a mountainous task?

'You leave it to me,' she says. 'You look peaky, and no wonder. I'd offer you a brandy but it's a bit early for that, isn't it?'

It is, and it's the last thing I need. The cotton wool in my head needs no encouragement to expand.

'It's nearly ten now,' she says. 'You go off and see the solicitors. You know where to find them, do you?'

'I do.' My self-esteem picks itself an inch or two off the floor. I have googled Hart and Lyman and I have an address and a map. I give her another hug and go across the hallway to my mother's flat.

There is an absence, of course, but what actually hits me more is how scruffy the place has become. Without my mother to focus on I see what I have missed before: the patch of carpet worn bare in front of her chair, the chipped paint on the doors where her stick has hit, a strip light hanging by its flex in the kitchen, a missing handle on a chest of drawers. And I can hear her voice, *Not worth replacing it at my age.* I haven't really come to see the place; it's her address book I'm after. Tomorrow I shall have to start letting people know. I find it in the drawer where the unopened bills were tucked away. *Farewell cruel world*, I think.

Outside I look at the map, decide that I'm not, after all, up to navigating my way to the solicitors and walk back towards New Cross, where I find a taxi and am dropped outside a small, discreet slip of a house, squeezed between strident shop fronts like a prim, elderly spinster at a rather brash party. It takes a while for the door to be answered and I realise that I should have phoned ahead. When I announce my business, the receptionist is pleasant enough, however, and sits me in a pale green waiting room with copies of *Country Life*. In Lewisham? Really?

After a while, a young man comes in, shakes my hand, introduces himself as Roger Aggleton, and takes me into his office. I realise at this point that I have been harbouring a completely inappropriate picture of my mother's solicitor. Too much literature again. Without really thinking about it, I have been picturing the old family solicitor so beloved of golden age crime novels: the silver-haired, plummy-voiced gentleman who has known the deceased since she was a girl – possibly carried a torch for her at one time – and will now give wise and fatherly advice to me. This is stupid, of course. My mother didn't have a solicitor *looking after her affairs*; she didn't have *affairs*. She sold a house and bought a flat, and she made a will. That was it. Roger Aggleton clearly never met her and knows nothing about her.

He has the will in front of him, but instead of reading it out in time-honoured fashion he pushes it across the desk to me. Maybe this is because there is only me; it requires the gathering of eager would-be heirs to justify the solemn reading aloud, I suppose. I pick it up and scan it. No surprises in the first paragraph: five thousand each to Ellie and Annie, and five thousand to be kept in trust for Freda. Nothing for Nico, but then the date is 2008. The residue goes to me – just the flat, I imagine, once the girls have their legacies. But it's the next bit, of course, that I'm really interested in:

Instructions for my funeral: I wish to be buried in the plot reserved in St Olave's churchyard beside my son, Christopher. I have no views on the nature of my funeral.

The tone is instantly recognisable and the content unenlightening; I knew Christopher was her son, didn't I?

'What happens now?' I ask Roger Aggleton.

'There will be a delay until we get probate, but your mother's estate seems to be very straightforward, so that shouldn't take long.'

'Have you any idea where St Olave's Church is?'

'I haven't.' He flushes slightly. 'I don't live round here, and I don't really do churches.'

'Me neither,' I say.

The receptionist, Claire, tells me where St Olave's is, however, and kindly calls a cab to take me there. Solid and rather squat, it stands marooned on an island, with roads running all round it. I walk through the churchyard, looking to left and right, and realise that it will take me forever to find this grave without help. I look into the church in search of someone who looks as if they belong. A verger? A churchwarden? The extent of my ignorance embarrasses me. Anyway, the place is empty. A July Saturday and no wedding? Well, its position hardly makes this a prime venue, I suppose.

Outside, on the large notice board that declares this to be St Olave's Church, I find the vicar's phone number. I hesitate, but if I'm going to ask him to conduct the funeral I'd better get onto it, hadn't I? The phone rings and rings and I imagine it trilling away in a cavernous vicarage somewhere. Eventually, I get a message to say that my call is being transferred, a voice answers, and I explain my mission. 'So it's the funeral,' I sum up, 'but I would also like to see this grave, which I knew nothing about and don't know how to find.'

'We keep a plan of the graves in the vestry,' he says, and his voice is young but has the appropriate warmth for a vicar. *Good casting*, I think. 'Our verger's laid up with a back problem, otherwise he could show you. You're up from Kent, you say?'

'Yes.'

'Give me five minutes and I'll come over.'

'Oh that's r—'

'No problem.' And he's gone.

Five minutes later a motorbike roars up the path to the church door and Peter Michaels, vicar of St Olave's, jumps off and removes his helmet to reveal a buzz cut and bright blue eyes in a thirty-something face. No clerical garb, not even a dog collar, I notice. Perhaps arranging this funeral will be less excruciating than I feared. He shakes my hand, dashes into the church, emerges with a rolled document and leads me round to the back. He moves at speed and I have trouble keeping up with him, weaving among the graves, even with my sensible shoes on. He is wearing trainers, I notice, which reminds me of something and makes me wonder whether David has read my text yet.

Peter Michaels stops eventually, in a far corner, near a nicely ancient bit of mossy wall, and unrolls his plan. He glances around, moves a bit along the wall and stops. 'Here we are,' he says.

I join him and am furious to find that my heart is thumping. I look down and there it is, a small gravestone with a simple message:

In loving memory of Christopher James Sidwell
b. 6th May 1949 d. 17th January 1950
'Grief fills the room up of my absent child'

I stand in the cold drizzle with hot tears running down my face. The quote must have been my father's choice. It's from *King John* and he was the Shakespeare buff, not my mother, who had no time for fiction of any kind. *1949*. I had a brother born in 1949 – a baby boomer, really. Aeons away, it seems to me, from my birth in heady 1962. Twenty-six my mother would have been, newly qualified and newly married, ready for her grown-up life.

I look at Peter Michaels, making an attempt to wipe off the worst of the tears, noticing that some have dripped down to make stains on my pale grey jacket. 'Where will she go?' I ask.

He squints at the map. 'Just here,' he says, indicating a patch to the left of the headstone. 'Your father is here, you see.'

And I do see, to the right of the headstone, an urn and a plaque:

Harold James Sidwell
15.11.17 – 4.8.74
In loving memory

No quote for him, then, though if she had asked me I probably could have come up with one. I was twelve, after all, and had read quite a lot. Did I know he was here? I don't think so. I remember the crematorium, the coffin sliding behind the curtain, my mother's hand on my arm, but I don't remember what happened after that. I suppose my mother came here alone to place the ashes and commune with Christopher.

'Would you like me to leave you alone?' Peter Michaels asks.

'No,' I say. 'That's all I need to see.' In spite of the giveaway tears, I am aiming for bright and businesslike, and I turn briskly away to accompany him back to his bike. 'I suppose there's plenty of room in your church?' I ask as we go. 'She was a GP locally and I think there'll be quite a turnout.'

'Oh, yes, she's quite a monster,' he says. 'The church, I mean,' he adds as he sees my startled face. 'Have you any idea of the day you would like?'

'Soon,' I say. I have thought about this. 'My daughter will be up in Edinburgh but she'll be back on Thursday. Would Friday be possible?'

We go into the church and while he goes to check the diary I take in its chilly grandeur. *Victorian, designed to impress and intimidate,* I think. *God, Mother, what have you got me into here?* He returns, we agree on Friday afternoon, he shakes my hand in both of his, and I watch him roar away. I remember an Indian friend saying to me once, 'Whenever I meet an only child, I always think, *Who will walk beside you behind your parents' coffins?'* Well, Ellie and Annie will be with me won't they? I might have expected David to be there too, but not now. Too bad. And, anyway, do I really have to walk behind the coffin? Does it have to be that theatrical? I have led a sheltered life. I've reached the age of fifty without having to think about funerals. Now I'm going to have to think fast, and this bit, at least, I shall have to do on my own.

I realise, standing outside the church door, that I am getting very wet. The rain didn't seem heavy enough to warrant getting my umbrella out but it is persistent and penetrating and I'm beginning to feel clammy inside my jacket. I go into the porch and fish my mother's address book out of my bag. Dawn is the person I'm looking for; Dawn might just be able to tell me about Christopher. She is the daughter of Betty, who was my mother's receptionist for years. Betty is dead but she, if anyone, was close to my mother. I can't remember Dawn's surname but I find it eventually – Reilly, so it takes a while – and I call her.

'Where are you?' she asks when I broach my business with her. 'Oh God, Alcatraz,' she says when I tell her. 'There's a café. Turkish. Down the road to your right if you're standing at the church gate. I can meet you there in fifteen minutes.'

It takes me a while to negotiate my way across the roads, but I find the café and cheer up at its robust aromas of coffee and cardamom. I'm ready for serious caffeine now and a good dose of carbohydrate, so I order a Turkish coffee and a piece of baklava. The café's proprietor seems to smile at me with particular kindness and I wonder if he has spotted the tear stains on my jacket (I hope the rain has dealt with my face). *I have always depended on the kindness of strangers*, comes to mind as I lean back in my chair, close my eyes and wait for my order. I'm no Blanche DuBois and I don't solicit or elicit kindness as a general rule but strangers have been kind to me this morning: Claire at the solicitors', Peter Michaels, this smiley man with the black moustache. Not to mention Margaret and Dawn, having me intrude on their Saturday morning, willing to help. I have to battle with the idea that all this kindness comes because I seem to be pathetic. It occurs to me that self-sufficiency is a kind of selfishness; it deprives other people of the opportunity to exercise the thoroughly desirable human instinct to be kind. I consider at least forty years spent marching through life, coping, and think how much thwarted kindness I have trampled underfoot.

My coffee and baklava come, and so does Dawn. She gives me a hug and says she's so sorry about my mum. She is a few years older than me, rather muscly and leather-skinned. She runs marathons for charity, I know, and spends her summer holidays climbing mountains. She orders a mint tea and gets straight to the point. 'Your mum really never told you about the baby?' she asks.

'Not a whisper. I had no idea. Did she talk to you about him?'

'Not to me. To Mum. She called my mum when it happened – when she found him.'

She looks at me as though she expects me to know what she's talking about. I stare back, dumb.

'It was a cot death,' she says, 'only I'm not sure they called it that then. She went to pick him up from a nap and he wasn't breathing. She called an ambulance, tried to revive him and rang my mum, who lived round the corner. By the time Mum arrived the ambulance was there but she wouldn't let go of him. Just kept trying to get him to breathe. Mum said it was the most dreadful thing she's ever seen. And she spent the whole of the war in Lewisham, so she'd seen a few things.'

'And there were no more children, until me?'

'No.'

'Was that deliberate, do you know? Or did it just not happen?'

'I don't know. I'm not sure that Mum knew that. She had a sort of nervous breakdown afterwards, your mum, I think. Didn't work for a while. Then she went back and just poured everything into her work, Mum said.'

'Well, that explains some things,' I say. I take a swig of my coffee, like a dose of medicine, but I can't face the baklava now. I offer it to Dawn, who shudders her rejection. We finish our drinks without saying much more. Dawn offers to *get the jungle drums going* about the funeral and gives me a lift to New Cross Station. We part with another hug.

As I go onto the concourse to look for the next train to St Pancras, my phone cheeps with an incoming text.

How did you know about Leanne's boyfriend? it asks.

Elementary ... I reply.

My phone rings. 'Where are you?' David asks. 'You sound as though you're in a station.'

'That's because I'm in a station.'

'Why? Where? Aren't you supposed to be doing your thing at the abbey?'

'Actually not. Long story. I'm at New Cross.'

'Going where?'

'Coming home.'

'Wait there. I'll drive you home. Give me twenty minutes.'

'Where the hell are you, then?'

'I've been at Wormwood Scrubs.'

'Lovely.'

'If I drive you home we can talk.'

'We can?'

'Yes. This theory of yours.'

'Oh, that.'

'Yes, that. What did you think I meant?'

'Nothing. Nothing at all.'

19

28.07.12: 07.45

Information Received

Scott heard the incoming text as he surveyed the contents of the bread bin and contemplated a jog to the garage for something more appealing in the way of breakfast.

Had a thought about the murders but lost it due to circumstances beyond my control. Involves shoes, pronouns and idiolect, with something about Odysseus, I think. Will try to think further. Meanwhile, find out the name of Karen's sister's boyfriend. G

He sat down at the kitchen table, swearing softly. Her bloody mind games. What was he supposed to make of *shoes, pronouns and idiolect? Idiolect,* he knew, through prolonged exposure to Gina, was an individual's characteristic use of language, but so what? As for Odysseus, did that mean anything or was it just showing off? The thing that made him want to grind his teeth and beat his head on the table was that she was probably onto something. That was Gina. But she couldn't just come out with it, could she? She was going to make him jump through all sorts of hoops first.

As he made coffee, he looked at the message again. What were the circumstances that were beyond her control? He was supposed to guess that too, of course. Probably something to do with the play in the abbey water garden, which she would expect him to go and see, never mind that he was leading a high-profile murder inquiry. Well, the name of Leanne Thomas's boyfriend he could find out. They had been interested in any boyfriends Karen might have had, but Leanne they hadn't thought about, and he didn't see why he should be relevant but he had learned not to ignore Gina's questions. He rang Paula.

'Leanne Thomas. Do we know if she has a boyfriend?'

'I don't think we asked. She said the boy's father isn't around but we didn't think other boyfriends would be relevant. I suppose ...' She hesitated.

'What?'

'All those locks on the door – she seemed like a woman living alone.'

'Yes.'

'Why the sudden interest?'

'You're not going to like this.'

'What?'

'A text from Gina.'

A silence.

'I thought you said—'

'I know. All the same I want to f—'

'Actually, hold on! Hold on! There was something. She may just be right. There was something – something's been niggling since we were at Leanne's yesterday. Do you remember you sat down on the sofa next to her and you moved something off it to make room?'

'Yes?'

'What was it? Can you remember?'

'A jacket of some sort, I think. Black.'

'Man's or woman's?'

'Hard to say. It was leather – or fake leather.'

'A man's, then?'

'Probably.'

'Who do you know who wears a black leather jacket?'

He took a breath. 'Darren Floyd,' he said.

'God knows how Gina got onto him.'

'Possibly not even God.'

'What are you going to do?'

'He's due to go to The Scrubs with me this morning, leaving at nine. He's no early starter. We may well find him round in Kendal Way. I'll pick you up in ten minutes.'

'What are you going to do if it is him?' Paula asked as she buckled her seat belt.

'Put him on a disciplinary. He knows quite well that he should have ruled himself out of the inquiry.'

'You don't think it's more than that?'

'Why?'

'I've been thinking. Haven't you thought that he seemed to have an agenda? He always seemed to be steering us in the team meetings. Away from Leanne, when we thought she might have Doug Brody's loot, and towards terrorists and paedophiles.'

'You don't think he's actually our killer?'

'I don't know, but it'd be worth checking his whereabouts that evening.'

He was silent for a couple of minutes. 'If he turns out to be our man, I imagine that will be the end of my career,' he said.

'But you wouldn't let him get away with it?'

'What do you think? Get onto the station to send a couple of uniforms to Kendal Way to wait for me there. We'll throw *misconduct in a public office* and *conspiracy to pervert* at him for a start, and we'll check his alibi.'

He stopped round the corner from Leanne Thomas's flat and parked in the shadow of a large camper van. 'Don't want to risk him hearing the car,' he said. It took some minutes of banging and shouting to bring Leanne to her door, and when she opened it she looked white and scared. The flat offered little in the way of hiding places and Scott found Darren Floyd, wearing only his boxers, in the wardrobe in Liam's room while the boy lay wide-eyed and silent in his bed. Scott escorted him into Leanne's bedroom to dress and then into the living room, where the uniformed officers were waiting for him, alert with the excitement of the arrest of a CID officer. Read his rights, Floyd, for once, opted for silence. Paula and Scott stood at the window and watched him being put in the car. Leanne flung out of the room and into her bedroom, where she slammed the door. 'We'll let him stew a bit,' Scott said, 'while we have a chat with Leanne. I still want to go and see Doug Brody. I'll take Sarah with me. You tackle Floyd, with Mike Arthur. He may be less on his guard with you – thinks he can bamboozle women, I imagine.'

'Not this one.'

'Exactly.'

Leanne, when she emerged from the bedroom, was surprisingly defiant. She had taken valium, or some such, Scott thought, and she had brushed her hair and put on proper clothes. She sat in the armchair, rather than in her usual slouch on the sofa, and said she and Darren had been together for about three months and insisted that she had no idea that there was anything wrong with Darren being on the case. 'I liked it,' she said, 'like someone was looking out for Karen. That's what Darren said. He was like looking after us all.'

Could she really be that stupid? Of course she could; Darren was plausible enough, after all.

They got up to leave. 'I hope Liam's all right, Leanne,' Paula said. 'He's had a scare. I expect he could do with a bit of a cuddle and some breakfast, couldn't he?'

Leanne eyed her with venom. 'You really are in the wrong job, aren't you? Social worker, that's you, telling everyone else what to do.'

'We didn't think about social workers, did we?' Paula said to Scott as they descended the stairs. 'I guess she's got one. They might be able to tell us something about the set-up there. I'll look into it.'

Doug Brody, sitting at a plastic-covered table in a small interview room at Wormwood Scrubs, was a different man from the one Scott had seen in the infirmary ten days previously. The livid bruises were gone but his face looked gaunt, and without the ferocious anger that seemed to sustain him on the previous occasion his eyes looked empty and bleak. He did not respond to Scott's greeting but sat, hunched forward over the table, head lowered. Scott and Sarah sat down opposite him.

'How are you, Doug?' Scott asked.

Brody raised his head slightly.

'You got anything to tell me, get on with it,' he muttered. 'Else leave me alone.'

His speech was slurred. Still being kept sedated, Scott guessed.

'More questions, I'm afraid, Doug,' he said. 'We want to know who killed Karen and Lara and we think you know already.'

They watched as Brody lowered his head to the table and covered it with his arms like a man protecting himself from a kicking.

Scott went on. 'Karen came to see you on the Sunday before she was killed, and you phoned her on the Monday evening. The day before she died. What did you talk about?'

Silence. No sound or movement.

'Karen was ringing the Samaritans, Doug,' Sarah said. 'Did you know that? She was so worried about something. She must have talked to you about it, too, mustn't she?'

'She was scared,' Scott said. 'Scared to death for herself and for Lara. You knew that, didn't you? But she wouldn't go to the police. Why was that? Did you tell her not to involve us? Would it have got you into more trouble?'

Brody suddenly raised his arms and flung himself back in his chair. 'Jesus!' he said. 'Where do they find you people? Go round the spas classes do they? *Hey, you look stupid enough. Ever thought of joining CID?'*

Encouraged by this sign of life, Scott said, 'So tell us, Doug. If we're stupid and you're clever, tell us. If Karen wasn't protecting you, who was she protecting? Who was worth risking Lara's life for?'

He was leaning forward now, trying to make eye contact but jerked back as Brody let out a howl. 'I made her promise!' he yelled. 'I made her promise and she never broke a promise, Karen.' He dropped his head and then looked up, straight into Scott's face for the first time. 'I killed her,' he said, suddenly quiet. 'I killed her. You don't need to look for anyone else.' He turned to the prison officer sitting by the door. 'I want to go now,' he said. 'I've got nothing more to say.' As Scott protested, he turned back to him. 'You can keep me here all day if you like,' he said flatly. 'All night too. I'm not saying another word. I can keep promises too. Not another word.'

Scott gave a stone a vicious kick across the courtyard as they were leaving. 'Damn!' he said. 'We must be able to find out who he's protecting. He loved Karen. He's destroyed. Why won't he talk? It can't be that he's scared for himself. He doesn't care if he lives or dies.'

'They've got him on a twenty-minute suicide watch,' Sarah said.

'Well, there you are.'

'It's got to be family, hasn't it?' she said. 'That's the only tie strong enough.'

'You can take the girl out of Family Liaison but ...'

'I suppose.'

'Do we know anything about his family?'

'He grew up in care, I think. I'll find out more.'

'Priority.'

They arrived at the car. 'You drive,' he said. 'I want to make some calls.'

'I'm not much good at London driving.'

'I'll direct you. Past the hospital and get onto the A219.'

He got out his phone and found Gina's message still on the screen. Well, she was owed credit for knowing about Leanne's boyfriend. Did she actually know it was Darren, he wondered, or did she just know he was a police officer?

How did you know about Leanne's boyfriend? he typed.

Elementary... came the reply.

There was nothing for it but to ring her.

Gina was waiting for them near the taxi rank. Sarah pulled up and turned to Scott. 'I'm quite happy to get a train home, sir. If you'd like some privacy.'

He started to protest but then took in Gina's face as she advanced towards them. Something was wrong and the chances were he was about to be blamed.

'If you don't mind, Sarah. It might be best. I want to talk to her about the case – because she was one of the last people to see Karen – but –'

'It's fine, sir,' she said. 'No need to explain.'

She climbed out of the driving seat, gave Gina an awkward half-wave and disappeared into the station. He watched her go. Tact? Or just frightened of Gina?

'Don't send her away on my account,' Gina said as he got out of the car. 'You've made it clear that this is strictly business.'

'Are you all right?' he asked.

'Don't I look all right?'

'Not really.'

'Thanks a lot.'

'I meant—'

'Let's just go, shall we?' she said, getting into the passenger seat.

He was silent as he negotiated his way through traffic. Then he asked, 'So, tell me. How did you know Leanne's boyfriend was a CID officer?'

'What?' He could feel her astonishment without needing to look at her. 'You mean he's a policeman?'

'Yes.' He glanced at her. 'I thought that was what you meant.'

'What's the guy's name?'

'Darren Floyd.'

'Well that's not right.'

He laughed. 'You think I don't know my own team?'

'He's on the murder inquiry?'

'Yes. But this goes no further, Gina, you understand? If the media get hold of it …'

'Quite. So do you think he's the killer?'

'The killer? No. I think he's broken rules by not declaring a personal involvement, and I think he may know more than he's let on, but we don't have any reason as yet to think—'

'Has he got an alibi?'

'We're checking that.'

'And you're certain he's Liam's father?'

'No! No. Liam's father left long ago, so Leanne says. Darren's only been around for a few months.'

'Well, that's what I meant when I said *Leanne's boyfriend* – I meant Liam's father.'

'Why?'

'Because I think Liam's father is the killer.'

'Why?'

'I told you in my text. *Shoes, pronouns, idiolect and Odysseus.*'

'Oh, yes! Of course. That really clarified things.'

She sighed. 'Do you want me to explain?'

'If it's not too much trouble.'

'If you knew the trouble I've had already today you wouldn't be so cavalier about it.'

He took a look at her again. His first impression had been right. She didn't look like herself. She looked pinched somehow, and deflated, actually smaller, without her usual bounce. 'Are these the *circumstances beyond your control* we're talking about?'

'You could say.'

'Tell me.'

'My mother's dead.'

He ought, he knew, to find somewhere to pull over and stop but the tidal flow of traffic was bearing them on relentlessly. 'Why didn't you tell me?' he asked quietly.

He could feel that she was turned away from him. 'I didn't think you'd be particularly interested,' she said.

'And that's because …?'

'You're not particularly interested in me, I suppose.'

He gave that a moment before he said, 'Well, I think I can persuade you that that's not true but it will have to wait until I'm not battling London traffic, I'm afraid.'

'OK.' She was still turned away from him.

'I am really sorry about your mother,' he said.

'Thank you.' He saw her wipe away tears with the heel of her hand.

They drove on in silence until she said, 'So you need to find out whether Liam's father is called William. Or Billy.'

'Why?'

'Because then we can be sure that he's the killer.'

'Didn't you tell me that Karen's dog was called Billy?'

'Yes. That's the whole point. That was my mistake.'

Risking killing both of them, he turned to look at her. 'Do you think,' he asked, 'you could just tell me what you're on about?'

'All right.' He felt her shift herself in her seat and lean back against the headrest. 'It's about what I saw on the afternoon Karen and Lara were killed. I always felt certain that the answer was there somewhere but I didn't get it until Freda gave me a piece of information, and then there was Friar Francis.'

He resisted asking what the hell she was talking about. Let her talk. She would get there eventually. The flat tiredness in her voice alarmed him. This was not Gina with a theory as he knew her, fizzing with the excitement of a challenge and the triumph of meeting it. He waited.

'I told you the dog was called Billy because I heard Karen call out "Billy!" when the dog attacked the "woman". Then Freda told me the dog was female. I hadn't thought of that. Dogs are male by default, aren't they? In all European languages, I think. Dogs are male, cats are female. There are those treats you can get – *Good Boy* treats for dogs and *Good Girl* treats for cats.'

Scott took a couple of deep, calming breaths, *Let her talk*, he told himself. *Just let her talk.*

'Anyway, when Freda told me the dog was female, I just thought, *Oh Billie, then, as in Holiday*, but that was sloppy thinking. And then last night I was watching the guy who plays Friar Francis in *Much Ado*. I was watching his feet and the way he walked and I remembered the man in the niqab and the shoes he was wearing. For some reason I'd forgotten them, but they were black trainers, quite distinctive, with a red flash, and I pictured it all again and I realised why the child – Lara – seemed to be behaving so oddly. She was laughing and pointing at the niqab woman's feet, where the dog was snuffling around, and it seemed just rude, but then I remembered what she was saying: *She's getting him. She's getting him.* I thought that was because the "woman" was kicking out at the dog but Lara knew the person in the niqab was a man, didn't she? She obviously must have known the dog was female so *she's getting him* was the other way round. The dog was getting the man. Except then I thought about the way Freda uses *get*. She uses it to mean *understand* or *know*, and that's where Odysseus comes in. Have you ever read *The Odyssey*?'

'At school, I think. Bits of it.'

'Do you remember his homecoming?'

'Why don't you tell me about it?'

He was prepared to be patronized. He was glad to hear some animation in her voice, some of the old Gina back in action.

'Well, when he returns to Ithaca after twenty years away, he disguises himself as a beggar so he can spy on everyone and find out what's been going on in his absence. He's really trying to catch his wife out, of course, poor bloody Penelope, who's been sitting there weaving and unpicking her endless tapestry and staving off her slavering suitors – though, come to think of it, she must be at least fifty by this time, so you'd think the slavering might have stopped. Anyway, he disguises himself in a covering of beggar's rags and no-one recognises him except his old dog, Argos, who is at death's door but manages to wag his tail and lick his master's hand before expiring.'

'And Karen's dog had previously belonged to Leanne – possibly to Leanne and her previous boyfriend – so the dog could have been greeting her old master, not attacking a woman in a niqab?'

'Exactly. Dogs have limited means of expressing their feelings, when you come to think about it. They bark to intimidate but they bark in excitement too, and in greeting. And jumping up and pawing someone can be aggressive but it can be excitement or delight too. People who know dogs can tell the difference, I'm sure, but the rest of us are left guessing and, frankly, most dog behaviour seems to be on the aggressive side.'

'So you're saying the dog was greeting her old master, and Karen and Lara knew that she was?'

'Yes.'

'And they recognised the niqab-wearer by his shoes?'

'Yes.'

'Do you have a theory about why the guy had decided to wear a niqab?'

'Well that's your department. You can't expect me to do all your work for you.'

He was silent. She would go on, he knew. Give her a verbal vacuum and she'd be in there, filling it.

'For what it's worth,' she said, 'I think he wanted to see his son and hear him sing, and for some reason he couldn't do that in plain sight. Maybe there's a restraining order on him not to approach Leanne or Liam. If she's living with a policeman, all the more reason for him not to risk it.'

'That would make sense of all the hardware on Leanne's front door – if she was trying to keep him out. But you're saying he killed Karen and Lara because they recognised him? He wouldn't have done that just because they knew he'd broken a restraining order, would he?'

'Well, I don't know, David,' she snapped. 'Don't just sit there picking holes in my argument when I'm doing your work for you. Maybe he's a wanted man. Wanted by you lot. He's in hiding but he needs to see his boy. It wouldn't be hard to find out, would it? On television they have all that stuff at the click of a mouse. Find out his name, why don't you? If it's Billy then admit that my theory has credibility at least.'

He fished his phone out of his pocket and handed it to her. 'Call the station, will you? And then put it on hands free.'

When he was put through to Steve Boxer, he said, 'Steve. Leanne Thomas's son – Liam – find out what you can about his father, will you? Name, background, record.'

The silence at the other end went on for so long that he

assumed that they had lost contact. Then Steve Boxer's voice came through. 'So you've heard, boss?' he said.

'Heard what?'

'About Liam.'

'What about him?'

'He's been snatched. His mother thinks his dad's got him.'

'When did this happen?'

'Just over an hour ago.'

'And when were you going to tell me?'

'I-it's-it's been all go here, boss. Emergency stations. Road blocks, and all-cars alert for the guy's van. DS Powell took over. We knew it would take you a while to get back from London – she talked to DC Shepherd – and –'

And knew that I'd sent a police officer back by train and was driving my girlfriend home, Scott thought. *She thinks I've lost the plot.*

'Where is DS Powell now?' he asked.

'They've got him, the guy, just ten minutes ago. Stopped at a road block on the A2 London-bound. He turned off into a field and got bogged down in mud – reckoned without the summer from hell. He's in a camper van with the boy. DS Powell's called for armed back-up.'

Scott's stomach plunged. 'Don't tell me –' he said.

'Yep. He's got a gun, boss. And he's making threats.'

'Against the boy?'

'Yep.'

'Where exactly on the A2 are they?'

'I can give you the coordinates.'

'OK. And Steve?'

'Yes?'

'What's his name, Liam's father?'

'Ah, that's the surprising bit. Brody. Billy Brody. He's Doug Brody's brother.'

20

Saturday 28ᵗʰ July

Common Ground

I keep quiet while David digests the news from the front. Road
blocks and armed response units are way out of my league. I
don't even – and this is pretty heroic – demand
acknowledgement of my brilliance in sussing out who Billy is.
I don't belong in this bit of the operation, I know, and if I draw
attention to myself it is just possible that he will turf me out
and leave me to walk back to Marlbury.

After a while, it's he who starts talking. 'This must have
been what Karen was worried about,' he says. 'She must have
known that Billy was back and was threatening to do
something like this. But he's Doug's brother and Doug made
her promise not to involve the police. And Leanne wouldn't
involve us because Darren wouldn't want that. If Leanne was
stopping Billy from seeing the boy, it's likely he tried to see
him at Karen's house – she seems to have looked after Liam
more than his mother did. He wouldn't have known about her
promise to Doug, but what I still don't see is why he was
prepared to kill to stop her from identifying him. You must be
right about him being wanted for something, and something
big.'

He eyes his phone in its little cradle on the dashboard.

'Do you want me to get Steve back?' I ask.

'No. Paula will know. I'll wait and get the gen from her.'

I restrain myself from saying something sarcastic about the indispensability of the multi-talented DS Powell and look out of the window. David is driving extremely fast now and it will be unwise to distract him.

We see the open-air stage set for the drama that's being played out from some distance away, lit as it is by the flashing lights of a ring of police cars. We slide off onto the slip road until we're nearly level with the place where, presumably, the camper van plunged off the road, and where the churned mud shows that the police vehicles have followed suit. David stops the car.

'You really can't be here,' he says, and I think for a moment that he is actually about to dump me. How far are we from Marlbury? Twenty miles? Tears threaten again. I am prepared to beg. 'You'll have to get in the back and lie down,' he says. 'I can't have you visible."

I don't argue. I do as I'm told. I feel quite sick as the car bumps its way off the road but I say nothing. I efface myself. David stops the car and shortly afterwards Paula arrives and slips into the passenger seat.

'Sorry I didn't inform you right away, boss,' she says, not sounding at all sorry, I think, 'but things were moving so fast. We needed to get the road blocks out and —'

'We'll talk about it later,' David says, in a tone I recognise – polite but ominous. 'Fill me in on this, quick as you can.'

'At 13.05 we got a call from Leanne Thomas. Liam had been playing with a friend in the front garden of a house just round the corner from Kendal Way. The friend ran in and told his mother that a man had taken Liam and driven him away in a big white van.'

'We saw it. We parked behind it this morning, didn't we?'

'I think he's probably been watching, waiting for his chance.'

'Then he saw us take Darren away, reckoned he'd talk and decided to act.'

'I guess.'

'Go on.'

'So we went into action: all-car alert, road blocks, back-up.'

'Did you know he was armed at this point?'

'Not right away but Leanne talked. Couldn't stop her, just blabbed the whole thing. I'd got nothing out of Darren, by the way, but Leanne has dumped him right in it. Funny, I thought she didn't give a shit about Liam but she was distraught – in pieces.'

'What did she tell you?'

'It was Billy Brody who did the petrol station job that Doug's doing time for. The visual on the CCTV, the partial DNA match – that was Billy. He knew he'd blown it with the CCTV so he did a runner right away, to Spain and then Morocco.'

'Where he got hold of the niqab.'

'I guess.'

'Doug Brody must have known Billy did it. Why didn't he finger him?'

'Steve dug out some stuff that may explain that. The boys were put into care when Doug was ten and Billy was five. Social workers' reports suggest Doug was always ferocious about protecting his little brother.'

'Why didn't Steve find him when he was trawling for Doug's associates?'

'No criminal record. Plenty of crimes, I imagine, but he got away with them. Doug always looked after him.'

'And Billy repaid him by killing his wife and daughter. Jesus. No wonder Doug looks as though he's going insane.'

He is silent for a moment. 'It must have been Karen calling out his name that did it,' he said.

'What?'

'Karen knew Billy was around but he thought he could trust her not to tell anyone. Then the dog ran to him and she called out his name – in front of a load of people. That was when he decided to kill her. What's he done with the money? Did Leanne say?'

'He's got it with him. Used some to buy off Darren. Helped to pay for that nice car.'

'And the gun?'

'Same one he used for the robbery, Leanne says.'

'Has anyone spoken to him yet?'

'He rang the station ten minutes ago. He says we have to let him take Liam to Spain with him or he'll shoot him. I've brought Leanne here. Thought she might be able to appeal to him. But someone needs to speak to him first, don't they? Find out what he expects to happen, assess the risks. Do you want to do that?'

Even from where I am, effacing myself on the back seat, I can hear the reluctance in her voice. And so can David.

'You're a trained negotiator,' he says. 'This one's for you.'

That's right, David. Anything for Paula.

I must make some sort of involuntary sound to go with this thought because Paula is suddenly aware of me. She twists round to look and I give her a little wave from my supine position. 'Don't mind me,' I say. 'I'm not here.'

She shoots a look at David; he makes a *we're not talking about this* gesture with his hand. 'Do you want to use my phone?' he asks.

She's about to say something but changes her mind. 'I've got his number in mine,' she says, 'but I'll call him from here if that's all right. It'd be helpful to have you listening in.' She shoots another look at me; I close my eyes and put my hands over my ears. 'Liam sings like an angel,' I say. 'That's why his dad went to the nursery concert. Might help. And now I'm not here.'

I don't keep my hands over my ears, of course, but listen

212

with avid attention. She fiddles around, putting her phone to speaker mode. Then it takes a while for her to get through, and it's not clear to me what the problem is, but then she starts gently, *low and slow*, just like you're advised to deal with recalcitrant teenagers in class.

'I'm Paula,' she says. 'How are you doing, Billy? The voice the other end is low and barely audible but she doesn't ask him to repeat. 'And Liam?' she asks, 'How is he?' Again I don't hear the answer but she goes on. 'Do you think I could speak to Liam for a moment, Billy? He must be quite scared. I think it might be helpful for him to know who you're talking to.'

There is some kind of movement at the other end – a scuffling, a bit of whispering. 'Liam?' Paula asks, very quietly, 'Is that you?'

'Yes.' The voice is tiny. Tears are seeping out from under my eyelids.

'Are you OK there with your dad, Liam? Have you got nice things to eat and drink?'

'I had crisps,' he says. 'And juice.'

'Not stocked for a siege, then,' David murmurs.

'That sounds nice,' Paula says. 'Have you got some toys there too?'

'Yes.'

'Good. Why don't you go and play, then, while I have a chat to your dad?'

There's a bit of a hiatus before Paula is back on with Billy.

'He sounds fine, doesn't he?' she says. 'And we want to keep him fine, don't we? Nothing that's going to frighten him.'

For the first time I hear his voice clearly. 'Course he's fine,' he says. 'Think I can't look after my own kid?'

'No. I think you love Liam very much, Billy, and you want the best for him.'

'And don't try telling me he's better off with that lazy cow and her bent boyfriend.'

'Have you thought about how it would be for Liam, Billy? In a strange country. Away from his friends. With everyone speaking a strange language. He's just about to start school, you know. That won't be much fun for him, will it, if he can't speak the language?'

'He'll be fine. The two of us, we'll be fine.'

'So what exactly is it you want, Billy?'

The voice at the other end is sounding more aggressive now. 'I've told you, I want out of here and out of the country, with my boy. Is that simple enough for you?'

'Well, actually, it's not that simple if you think about it. Is Liam on your passport? Because, if not, even the police can't overrule passport control. And then you're stuck in the mud there, aren't you. Even if we said, *OK, drive away*, you wouldn't be able to do it. You'd need someone to pull you out of the mud and I think you know we're not going to use police cars to do that.'

The silence when she stops speaking is absolute; the man seems to have stopped breathing. Paula must have pressed *mute* because she says to David, 'I think he's put the phone down.'

'Just wait,' he says. 'You've got armed officers in position?'

'Yes.'

We all wait. Then the voice is back, stronger this time. Maybe he's had a drink.

'I'm not doing any more talking,' he says. 'Liam goes out of the country with me or that's it. I'm not losing him again.'

'He's put the boy somewhere where he can't hear,' David mutters. 'That's why he put the phone down.'

Paula is very quiet, very concentrated. 'You're in a bad place, Billy,' she says. 'You're in a corner, and that's not a nice place to be. That's when people make bad decisions because they can't think straight. Don't let that happen to you. Think about Liam. Think about his life. I hear he sings brilliantly. You love him and you feel proud of him, and you can go on doing those things if we can just all keep calm and sort out this bit of trouble you've got yourself into.'

She is good, I have to admit it. She is good.

The answer when it comes is calmer. 'And how are we supposed to do that?' he asks, reluctantly.

'You wanted to see your son and spend some time with him,' Paula says. 'That's not such a terrible thing. Not against the law, that. The problem is the gun, isn't it? Carry a weapon and you're in real trouble. So step one is to get rid of the gun, Billy. Open the window and throw it out, and then it's all easy after that. You come out, Liam comes to no harm, and you get full credit for giving up the gun and behaving like a good father.'

She is saying nothing about the robbery, I realise. Does she think she can con him that he's got away with that?

'That sounds easy enough,' the voice says, and it has an odd ring to it. 'All hunky dory, eh?'

'Just give us the gun, Billy,' she says.

'OK.'

We wait. Then I hear Paula say, 'The door! He's coming out. He's got the gun.'

David is out of the car and I roll over, keeping low, my eyes just at window level. It takes a moment to orientate myself and then I see them, the man with the boy clasped in one arm, the other hand by his hip, holding a gun. 'You let us walk away from here,' he shouts, 'or I use this.'

David is walking towards him. My brain seems to freeze. *David is walking towards a man with a gun in his hand* I tell myself, but the meaning of the words seems lost to me. I get my head up higher, looking for the police marksmen, but I can't see them. I can see Leanne. She's on her knees in the mud, howling.

David keeps walking. 'Don't be frightened, Liam,' he calls.

'Your dad won't hurt you. He loves you. He loves you more than anything in the world.'

I'm not quite sure what happens then because I've got tears blurring my vision. I don't know whether Billy Brody chooses to put his son down or whether he's distracted and Liam makes a frantic effort to escape, but suddenly the boy's down and on his feet and running towards his mother. I see Billy Brody raise his gun and then there's the startling crack of a gunshot, Liam falls to the ground and I can hear myself screaming 'No!' into the hubbub around me.

I scramble out of the car on rubber legs and watch Leanne stumbling across the muddy grass to the little body, but I can't bear to see the moment when she reaches him so I look instead towards the other area of commotion, where a man lies bleeding on the ground and paramedics are bending over him. It must be David. I start running, but then I see that David's somewhere else, talking to a couple of uniformed officers, and he waves me away furiously as I approach. The man on the ground with the bloody head, I realise, is Billy Brody. Shot Liam and then shot himself, I suppose. But there was only one shot, surely? Unless I was so stunned by the first I didn't hear the second one. Slowly, reluctantly, I look back to where I know Leanne will be cradling her son, but some sort of magic has happened there. The paramedics are there too, and Leanne is kneeling in the mud again, but Liam is on his feet, dazed and bewildered, certainly, but completely alive. A paramedic is checking him over, gently, and Leanne is talking to anyone in earshot. 'Just threw himself to the ground,' she is saying, 'when he heard the shot. I thought I'd lost him. I really thought I'd lost him.'

Well, it doesn't have the elegance of the breath-catching returns to life in Shakespeare's late plays but it has its own poetry, I suppose.

I hover about, taking in the scene, because I shall never

experience anything like this again, until David appears at my side and propels me towards one of the police cars. 'What happened?' I ask.

'Can't talk about it. You're a witness. I need you to go straight to the station and make a statement.'

'But I didn't—'

'Just say what you saw. Don't embellish, don't interpret, just say what you saw.'

He puts me in the car and speaks to the uniformed policeman at the wheel. 'She's a witness. We need her evidence untainted. No discussion. Don't even talk about the weather. Straight to the station and into an interview room.'

'Well I hope they'll give me a cup of tea,' I remark as we drive away, but my captors are following orders to the letter and I get no response.

At the station, however, the kindness of strangers reasserts itself. I am put into one of the vulnerable witness rooms – soft chairs and soothing colours – and I am brought tea with sugar, a plate of biscuits and a blanket to wrap myself in because I'm clammy and shaky by this time. Then Sarah Shepherd turns up, showing no ill-will about having to surrender her place in David's car, and takes me very gently through the events of the past couple of hours. We arrive at a very respectable sounding explanation for my presence at the scene – material witness in the case of the murders of Karen and Lara Brody, called to London by my mother's death, being returned to Marlbury for further questioning, caught up in fast-moving events. Then she takes me, quietly and calmly, step by small step through the minutes before Billy Brody was shot. I have good recall in general, and this was a pretty intense experience, so I'm quite confident about my answers, but it isn't until we get to the bit where Billy Brody raised his gun and Liam fell to the ground that I realise that this – just this – is what it's really about.

'You're sure,' Sarah asks with an extra degree of calmness, 'that was the sequence. Liam started running, Brody raised his gun, Liam fell, Brody fell?'

'I didn't see Brody fall. I thought the man on the ground was David. I—'

'OK. OK.' She holds up a pacifying hand. 'I only need what you did see. The important thing is the sequence. Brody raised his gun before you heard the shot? You're sure of that?'

'Positive.'

'And when you saw Brody on the ground, what was happening?'

'There were two paramedics with him.'

'And that was how long after the shot?'

'It felt like immediately after.'

'Thank you.' She manages a small smile.

'Is he going to be all right?'

'No, he's not, I'm afraid.' She prints off the statement she has been typing up as we've talked and hands it to me. 'He was DOA, I'm afraid. Read the statement through, will you, and sign it if it's all right?'

'I wonder if he'd decided to kill himself when he came out of the van.'

'Oh, he didn't kill himself. One of the marksmen shot him. There'll be an inquiry. You seeing him raise his gun as Liam ran away from him is critical. A reliable civilian witness at the scene is just what we need.'

'Glad to be of service,' I say, and then I start to cry.

'What is it?' she asks.

'You didn't ask me about the boy,' I sob.

'The boy?'

'Christopher. He fell down dead and then he stood up.'

'Christopher?'

'Liam,' I say. 'I mean Liam. He fell down dead and then he stood up. His mother ... his mother ...'

She passes me tissues and waits for me to pull myself together. 'I hope you feel we've looked after you all right here,' she says. 'I'm sure DCI Sc —, David would want —'

'He's got other priorities,' I say, blowing my nose. 'As have I. I've got my daughter's play to go to this evening. I should have been there this afternoon. It's about love and sex, treachery and trust, life and death, hope and despair – oh, and the search for identity. It's just the kind of light entertainment you need after a heavy day.'

21

Monday 30th July to Saturday 4th August

Moanday to Shatterday

I read a novel once, of which I have only a hazy recollection, though I remember a rich but neurotic and dysfunctional family in which the teenage children had renamed the days of the week: they were, I think, *Moanday*, *Tearsday*, *Wasteday*, *Thirstday*, *Frightday*, *Shatterday* and *Sinday*. These come to mind as I recount to you the events of my odd week. I shall leave you on Shatterday; there will be very little chance, I fear, that Sinday will live up to its name.

So, *Moanday*. I decide to go into work although there is nothing I have to do and I could very easily take some compassionate leave on a variety of grounds. I'm too edgy to enjoy a day at home, though. I coped yesterday by wearing myself out with a huge clear-out once Annie and her posse had departed for Edinburgh in the terrifyingly ill-maintained Volvo. My efforts went well beyond just putting things to rights: I prowled the house with black bin bags, hurling into them anything broken, ugly or just in the wrong place; I discarded neglected toiletries in the bathroom and unused gadgets in the kitchen; I went through the fridge and freezer throwing out food I'm never going to eat; I rolled up rugs and bagged up cushions and hauled them up to the attic. They could have used me on television for one of those decluttering shows. In the midst of all this, David rang, but I didn't answer because if it turned out that he wasn't ringing to see if I was all right, only to bark some more orders at me and criticise my witness statement, I knew I might well have a tantrum and that would be energy wasted when it could be devoted to decluttering.

So, here I am at nine o'clock in my office, scanning my emails and surveying my in-tray. On the top of the in-tray is the application form for the directorship of the Unit for Specialist English Language and Enhanced Skills Support. I take a deep breath and I fill it in, conscientiously and neatly. Then I print it off, together with my enhanced CV and clip the two together. I address an envelope to HR and before I put the forms into it I read them through again. It is an excellent application, I think, and if there is any justice the job is mine. Why do I feel so miserable then? It is not just because I suspect that in this case there will be no justice, is it? It is actually that I don't want the job. I don't want it because the amalgamation is a stupid idea; I don't want it because managing the remedial bit will distract me from the work I'm good at; I don't want it because if, by any chance, the VC gets overruled and I am appointed, he will simply start looking for other ways to get rid of me and I am just too tired for the fight. And that's the most alarming bit, really: Gina Gray – too tired for a fight.

On the other hand, the alternative is unthinkable: knuckle under? Accept demotion? Watch dreary sandal woman making a hash of my unit? I pick up the phone and I ring HR. *Human Resources*. Whoever thought that was an improvement on *Personnel*? *Personnel* makes it clear that you are dealing with people, individuals – persons. *Human Resources* works almost like an uncountable noun; it implies an undifferentiated heap of humanity, from which you scoop as much as you want, slicing and dicing as required. Does nobody but me think this sounds perilously like *Brave New World*?

When I get an answer from HR, I give my name and say I would like to discuss options regarding voluntary redundancy. I may be paranoid but I get the feeling that they are expecting to hear from me. 'Why don't you come over in half an hour?' the bright young woman on the other end invites me. 'Derek can take you through it.'

Derek is neither bright nor young; he is small and grey and possibly lives with an elderly mother. He is a process man. He prepares to take me at length through the procedures. He has used his half-hour's notice to get up to speed and he knows about the USELESS proposal, though he blenches at my calling it that. 'How long do you reckon it will take,' I ask him, 'for them to change that name? Would you like to take a bet on it?' He declines my wager. Redundancy, he explains, has to be initiated by the university; employees cannot ask to be made redundant – they can only resign. He can find no record of my being offered voluntary redundancy; is that right?

'Not in so many words,' I say.

'But in your case,' he says, 'I imagine it would not be a problem.'

'Why?' The question comes out sounding quite aggressive and he shrinks from me a bit.

'I-I meant only that with an amalgamation of this kind one of the benefits hoped for is some savings on staffing, so if anyone is willing to—'

'Yes. Well, I might be willing. What sort of a deal would it be?'

'That depends,' he says. 'It varies with individual cases and it's usually a matter for negotiation. If I may say, you don't put yourself in a strong position by letting it be known that you want redundancy. It gives you nothing to bargain with, you see.'

Stupid, stupid woman! Of course that's right. What was I thinking?

'So perhaps you could forget that we had this conversation?' I ask, smiling winningly, 'and tell the vice-chancellor that I am determined to hold onto my job at all costs?'

'Oh, I don't speak directly to the vice-chancellor,' he says.

'That's all right.' I say. 'I do. So, let's put it another way. Given my current salary and assuming I am not made head of the new unit, how much is the university likely to pay me to go away?'

After a bit of havering, he names some minimum and maximum figures which sound to me pretty generous.

'All right,' I say. 'It's an option. Thank you for your help. I can take it from here.'

I get up to go but he stops me.

'Just one thing,' he says. 'You would be required to sign a non-disclosure agreement.'

'Non-disclosure of what?' I ask, sitting down again.

'Of the amount of the redundancy payment, and in some cases, the reasons for the redundancy, as well as an undertaking not to take any action against the university in the future.'

'And you think mine would be such a case?'

'I think so, yes.'

'Because I might take the money and then sue the university for constructive dismissal or some such?'

'That sort of thing, yes.'

'A gagging order! I would be the subject of a gagging order. Doesn't life get exciting round here?' I say as I get up and leave.

I almost run back to my office, where I take my application, rip it through and stuff it in the bin. Then I sit down to write a letter.

Dear Vice-Chancellor,

Though tempted by the challenge of running the aptly named USELESS, I have decided that it is time for me to seek wider horizons in a place of learning less parochial, less temporising and less academically compromised than Marlbury University.

If required, I am prepared to work out my period of notice until the end of October but, given the proposed reorganisation of my unit, I assume that the university will prefer an earlier departure date.

I wish the university well. You yourself will, I am sure, go from strength to strength in moulding it in your own image. I shall watch with some interest the progress both of the university and of the new unit, should you decide to press ahead with the reorganisation in the light of my departure.

Yours sincerely,

Virginia Gray

I am not altogether satisfied with this but you can go on polishing this sort of thing forever, so I don't. Without pausing to reread, I bundle the letter into an envelope, run down to the office and drop it into the internal mail. Then I take myself out for lunch.

I lunch in the bar of the Aphra Behn Theatre, a pleasant space with walls adorned by signed photographs of minor actors, mainly known for their roles in television soaps. I order a smoked salmon sandwich and a glass of Prosecco because I am determined to be upbeat about my new freedom, and then I feel acutely self-conscious as I work my way, without much pleasure, through this solitary celebration. I almost persuade myself that a second glass of Prosecco will do the trick but in the end I don't linger. I return to my office and trawl for the website I need.

The site is a gov.uk one, labelled helpfully *What to do after*

Someone Dies and it is, in fact, remarkably helpful. It tells me exactly what I need to do and I learn that I have already failed to do the crucial thing, which is to get hold of the death certificate. This, I assume, was issued by the hospital. *You will need this for the undertaker and to arrange the funeral*, I am informed. I ring Margaret.

'Ah, Gina,' she says. 'I was going to ring you later – after work, you know. How are you doing?'

'Oh fine,' I say, as one does. 'I realise, though, you can't do anything about the undertaker until I get the death certificate, can you?'

'Well, no. I have booked them provisionally for Friday but they can't – you know – collect her until you show them the certificate.'

'I was thinking of coming up on Wednesday to do everything – the register office and so on. Is that soon enough?'

'Oh yes, I think so. But they do want to know what sort of coffin.'

What sort of coffin? 'Well, the usual, I suppose,' I say vaguely. 'Can you just tell them whatever they think?'

There is a pause. 'I think,' she says, 'that you ought to speak to them yourself, dear.'

So I do. I ring them and they address me with professional sympathy nicely calibrated for a woman who has lost an eighty-nine-year-old mother. They run me through the coffin choices and I opt for the ecological credentials of wicker, though this would hardly have been a concern of my mother's. She belonged to a generation for whom the harnessing of the natural world to the human will was nothing but positive; I don't think the idea that we were wearing the world out ever really impinged on her.

I return to the website and find that local councils offer a brilliant service called *Tell Us Once*. One phone call to the council and income tax, council tax, state pension and a whole lot of other things will be dealt with. I do think this is wonderful and if the Bullingdon boys' public sector cuts mean that it disappears I may actually assassinate one of them.

I make a list of jobs and phone calls and put them into a logical order. Then I go home and drink half a bottle of red wine, left behind by my house guests, and eat several slices of toast and marmite. This is a bad combination and I feel sick. I try to watch television but can't concentrate. I go to bed. At some point in the night, I go to the bathroom and throw up. In the morning I am light-headed and exhausted.

Tearsday. It is mid-morning before I haul myself into work and when I pick up my mail I find that HR have already sent a response to my letter of resignation. Fast work, I must say.

Dear Mrs Gray,

We have today received notice from the vice-chancellor's office of your intention to leave your post as director of the English Language Unit.

We note your willingness to be flexible in the matter of notice, and in view of the imminent dissolution of the ELU in its present form, we propose that your resignation takes immediate effect from the date of your letter, that being the 30th July. You are offered two months' salary in lieu of notice.

Please reply in writing immediately to indicate your acceptance of these terms.

So there it is. I've resigned, but they've somehow managed to sack me anyway. I'm done. No last this or that. I'm out. I half expect someone to appear with a couple of cardboard boxes to put my stuff into. I look round my office. There's enough here for a pile of movers' crates, never mind cardboard boxes. Better get started, then, before I find someone else is moving in.

I start with the filing cabinet: I select two box files with official stuff in – exam results and so on. Student Records have all this information, I'm sure, but I'm not comfortable about throwing it out, so I take the files down to the office and ask Gillian if she can give them house room. I don't tell her I'm leaving. I haven't found a satisfactory way of telling it yet. While I'm downstairs, I go into the cleaners' cupboard and take a roll of black bin bags. It seems to be my week for bin bags. I pile files and papers into the bags, sweeping stuff off my desk to join them and tearing down the theatre posters that adorn the walls. I pull out the drawers of my desk and empty them into another bag. I survey the bags, which are now taking up most of the floor space. They are heavy and they will have to be dragged downstairs one at a time. I shall be asked what I am doing. I am hot and furious and close to tears again. I go over to open the window and conceive a brilliant idea. My office is on the first floor and the window is low, with a wide ledge that can be used as a seat. I push it up as far as it will go, take one of the bags, tie it tightly at the neck, haul it over to the window and push it out. It splits a bit as it hits the ground because it has sharp-edged box files in it but nothing falls out. I repeat the process until eight bags are deposited there. I did intend to drag them round to the bins at the back but I'm really too tired for that now. I have to think about the books. I have a small inner office which is lined, floor to ceiling, with books. These are not being binned – not even the out-of-date teaching books from the 1980s. I phone a removal firm and tell them I have several hundred books needing to be packed up and put in storage. They will come tomorrow. I take a last look round the room and walk over to the SCR.

There I find Malcolm, who is actually just the person for such an occasion. I tell him the whole story, minus the events of Saturday, since I think these may still be confidential. I tell him about the amalgamation, the resignation, the clear-out.

'Could you tell the others?' I ask. 'They'll know something's up; the bin bags are a bit of a giveaway.'

He laughs, and I do too but I have to be careful. Anything can tip me over into hysteria these days. I take a deep breath. 'I need to say goodbye to you all properly, of course,' I say. 'Lunch time Thursday at The Old Castle? I'll have had time to work out how you're going to manage the summer courses without me.'

'Not your problem,' he says. 'HR made the problem. Let them sort it out. Bin the worries along with everything else.'

He is a surprising man and I realise that I have always underestimated him. He is actually quite envious of me, I think. A fantasy bolter himself, maybe?

In the afternoon I have a scheduled class with my wives, who won't know that I am not actually their teacher any more. I go to say goodbye, taking some strawberries with me as a festive touch which cannot, I think, possibly be non-halal. I can see immediately that there is no chance of our being festive, however. Athene has gone, her husband's money from the Greek government having been cut off; Juanita says she will have to leave early as she has packing to do for their return to Venezuela for the rest of the summer; Jamilleh is not there, of course, though Farah is, looking severe and unsmiling in her darkest jilbab, with her khimar, it seems to me, wound more tightly than usual round her strained face. Only Ning Wu looks as usual, but her usual is not life-and-soul-of-the-party.

Unwilling to tell them that I have been sacked, I say that someone else will be taking over the class as my mother has died and I have to go to London for a while. They make mildly sympathetic noises but don't seem sorry to be losing me. I ask Farah how Jamilleh is and she replies warily that she is all right, as though she believes that answering any question is a dangerous thing to do. Jamilleh will not be coming back to English class, she says, though I suppose she may change her mind when she hears that I have gone. She blames me because I brought Paula Powell along and got her into a sequence of events that nearly killed her. No-one official will apologise to her, of course; she is just collateral damage. We make stilted conversation about children and summer plans; they are not interested in my plans, which is a relief since they are unknown to me at present. I offer strawberries. Farah takes one and nibbles at it suspiciously as though it might have been injected with cyanide; Juanita comments that strawberries are the only good fruit that England produces; Ning Wu eats silently. After twenty minutes, I give up, wish them well and send them away. To my surprise, Ning Wu remains.

'I would like to thank you,' she says, 'for very good classes.'

I am ridiculously pleased by this. 'I'm so glad you enjoyed them,' I say.

'I learn at lot,' she says. 'Very good vocabulary.' *Vocabulary* is a difficult word for a Chinese speaker because of their difficulty in distinguishing *l* from *r*, but she manages pretty well. 'I hope to take degree course next year,' she says. 'Next week I start full-time summer course for my IELTS exam. Do you think I can get IELTS 6.0?'

'Do the eight-week course, Ning Wu,' I say, 'and I'm sure you can. You have good study skills and it's a very intensive course.'

'I hoped you would be my teacher,' she says.

'All the teachers will be good,' I say. 'I can guarantee that – I chose them.'

'But we laugh in your class. You make us cheerful.'

'Oh yes,' I say, giving her my biggest smile. 'Cheerful – that's my best thing.'

I give her an awkward sort of hug, wish her luck, press the remaining strawberries on her and go home.

Wasteday.
Hospital
Register office
Undertaker's
Bank
Council offices
Vicar
Flat

These are the jobs for this morning and I may not do them in exactly this order but the first two have to come first. I wait for the rush hour to subside before I set off and when I get to New Cross I engage a taxi. This is, I have decided, the only way to manage this morning's tour of the London boroughs of Southwark and Lewisham. They aren't places where you can flag down a taxi any old time – they are, after all, south of the river. 'I shall need you for possibly a couple of hours,' I tell the driver. 'I have seven different places to go to.'

He looks at me, weighing up my trustworthiness. Is he going to ask for a deposit?

'Have to charge you waiting time,' he says. He is evidently the grumpy kind, which suits me fine. I don't want him to take an interest in me; silent contempt will be very restful.

And so we go, and all is remarkably smooth: this has an air of unreality for me but I'm engaging with people for whom it's totally mundane. At the hospital they are chilly – deaths go on their debit side, after all; at the register office they are kindly and gentle, at the bank cool and brisk, at the council offices slow but competent, at the undertaker's calm and reassuring. By then I'm in need of a cup of coffee and I get my driver to take me to the Turkish café near the church, where the proprietor welcomes me like an old friend. I offer the taxi driver a coffee but, to my relief, he prefers to sit in his cab and smoke. In the café I phone the vicar to tell him I have the documents he needs for the funeral and he says he will come and join me. He breezes in, charming and energetic as before, orders a double espresso, casts a look over my documents and makes a couple of notes, says he has had email exchanges with my lovely daughters and *we're getting there*, and rushes off again. I get back in the cab and go to my mother's flat, where I pick up the unopened correspondence from the kitchen drawer, assuming that this will give me access to her utility and pension providers, and anyone else who needs to be notified. I ring Margaret's doorbell, because I feel I should, but am relieved to get no reply. I get back in the cab, return to the station and hand over to my driver a huge wodge of cash, drawn earlier for that purpose at my mother's bank.

On the train home I get a text from David. *Time to talk?* He asks. *Dinner tonight at La Capannina?* I regard this message with misgiving. It had to come, of course, the *coup de grâce*. I think he hoped that he could treat me so badly that I would dump him, but since I haven't done that he feels the need to draw a line. He doesn't like untidiness, David. The choice of *La Capannina* is tactless, I think. It's not *our restaurant* in a pathetic, sentimental way, but it is a place that we've gone to when we've been feeling harmonious. I text back. *Do we really need a meeting? How about email? Doing it by text is also fashionable.* My phone rings. 'I'm on the train,' I say.

'Quiet carriage?'

I look around. 'No.'

'Fine. Why not dinner? I have things to tell you.'

Why not dinner? Because either he dumps me at the start and then we have to do *still be friends* for the rest of the evening, which will be excruciating and give me indigestion, or he waits to the end and I have to munch my way through three courses, waiting for the moment, also giving myself indigestion.

Into my silence, he asks, 'Were you planning to do something else this evening?'

231

'Yes,' I say, clutching at the lifeline. '*Much Ado*. I got sacked from it but I ought to go and see it – see just what sort of a hash they've made of their costumes without me.'

'Well, I'd better come and see it too,' he says. 'It's Beatrice and Benedick, isn't it? The pair you like to compare us with.'

'Except it has a happy ending,' I say.

'Really?' he says.

So we go to see *Much Ado*. We arrange to meet for a drink beforehand and David arrives looking quite bouncy and pleased with himself. Is he already dating Paula, I wonder?

'You're looking smug,' I say, accepting a gin and tonic.

'Professional pride,' he says. 'We've got good evidence that Billy Brody robbed the petrol station and killed Karen and Lara. Doug Brody's conviction will be quashed and the coroner can give a clear verdict on the murders, which is the best the family can hope for. But the big news you'll read in the papers tomorrow. The drugs and people trafficking ring I was working on with the Met – we made ten arrests overnight, in London and here. It's a major breakthrough and the Met have offered me a job.'

'In London?'

He looks at me. It is a stupid question.

'Well done,' I manage. 'Jolly good.'

So this is how he's going to do it. *In London for good – huge responsibility – married to the job – long-distance relationship not really viable, blah blah blah.*

I drain my drink much too fast. 'I, by contrast,' I say, 'have lost my job.'

'You're not serious! Why? How?'

I wave an airy hand as the gin surges dizzily through me. 'Too boring to explain,' I say. 'University politics, crap vice-chancellor, unwise me.'

'What are you going to do?'

'Well first I'm going to bury my mother.'

'Of course. Sorry. When's the funeral?'

'Friday afternoon.'

'Would you like me to come?'

'I don't … let's see, shall we?'

'OK.'

We are silent. He drinks; I watch him.

The play is all right but the dank chill of the evening seems to cast a gloom over cast and audience alike and it doesn't really take off. They have found a teenager, it seems, to play Ursula – quite well, actually – but the costumes suffer from the absence of a watchful eye – a hem here, a bra strap there, and some outrageous footwear from a couple of the men, who have, presumably, lost the shoes they were issued with. David seems to enjoy it, though; nothing can dampen his good spirits. He suggests another drink afterwards but I propose tea and a pudding at the pizza place next to the abbey. More alcohol is likely to make me cry. If we've got to get this over with, a ballast of carbohydrate may help.

When we're settled, he says, 'I know you've got a lot to think about at the moment but have you thought at all about what you're going to do job-wise?'

'Not really. Why?'

'Might you move away from Marlbury?'

'What?'

'I mean, without the job and with Annie launched and Ellie settled, you could move, couldn't you? Somewhere with more opportunities professionally?'

'Why are you being my career consultant?'

'Well, you know the riff you do about us not knowing what to call each other – *partner, boy/girlfriend, lover, other half, significant other* all unsuitable? I was thinking that there is a solution to that.'

'Just not see each other, you mean?'

'I was more thinking of marrying each other.'

'What?' I choke on my mouthful of plum and almond tart and stare at him. 'Do what?'

'*Get thee a wife, get thee a wife.* They're nearly the last lines of the play. We could move to London. There'd be loads of colleges for you to teach in. A new life.'

'Hold on,' I say. 'I must just—' and I rush off to the ladies, where I stare at myself in the mirror for a long time and wash my hands before returning.

'No,' I say. 'No.'

'Look,' he says, 'if this is just punishing me because I've been preoccupied with work, don't you think you ought to—'

'It's not that.'

'Well, what then?'

'I'm nearly fifty, David. You're forty-two. Yes, it's time for you to get married. It's not too late but it will be soon. You shouldn't be hanging around with a menopausal woman, you should have a family – have a son – have a life.'

'I can have a life with you. And I'm fond of Freda and Nico and the girls. I don't need more family.'

'You do! Being fond isn't good enough. You can't opt for being an honorary grandfather at the age of forty-two. Marry Paula, why don't you. She'd have you like a shot. And have your babies.'

'I don't want Paula, I'm not at all sure she wants me and I know she doesn't want babies! You of all people shouldn't assume—'

'Well, find someone else then, but not me. I'm on the downward slope, David, and not even HRT can stop it. In ten years' time you'll still be a good-looking man and I'll just be an old bat.'

There is a silence. 'I did think,' he says, 'that you loved me.'

'I do love you!' I say this so loudly that heads turn from nearby tables. 'That's why I won't stay with you,' I hiss, 'because in ten years' time you won't love me and I won't be able to bear it.'

I pick up my bag and coat and I go round behind his chair. I drop a kiss on the top of his head and lay my cheek for a moment against the rough texture of his hair. 'Get a life,' I say. 'Just get a proper life.'

Thirstday. Well, I cry a lot in the course of the night and am horrified in the morning at the state of my face. I try all sorts of repair tactics – even cucumber slices on my eyelids – in the hope of not looking completely pathetic when I meet my ex-colleagues at lunch time, but in the end I have to dig out some old light-reactive sunglasses which don't look too ridiculous when worn inside but do disguise the ravages to some extent.

I get to The Old Castle early but find Malcolm already there, nursing a glass of coke with a lot of ice in it and looking miserable. 'Are you all right?' I ask.

He looks at me as though he can't quite focus on me. 'I've had a bit of a shock,' he says. 'I did night duty at the Sams last night and Estelle – our director – was there in a terrible state. I don't think it's confidential – she says the media are all over it. Her husband has been arrested on people and drug trafficking charges. There were a whole lot of them arrested apparently, early yesterday morning. Estelle's distraught.'

'And I suppose she had no idea what he was up to? Wives never do, do they? You acquire it when you sign the register, the blind eye, available to be turned as necessary.'

'You're very cynical,' he says.

'Me? No. Disappointed idealist, that's me.'

'Actually,' he says, 'I think she did suspect something. Karen Brody rang us because she had information she said she wanted us to pass to the police. She kept asking to speak to Estelle about it and Estelle got rattled. I think she was afraid that Karen's information was about Bruce – her husband.'

The others arrive and I buy drinks. This is turning out to be an expensive week, but I have been on property websites and am amazed at the price I can expect to get for my mother's flat. Everyone makes an effort to chat brightly and I fend off enquiries about my plans by declaring that I'm thinking of taking a gap year. 'Thailand, India, Australia,' I say. 'You know the kind of thing.' They do, and I see the same look of longing in their eyes as I saw in Malcolm's. They were all once EFL teachers, after all, teaching abroad before they upgraded to UK universities and teaching academic English. They've known the delights of freedom, of moving on when they got bored, before prudence told them it was time to come home and take out a mortgage. Travelling abroad actually has no appeal to me whatever but it's a fantasy that satisfies them.

We part with hugs and promises, in the usual way of these things, and I go home to find something to wear tomorrow.

In the evening I meet Annie and Ellie at Monks, Marlbury's only cocktail bar. Annie is just off the train from Edinburgh and is edgy and sleep-deprived. They buy me an alarmingly green drink in a tall glass. I fear that it's going to be sticky with crème de menthe but it turns out to have a lot of lime juice in it and to taste treacherously fruity and harmless. 'I really mustn't have a hangover tomorrow,' I say.

'Talking of which,' Ellie says, and produces a piece of paper. 'Order of service for tomorrow.'

I look at it. They have chosen the sort of theology-light hymns that the non-religious do choose: 'Morning has broken' and 'Who would true valour see', finishing with 'Jerusalem'. Then there are a couple of readings – Prospero from *The Tempest* for Ellie and Swinburne's *Garden of Proserpina* for Annie. I ask if this latter isn't a bit ostentatiously non-Christian, but she says, 'Pete says it's fine.' I am puzzled about

Pete for a moment until I realise that she means Peter Michaels, vicar of St Olave's. *Of course he's Pete.*

He will, I'm told, do the eulogy. Dawn has been gathering testimonials from old friends and patients and he will weave these into something. We shall say the Lord's Prayer and be sent away with a blessing. 'It looks fine,' I say. 'It's just all a bit odd, knowing Granny.' They know now about Christopher; I told Ellie and she has told Annie. Ellie wept when I told her, but she is the mother of a baby boy and probably still a bit post-partum hormonal. Annie is not very interested except insofar as he necessitates this funeral.

'Are we processing behind the coffin?' she asks. Neither of them has ever been to a funeral, but they've seen them in films.

'I told the undertakers not,' I say. 'It seems a bit black veils, if you know what I mean.'

I return the paper to Ellie. 'And now I have some news,' I say. I tell them about the job but not about David, because they are young enough to think that a wedding is lovely under any circumstances and will berate me for turning him down. 'So, I'm free,' I conclude. 'I don't need to get another job right away because I'll have Granny's money, so I shall go away somewhere. I fancy somewhere by the sea but a bit remote. The east coast somewhere, damp and blowy.'

'How long for?' Annie asks.

'I don't know. A few months, I suppose.'

'What about the house? Who's going to keep an eye on it?'

'I'm thinking of letting it.'

'It's my home!' Annie protests. 'You can't let other people live in my home!'

'It's not really home any more, Annie, is it? You've got your flat in Oxford that Pa bought for you at great expense. My house is just a convenient youth hostel these days. Wherever I go I'll have a spare room and you'll always be welcome. And I'll have Freda to stay. I think she'll love being by the sea.' I turn to Ellie. 'I'm sorry about not being available for babysitting,' I say.

She picks up my empty glass. 'We'll cope. I've got a couple of year twelve girls who are dying to babysit for me, though they won't do it for free, of course. And if you can manage three bedrooms, we'll all come and stay,' she says. 'Refill?'

After that, when everyone has had another drink, we quite enjoy ourselves constructing the fantasy of my new life.

'A dog, definitely,' Ellie says.

'Eccentric clothes,' Annie proposes, 'long and floaty – with turbans.'

'I was thinking of letting my hair grow,' I say. 'Long and witchy.'

'And you'll keep chickens.'

'And pick samphire from the cliffs.'

'And talk to myself when I'm out with the dog.'

We part with arrangements for the next day. Ben is going to stay with the children and Ellie is going to drive us so that we can go to the flat afterwards and take away any mementoes people want. They leave me at my front door; it is early still and Annie is having supper at Ellie's. I was invited but I pleaded things to do. I make myself some beans on toast and go to bed.

Frightday. The church is filling up behind us. Since we are not walking in behind the coffin, Peter Michaels suggested that we go in early and settle ourselves in our front pew. 'Plenty of time to greet people afterwards,' he said. So we can't see people arriving without craning our necks in an unsuitable way but we can feel them. We can hear the buzz. It's a bit like being in a dressing room backstage and hearing the audience arriving over the Tannoy. Annie gets a text message.

'Mobiles *off*,' I hiss, but she gets up and heads off down the aisle, returning a minute later with Jon. He looks tired and he should be sleeping because he's on nights, I know, but I am very glad to see him. He will keep us all steady, I feel, and steadiness is needed because I sense a latent hysteria in the three of us. It's the strangeness, I suppose. I am reminded of a recurrent dream I have in which I find myself on stage in a play I have never rehearsed, in a role for which I haven't got round to learning the lines.

I allow myself one look round the church under cover of the business of greeting Jon and realise that it is packed. There must be a couple of hundred people here. And they all know what to do, even if we are bewildered. They sing 'Morning has broken' with extraordinary sweetness and laugh and weep at Peter Michaels' tender account of Dr Jean Sidwell as her patients knew her. I am touched by these reminiscences but not moved to tears. It is when Ellie reads Prospero's speech from *The Tempest* that the tears come.

We are such stuff
As dreams are made on; and our little life
Is rounded with a sleep.

Not such a little life, I think. A girl fighting to go to medical school in the 1940s; treating bomb victims in the East End while still a student; losing her son and nearly being broken by the loss; putting herself together again and devoting herself to mending other people for another forty years; this packed church a testament to her energy and skill and determination. And I never appreciated her because I wanted more of her for me. The girls, either side of me, squeeze my hands. They don't know what I'm weeping for but I am grateful for the comfort.

We finish with a rousing rendition of 'Jerusalem' and the blessing that exhorts the Lord to make his face to shine upon us, which I do think is rather lovely, and we step out into feeble

239

sunshine to greet and thank and smile. We bury her next to her son and return to the church hall for tea. Much later, Ellie, Annie and I go to her flat and take home mementoes, more because we feel we should than because we really want them. She was always frugal, and more so as she got older. Annie takes a pair of eggshell china cups with a faint blue wash to them, which must have been a present and probably never used; Ellie takes a photograph of her at her graduation and a set of Russian dolls that we find in the bedroom – also a gift, I suppose; I take a little opal pendant, the only jewellery I ever saw her wear, apart from her wedding ring.

Annie is staying in London, spending the weekend with Jon, so Ellie and I drive home alone. She rings Ben, who says the children are fine and in bed, so she suggests we go out for supper. She proposes the pizza restaurant next to the abbey, but I veto this for reasons I don't explain, and we go for a curry instead. We drink some beer and get quite cheerful. I go straight to bed when I get home and, for the first time in weeks, it seems, I sleep well. Like the dead, in fact.

Shatterday. I wake to sunshine streaming through the curtains and a feeling of lightness that astonishes me. I get out of bed, push up the window, and lean out to savour the morning. *The pathetic fallacy*, I tell myself, but nothing can quell this astonishing feeling of buzzing aliveness that has taken hold of me. The albatross of failure – professional, personal, maternal and filial – that has sat on my shoulders for days appears to have flown off in the night, leaving in its place nothing but a light-headed irresponsibility. I am humming as I dress and make myself cinnamon toast and milky coffee. I eat and drink, pacing the kitchen, too light on my feet to sit down. I pack an overnight bag with a minimum of requirements – toothbrush, nightie, knickers, book, laptop.

I ring Ellie's house and ask to speak to Freda.

240

'Hello, Granny,' she says.

'Freda,' I say, 'I'm going away for a holiday.'

'Where?'

'I'm not sure yet. Somewhere by the sea.'

'How long?'

'Quite a long time, actually.'

'Why?'

'Well, I'm very tired, so I need a rest.'

'All right.'

'I thought you might like to come and visit me for a bit, and play on the beach.'

There is a silence.

'Are you good at building sandcastles?' she asks.

'Brilliant,' I say.

At ten o'clock the estate agent arrives to discuss letting the house. *Cosy* and *nice family feel* are epithets she uses several times as she looks round, but I suspect this is code for *scruffy* and *old-fashioned*. When she has finished, she sits down on the saggy sofa and sighs. 'To be absolutely honest with you,' she says, 'a house of this kind isn't easy to let. If you're planning to come back to it, I wouldn't recommend letting it to students – student lets get very hard wear. And couples who are looking for a four-bedroom house are usually in a position to buy. We can do our best, set a reasonable rent, but I'm not very hopeful.' She looks around. 'You are planning this as a short-term let, aren't you? I think that's what you said on the phone.'

'I'm really not sure,' I say.

'Only I could sell this for you just like that,' she says, clicking her fingers.

'Really?'

'Oh yes. It's a lovely family house in the catchment area for good schools. We have people queuing up for houses like this.'

'Even houses in the condition this one's in?'

'Oh yes. People like the opportunity to refurbish – put their own stamp on a house.'

'Well, sell it then,' I say.

When she has gone, I write a note for Annie and leave it on the hall table.

You may find For Sale notice on house, I write. *Expert advice says it makes sense on financial grounds. House is all yours for rest of summer, though. Have phone and laptop with me for emails. Lots of love. Ma*

I take a look round the house, checking doors and windows, then pick up my bag and walk out. I am stopped in the porch by the sight of my bike. I pat its worn seat. 'Don't go anywhere,' I say. 'I'll be back for you.' Then I slam the front door and head off down the road. If I didn't know I would look ridiculous, I would run. I actually feel as though I could fly. I have a great bubble of elation in my chest. I feel untethered, like a hot air balloon that is being released from its guy ropes one by one and is straining to float away. I jump up and touch a tree bough that overhangs the pavement.

In the short term, I know where I'm going. I'm heading for the station, then London, where I shall see another estate agent, about selling my mother's flat, and spend a few days doing theatre, galleries and some shopping, since what I'm wearing and a spare pair of knickers won't take me far. When I've had my fill of metropolitan cultural delights I shall go to St Pancras and choose a train. I have a picture of where I want to end up; it's just a question of finding it. I picture a small grey cottage on a cliff and myself inside it, sitting by a driftwood fire, a dog at my feet, reading a book and glancing occasionally at the foaming sea beyond my window. The picture is intense and I see it like a Vermeer interior: the yellow light from the fire and the pale square of a winter afternoon at the window;

the rough texture of the dog's coat and the graceful line of my bent head as I read. There will be false starts, no doubt, and a lot of nights spent in unlovely B&Bs, before I find something that can be moulded to match this Platonic ideal of a retreat from the world, but I am confident that I shall find it.

I stride on, gathering pace, swinging my bag. There is an odd roaring sound in my ears and I think I know what it is. If I were just to turn my head and look over my shoulder I could be certain. It is the sound of bridges burning behind me.